Vicki Covington

SIMON & SCHUSTER
New York   London   Toronto   Sydney
Tokyo   Singapore

NIGHT RIDE HOME

SIMON & SCHUSTER
Simon & Schuster Building
Rockefeller Center
1230 Avenue of the Americas
New York, New York 10020

SIMON & SCHUSTER and colophon are registered trademarks
of Simon & Schuster Inc.

Designed by Levavi & Levavi
Manufactured in the United States of America

10   9   8   7   6   5   4   3   2   1

Library of Congress Cataloging-in-Publication Data

Covington, Vicki.
Night ride home / Vicki Covington.
p.   cm.
I. Title.
PS3553.0883N5   1992
813'.54—dc20   92-15907
                                        CIP

ISBN: 0-671-74345-7

Acknowledgments

Special thanks to my editor, George Hodgman; to Dr. William Hull and Samford University; to the Birmingham Public Library's Southern Collection; to the work of Jean Patterson Bible and Kathy Kahn; to Ouida Kinzey, Ron Bethard, Raymond and Myrtle Burton, Jack Marsh, Lucile Lovell, Mary Nell Burton, Katherine Marsh, Dennis Covington, Ashley Covington, Laura Covington, Amanda Urban, Nancy Nicholas, and especially to Gene Burton for showing me the place that opened the door.

On the rough wet grass of the back yard my father and mother have spread quilts. We all lie there, my mother, my father, my uncle, my aunt, and I too am lying there. First we were sitting up, then one of us lay down, and then we all lay down, on our stomachs, or on our sides, or on our backs, and they have kept on talking. They are not talking much, and the talk is quiet, of nothing in particular, of nothing at all in particular, of nothing at all. The stars are wide and alive, they seem each like a smile of great sweetness, and they seem very near. All my people are larger bodies than mine, quiet, with voices gentle and meaningless like the voices of sleeping birds. One is an artist, he is living at home. One is a musician, she is living at home. One is my mother who is good to me. One is my father who is good to me. By some chance, here they are, all on this earth; and who shall ever tell the sorrow of being on this earth, lying, on quilts, on the grass, in a summer evening, among the sounds of night. May God bless my people, my uncle, my aunt, my mother, my good father, oh, remember them kindly in their time of trouble; and in the hour of their taking away.

James Agee
A Death in the Family

I

Warrior Road led to the river or to town, depending on which way you were going. Most people never made it down to the dark, muddy waters—maybe brave lovers or drunks or farmboys bent on killing a water moccasin. So for most folks it was just a lane to somebody else's house, a way to go places, a way to go home. From the river, the road led first to farmland where fathers grew vegetables and didn't question happiness. Curiosity took their sons up the road to the mines, where the men arrived from home at dawn in their overalls, carrying safety lanterns and black dinner buckets with biscuits that'd been cut in half and filled with stewed fruit. They'd trudge past the dance hall and cross the creek to uptown camp, where the land rose to herald the mine superintendent's brick home, the sheriff's office, commissary, post office, and school.

A few dusty yards had pigs, dogs, and a goat. Chickens am-bled around the neighborhood like lost vagabonds, squawking with hunger and lack of purpose. They might wander over to Warrior Road and get caught in the headlights of a truck bound for the coke plant farther up the road, or the steel mill beyond, or the city. Warrior Road marked the progress—or perhaps the demise—of the community. For it began with the river, snaked to the farm, and led to the mine, the plant, the mill, and ultimately to the city of Birmingham. The traveler had one respite—Scotty Sandifer's filling station. The Sandifers allowed neighbors to purchase gas on credit, with special discounts for miners who'd fallen prey to bad fortune—a lost leg, a bad lung. Condoms were free on holidays that didn't involve Jesus. Nehis were a given. And Grace Sandifer kept a supply of Hershey bars in the icebox under the air compressor to give to lactating mothers or screaming children distraught with breast weaning or summer's blistering heat.

In the afternoons, Scotty and his hunting buddies sat on crates behind the red brick establishment, where the cornfield beyond lay in splendid harvest. They'd shoot skeet, tossing the clay pigeons up against the blue sky dome, then fire and yelp like boys whenever they hit their mark. Overturning the Nehi crates, Scotty made barstools where they all drank beer until the sky turned orange, then indigo, as a crescent moon rose over Warrior Road.

For Keller Hayes, the Sandifers' station was not a roadside stop but a final destination.

Laura, Scotty's daughter, stood beside the concrete island in front of the station, pumping gas. Her cropped hair fit like a light-colored tam. She wore green workpants gathered at the waist by a belt, and a mustard jacket. Keller had loved her the first time he realized she wasn't a boy.

"Ethyl, regular, or benzol?" she asked, laying her hand over his. She knelt beside Keller's dark-blue Studebaker. Scotty, her father, sat on a crate beside the station, and Laura peered over at him with hooded eyes, like a convict escaping the law.

Keller reasoned that Scotty's hate for him was rooted in the fact that he was a miner's son—as if Scotty had room for vanity, sitting on crates and drinking all day behind his family business while his daughter pumped gas. Yet the very sight of him—his tiny, muscled body—caused Keller to quicken. Scotty was mean when he was drunk, and Keller was, in the end, scared of him.

"Mother needs to talk to you," Laura told Keller.

"Where is she?"

"Inside," she said, gesturing to the brick station.

Keller hopped from the Studebaker and pumped his own gas while Laura washed his windshield. Scotty moved closer, close enough for Keller to smell the liquor.

"Hello, Mr. Sandifer," he said.

Leaning against a gas pump, Scotty smiled, his blue eyes staring haughtily. He was wearing a green baseball cap and jeans, and holding a rifle, the barrel pointing toward the earth. He hadn't always hated Keller. In the early days of Keller's friendship with the Sandifers, the boy had spent his afternoons at the station, helping pump gas after school. Scotty had even taken Keller hunting over in Praco. They'd hit quail. But when it became clear that Keller was falling in love with Laura, Scotty grew distant, then surly, then mean.

Now Keller stood pumping gas, trying to avoid Scotty's eyes. Scotty tossed a clay pigeon disk in the air and fired, then adjusted his baseball cap. Hissing appreciatively like he'd just witnessed a deer crossing Warrior Road, he reloaded, and for a moment Keller feared he might fire at passing cars. But instead he turned back to face the cornfield behind the station, where the sun had fallen below the horizon, leaving crimson stains in its wake. Keller wanted to ask him something but he didn't know what. An ordinary fistfight, a black eye, a decent scrambling in the dirt would be just fine, but this silence was like fighting wordlessly with a woman.

After he'd finished pumping the gas, he went inside.

Grace Sandifer sat on a red stool behind the cash register. Beside her, the air compressor made an exhausted noise. She rose and took Keller's hand in hers. Grace had blond hair, cut short, like her daughter's. She was strangely attractive, but with one hazel-colored wandering eye and the other one stationary, and blue like Scotty's.

"I was going to come see you and your mama and daddy," she said to Keller. "We've changed the wedding plans." She moved the clay pigeons—Scotty's skeet-shooting devices—to the far side of the cash register, leaning over the counter. Keller tried to look into Grace's steady blue eye, but his instinct was to follow the roving hazel-colored one that surveyed Warrior Road.

"Scotty's drinking," Grace said as if this were news.

Keller nodded. "Yes, ma'am, I know."

"I've talked it over with Brother O'Flynn and he agrees. Rather than tomorrow, we're going to have the wedding on Sunday afternoon directly after preaching, if that's all right with you and your folks."

Laura came in, pulled off her gloves, and began eating a Hershey bar beside the old laundry heater. She smiled. Standing in the light of late afternoon, she raised an eyebrow in criminal charm. He didn't yet know what lay under her boylike façade, but he wanted whatever it was.

Keller looked at the green drink box, hoping Grace was going to offer him a free Nehi like she always did. He moved closer to the heater to warm his hands.

"We'll all just move on over to Sister's house for the ceremony. Scotty never shows his face anywhere on Sundays, but just in case, we'll all be up at Sister's," Grace went on. "Supposing there is trouble, we don't want Scotty burning the sanctuary," Grace said flatly, without a trace of apology or fear. Keller knew he was in for a good life. Girls always turned out like their mothers.

"So, it's going to be at Sister's," she affirmed as she stacked quarters in piles of four.

"You mean Lila's?" Keller clarified.

"Over on the crest. You know where she lives, don't you?"

"Yes, ma'am," Keller said, studying Grace's beige work-clothes. Laura and her mother were always dressed like boys.

"Now, we've taken care of everything—the flowers and the food and all that," Grace went on, brushing dust from the counter.

"Dad's paying the preacher," Keller said.

A car turned in to the station, causing headlights to penetrate the smoke and dust.

"We're closed," Grace called from the brick station where she sat on her red stool, counting change. But Keller knew she didn't mean it. The station's hours were hardly fixed.

Grace leaned forward, and momentarily the hazel roving eye worked along with the blue one, causing her to stare squarely into Keller's face. "You need anything besides gas today?" she asked, which meant cigarets or condoms, although Keller knew she meant only the former in his case.

"No, ma'am."

"Don't forget your Nehi," she said, gesturing to the green drink box, and went outside to wait on the customer whom she'd just informed that the station was closed.

Laura took off her man's gloves and held both of Keller's hands inside her palms. She leaned over the counter, and her blue eyes unabashedly searched his face as she kissed him. She always did it this way, like a scientist studying something precise yet distant.

After it was over, she backed away and tilted her head to the side, causing her hair to fall over one ear. She never said a word, just smiled.

"I love you," he told her.

"I know that," she replied, putting her gloves back on. "I love you, too."

Glancing down at Grace's business ledger, he read familiar names of neighbors who'd charged gas that day. Laura often didn't know the name of the customer and, rather than asking, would write *preacher in brown Ford*, or *old lady in Chrysler*—or, Keller noted here on this afternoon's ledger, *nigger in red pickup*.

"See that?" she said, gesturing to the column that read *mer-*

chandise rather than *gas, oil,* or *tires.* "Do you know what that means?"

"No," he said.

"Rubbers."

"I've got some," he told her.

She smiled. "But not till Sunday."

"I can wait."

She raised her chin.

"You're not worried over Daddy, are you?"

"No," he lied, turning to face Warrior Road, where Grace was leaning over into an old pickup, talking to the customer whose tank she'd just filled. He imagined the person inside the cab trying to decide which eye to look in—the wandering one or the one standing still. She waved goodbye to the people in the truck, turned and walked back toward the station, carrying an oily rag in hand.

Keller got a grape Nehi from the drink box and looked at his watch. He was supposed to pick his daddy up at the mine. The shift was over at three-thirty, but because his daddy was a foreman, he always lingered at the bathhouse and mine until sunset. He thanked Grace for the Nehi and told Laura he'd see her later in the evening. Just as he stepped back out into the winter cold, he heard Scotty fire his rifle.

Standing on the concrete island, Scotty smiled languidly at Keller. "Shooting skeet," Scotty said. "Practicing," he added, giving Keller a piece of his blue eyes. "Got to have a perfect mark," he went on. "Wedding day," he said, his thin lips bending to smile.

"Scotty, go on," Grace said. She was standing behind Keller.

"Now, I'm just letting the boy know where all the hunting's gonna be this weekend. Some good game," he said. "A fine season, pretty boy. Now, give me one of those Clark Gable smiles of yours." Scotty pulled his green baseball cap over his eyes like a kid in the dugout, killing time.

Keller jammed his hands into his pockets.

Reloading his rifle, Scotty glanced up. "Nice weekend for hunting, ain't it?" he asked Keller.

"Yes, sir."

"Want to hit quail over in Praco?" Scotty asked, grinning.

"No, sir."

"And why's that?" he asked, his snake-thin lips alive as he reached down to pick up his amber beer bottle. He took a sip.

"Getting married," Keller answered unwaveringly.

"Marrying who?" Scotty asked, taking another sip of beer.

Keller looked away. He wanted to pin Scotty's hard body to the earth, the way you might seize a steer for the branding iron. He'd once watched his own father almost kill a superintendent with his bare hands. The man had beat a striking miner in the presence of the miner's daughter. It was, for Keller, a good memory.

Now Keller stood beside the gas pump and fumbled for a cigaret, digging his boots into the slag and mud that surrounded the concrete island, not wanting to formally sever the possibility of civility with his future father-in-law.

Scotty tipped the green baseball cap to Keller. "You come back now, pretty boy. We appreciate your business, don't we, Dancer?" he asked Grace. Keller had heard him call her this before. He had nicknames for everybody when he was drunk. "Don't we, babycakes?" he called to Laura, who had begun tinkering with an engine on the side of the station, under the water oak.

Keller drove back down Warrior Road, furiously smoking a Lucky. The winter sun bent westward, causing the shadows of tall trees to darken the yards alongside the road. A few homes burned wood, and the smoke rose from the chimneys, gusting gray against the indigo sky.

His own neighborhood, Sweetgum Flat, lay to the north of Warrior Road. Unlike the places where they'd lived in Kentucky and West Virginia, the Alabama camps were located apart from the mines. Sweetgum Flat was a series of company houses, lined in rows facing an alley with outhouses. Each home had a tiny garden for growing corn, okra, tomatoes, and beans. Big washtubs held dirt in winter, plants in summer. Tire swings hung from oak trees. Crepe myrtle kissed the sides of houses where, on spring mornings, women scrubbed the whitewash with a mop to erase coal dust.

He parked beside the dormant garden in his own yard and honked for his mother, Tess. She liked going to the mine. Tess tossed her long, wild honey-colored hair to one side and ran to the car, her shawl flapping in the wind like wings.

Keller felt his mother was crazy. She was a performer. She played the mandolin, banjo, and piano. Her voice had carried them all over Kentucky and West Virginia. She had sung in rollicking churches where grown men and women wailed like animals just coming into season and children crawled the aisles on all fours, naively drunk on the crooked spectacle. In fact, his father had met her at a revival over in Wegra, Alabama. They'd married and moved to Praco, where Keller was born. When they boarded the train for Kentucky, Tess carried her musical instruments and her revival dress, a white eyelet with pearl buttons that, along with song, transformed her wild nature into tranquil purity. She worked a deal with the pastor so that a piece of the offering went to pay those who served the Lord with song—meaning her. In this way, her family secretly rose above the clacker system. Tess dropped pennies into a cup she kept in the cubbyhole kitchen that overlooked the Kentucky hills, where the miners, in their kerosene lamplit hats, could be seen scurrying like fireflies in and out of the mines. Years later, when they came back to Alabama, she had a nest egg cushioned in the folds of her revival dress and big plans to hit the churches along Warrior Road where Sweetgum Flat lay to one side like ripe fruit. The first thing she did was look for a car. She wanted to buy the family a tan-colored 1935 roadster convertible complete with wooden steering wheel, rumble seat, and fashionable two tires on the front body. But since she couldn't afford it, she settled for a used Studebaker, and that's what Keller was driving this afternoon.

——

Leaving the neighborhood, Keller and Tess drove up Pinegar Hill in the direction of the No. 3.

"They changed the wedding," he said, lighting a Lucky.

Tess turned. "What?"

He glanced in the mirror, brushing his fingers over his brown hair, making it go to the right side. "Sunday, instead of Saturday. At their Aunt Lila's place rather than the church," he told her.

Tess clutched her pocketbook. He knew she'd do this. She always clutched her pocketbook when she was mad.

"Well," she said, getting a tissue from her pocketbook and blowing her nose, "I guess I'm the last to know." The thin, colorful bracelets on her wrists clinked together when she moved her hands.

"Scotty's drinking," he said.

"The bastard," she replied.

"You know, they're afraid he'll mess things up."

"And he would."

"So you need to tell everybody it's been moved," he said.

"I'd like to blow his brains to Birmingham and back," she said.

"If he doesn't blow yours first," he said and examined, in the mirror, a tiny scab on his neck from shaving.

Tess began putting clasps in her hair. She had lots of clasps at home, shaped like all kinds of animals. She had duck, flamingo, and bear cub clasps. She said they were from Spain. He didn't know where she'd gotten them or why she wore them, but Laura and the other girls he'd dated said his mother had class.

They drove past the white Baptist church where Tess sometimes sang when she wasn't working the Holiness, where they liked snakes and spoke in tongues. The people in the new, staid sanctuaries were richer, but the money often flowed more freely from the poor, who lost their minds over her voice and gave their last coins. She felt, she said, less guilty in the rich churches.

They passed the cemetery, and came to the mine. The coal shaft's being near the graveyard was fitting, Tess had said over and over, almost every time they went by. But she didn't say anything today. Keller knew she was still fuming over Scotty Sandifer. She hated him.

Keller parked the Studebaker by the fence where the loan shark stood like a big animal, nursing a cigar. Behind him, coal fell from the big tipple to the flatcars below. Keller watched men stream from the hole in the earth to the brick bathhouse. They came out the other door, clean and strong as horses.

Ben Ray emerged from the bathhouse, wearing his hard hat and jeans. He was growing a beard.

Keller hopped from the car, moving to the passenger side so that Ben Ray could drive. Ben Ray reached over Tess to pop Keller affectionately on the knee. "One more day of civilian life," he said to Keller, referring to the wedding.

"Two more days," he said.

Ben Ray stroked his beard.

"Did you hear him?" Tess asked, looking up at Ben Ray. "They had to move the wedding till Sunday because Scotty Sandifer's ass is on his shoulders."

Keller smiled. Evening was falling teal-blue. A thin coppery band of sunset painted the sky's edge. For as long as he could remember, he'd made this night ride home with his parents. The sulphur scent of the scrap hill this time of day mixed with Ben Ray's after-shave. He was getting married on Sunday. He hung an arm out the window.

"Last night ride home," he said quietly.

Tess didn't hear him. She was studying Ben Ray's handsome face with accusatory surveillance. "You having an affair?" she asked Ben Ray.

"You just say that when I'm looking good," he replied.

"Men who grow beards at forty got something up their sleeve," she said and paused a moment. "Well," she said. "Are you?"

"If only," he said, running his hand down his neck to where the dark chest hairs grew up over his collar.

When they passed Bolivia Ivey's shack, they all stared. Bolivia was the newest of the camp whores, a smallish girl with Indian-looking braids and wobbly legs, now pregnant. All the women were curious about her, especially since she'd started showing.

This evening, she sat on her porch steps, holding a calico cat, wearing a dingy gray overcoat and an oddly contrasting bright yellow broomstick skirt. She'd moved to Sweetgum Flat with her daddy only a year ago, and he'd been immediately killed in the No. 3 mine. Keller looked at her dark braids and skinny body with the basketball belly. She was supposedly a Melungeon from Tennessee. The Melungeons were believed to be part Indian, or maybe from Portugal, though the latest theory was that they were Jewish, Mediterranean-bred.

Bolivia waved, and the cat leapt from her arms in one perfect arc.

"Is that who you think I'm sleeping with?" Ben Ray asked Tess affectionately.

Keller looked away. The girl was disturbing to him, the way she lived all alone with the cats. Some people said she was a witch. He'd been with her once last spring, and he wasn't allowing himself to believe the baby might be his. It could be anybody's, he reasoned.

Ben Ray turned in to the dirt yard that held their home. They all stopped to look at the garden of turnip greens, and while they were standing there, Keller saw Bolivia coming down the road, holding a basket of eggs. Ben Ray took his miner's cap from his head in greeting, and Tess's face grew bright with curiosity.

"I'm going back to see Laura," Keller said.

"Be home for supper," Tess replied, her eyes fixed on Bolivia.

Keller spun from the yard, causing dust to fly. But in the rearview mirror, he saw his mother talking to her, accepting the basket of eggs, and he knew she was asking her in for dinner.

Women were a mysterious lot, Bolivia felt. Knowing their husbands so intimately—their spines, earlobes, and lips—she studied the wives curiously as they passed by, toting groceries from the commissary, and speculated what kind of lover each might be. She didn't ask for money. But since the accident had killed her daddy, all the miners were intent on paying. Most gave company clacker, which bought food at the commissary. Occasionally somebody dropped a real nickel in the metal cup on the table. When she realized she was carrying a baby, she had quit love altogether and relied on the commissary owner, who gave her free food. Her friend Charles—the scrap iron man, who was in love with her—donated other provisions. She wondered how long the company would allow her to live in her daddy's house now that he was dead.

Ben Ray Hayes had never visited her, except to deliver the

news that her daddy was dead. She liked Tess, his wife. When Tess sang in the church on the hillside above Sweetgum Flat, her voice carried like birdsong, all over the hollow.

Since she'd never had Ben Ray, Bolivia imagined Tess a good and earthy lover. And never having slept with Ben Ray also gave Bolivia reason to feel that her friendship with Tess was uncontaminated. She hardly knew Tess, yet she loved the sight of her—those white revival dresses and the funny things she wore in her hair. In spring, she'd wear a gardenia. During winter, it might be a spray of dried hydrangea secured with a tortoiseshell clasp, or one of her animal figures.

Now, as she followed Tess up the wooden steps to her house, Bolivia studied Tess's hair, left, this night, to its own devices. It fell over her substantial shoulders. Tess wasn't fleshy, just hearty and strong, like a carpenter had built her body well.

Bolivia stood at the door, taking in the Hayeses' place. The walls were freshly painted, the same color as the eggshells in Bolivia's basket. Tess's drapes were lightweight and ivory rather than olive drab. The red-hot coals in the fireplace cast a warmth over the entire room. Beside the table was a modest buffet where clay pots painted a rainbow of colors held sprigs of magnolia leaves. And there was a piano. It was hard to believe this was a company house.

"Where's your cat?" Tess asked, taking Bolivia's old gray coat and staring at her stomach.

"I have five cats," Bolivia told her. "They're at home. They don't like the cold."

"You were holding the calico when we passed earlier," Tess said.

Bolivia shrugged, tried to smile. The men hated her cats, which often crawled over their naked bodies, trying to interrupt the lovemaking.

Ben Ray threw some heart of pine into the fire, causing it to spit and rise in an orange blaze. He turned to Bolivia and smiled sweetly like a father might. Bolivia believed Ben Ray was the most handsome man in Sweetgum Flat, but maybe, she reasoned, that was only because she hadn't had him and therefore he still carried some mystery. And he'd come to her that day with the news of her daddy, his brown eyes full of the news.

"You looking forward to the wedding?" she asked him, standing to warm her hands by the fire. He stoked it, causing it to glow more brightly. He was wearing jeans and growing a beard.

"I hear they've moved it on account of Scotty Sandifer," Ben Ray said.

"He talks big, but he's harmless," Bolivia said.

"You know him?" Ben Ray asked, turning to her. He smiled, stroking the brown whiskers on his cheeks.

"Yes," she said, hoping he wouldn't embarrass himself by asking her how she knew him. He didn't.

Tess, standing in the doorway to the kitchen beside her rainbow-colored clay pots, was now wearing an apron. It had turquoise rickrack. She looked beautiful in the firelight.

"All we got is pinto beans and bread," Tess apologized, her eyes still fixed on Bolivia's pregnant belly. "Commissary didn't open today."

"Mr. Graham's wife's very sick, that's why he didn't open," Bolivia said. She knew absolutely everything that went on. She could fill a newspaper with what she knew. The men always talked while they prepared to leave, putting on boots, combing their hair at her mirror.

"What's wrong with Graham's wife?" Tess asked, reaching into the buffet drawer for forks and spoons. She set the table.

"Her joints," Bolivia said. "I told him to rub turpentine."

Ben Ray smiled at her. She could see her reflection in his brown eyes, and he held her gaze.

"Can I help you with dinner?" she asked Tess, breaking with his eyes.

Tess was lost in thought, standing in her tiny eating nook, her hair going in all directions. Bolivia fought the impulse to touch it.

"Keller won't be back in time for dinner," Tess said. "He's out with Laura," she clarified.

Bolivia knew Laura Sandifer. She looked like a boy.

"Yes," Tess answered her earlier question. "You can help."

Tess followed her to the kitchen—a replica of Bolivia's own tiny cooking place. A narrow space, the size of a butler's pantry, holding a stove, potbellied heater, and icebox on one side, and ceiling-to-floor shelves on the other. Rather than dry goods, Tess's shelves were lined with an assortment of musical instruments, toy animals, and painted figurines. Curious, Bolivia picked up the elephant, giraffe, plaster-of-paris bluebirds, and harmonica.

"Those are my toys," Tess said, holding a wooden ladle in her hand and staring into the pot of pinto beans. Her back was to Bolivia.

"Where did you get your toys?" Bolivia asked, wondering where Tess kept her sugar, meal, and canned goods.

"Church folks," Tess answered. She turned. "They pay me, you know, for singing."

Bolivia nodded.

"You ought to come on up sometime," she said, meaning, Bolivia knew, to the colored church up the snaking road.

"I've heard you sing," Bolivia said.

"Oh?" Tess turned once more from the pinto beans.

"Your voice carries all over the holler."

Tess put down her wooden spoon. "Honey, that baby's ready to be born," she said, shaking her head, running her hands up and down Bolivia's arms. Bolivia felt the baby kicking, its legs up in her throat and its head bearing down hard between her legs. Tess traced her finger over the spherical flesh as if studying a globe.

"Have you seen a doctor?" Tess asked, turning back to the pot of pinto beans.

"No, ma'am."

Tess turned, tossing her amber hair back. "Don't call me *ma'am*," she said. "I'm not that old."

Bolivia stood still and didn't say anything.

"We have milk," Tess said. "Can you get it from the icebox?"

At the table, Bolivia poured three glasses while Tess spooned beans onto each brown plate. In the family room, Ben Ray sat on the stone hearth, warming his back and reading a newspaper. She knew he was a day foreman. He didn't cough, though.

"You always worked the mines?" she asked him, while they ate. She was directly opposite him at the small wooden table.

" 'Fraid so," Ben Ray answered. He was reading *Life*. Bolivia had seen the magazine at the commissary. Mr. Graham read it. "Convention in Detroit," Ben Ray said and moved the magazine over so the women might see. John Lewis had called off the big strike last month. Bolivia knew this from the miners who visited her.

"He needs to get rid of this sister of his," Ben Ray said and took a big bite of beans. Bolivia looked at the photograph under the headline. In the picture, John Lewis's daughter, Kathryn, was sitting in a fancy chair. She was, Bolivia noted, very fat.

"She's opposed to U.S. war participation," Ben Ray said to Bolivia.

Bolivia studied his eyes. They reminded her of chocolate after you melt the butter in to make icing.

"We're not in the war," Tess said.

"We will be," Ben Ray said. "Look at them silk socks," he said to Tess, gesturing to Denny Lewis, the brother, who sat cross-legged next to fat Kathryn, his pin-striped-suit trouser legs rising to reveal sleek socks. In the photograph on the opposite page, the Lewis faction was glumly seated as union president Murray called for an affirmative vote on a resolution backing the administration's foreign policy, while Denny Lewis was indifferently reading a newspaper.

They ate in silence. The pinto beans and bread tasted good. Ben Ray thumbed through the magazine the way men do while they eat. He stopped at an ad that read "Defense News Warns Motorists—Find Out, How's Your Oil Filter?" A man in a filling station uniform was holding up a stick. "Save oil for defense," the ad read. "Let a Fram dealer test your oil with Fram Master Dip-stick."

"I wonder if Scotty Sandifer has those," Ben Ray mused.

"He's not a *Fram* dealer," Tess replied. "Whatever the hell a Fram dealer is." She paused. "Son of a bitch," she said.

Bolivia looked at her, then at Ben Ray, then picked up her fork and ate some more beans.

"Scotty Sandifer don't think Keller's good enough for his daughter," Ben Ray told her. "It makes Tess spit nails." He smiled.

Bolivia shifted her weight in the chair. She had to pee. The baby was pressing on her bladder. The room was growing cold, the firewood stack wearing thin beside Ben Ray's newspaper on the hearth. Soon, Tess went to the bedroom, returning with old overcoats that smelled of lavender. Tess draped one over Bolivia and kept the other for herself.

After dinner, Bolivia washed the dishes. Tess let her.

Ben Ray got more firewood. Tess played the mandolin. Over the sofa was a framed photograph of Keller. Bolivia studied it. She'd been with him shortly after her daddy died. Guilt and regret swept her. She was certain Keller was the father of the baby, and she hated herself for being in his house, carrying this sordid secret in front of his mother.

"He's handsome, isn't he?" Tess asked.

"Yes," she said. "He is handsome."

"Everybody thinks he looks like Clark Gable," Tess said.

Bolivia agreed. He did.

"The wedding's been moved," Tess said, "to Sunday, at Lila Green's house. You're coming, aren't you?"

Bolivia shrugged. "I guess so," she replied, stunned with the sudden invitation. "Where does Lila Green live?"

"On the crest," Tess told her. "But don't worry. You can ride with us."

"All right," she said, wondering what had possessed Tess Hayes to strike up this unlikely familiarity. It was as if she knew the truth, but of course she didn't. Bolivia didn't know how to refuse the invitation.

When it was time to leave, Ben Ray helped her into her coat

and walked her home. On the way, they smoked his Chester-fields.

The time he'd come to tell her that her daddy died was in late spring. Passionflower grew along the stone wall separating her yard from the creek that lay in the heart of Sweetgum Flat. She'd picked blackberries that day, and her fingers were stained purple. She was sitting on the porch with her cats underfoot, waiting for sunset to come before making a cobbler. The sulphur stench from where the scrap hill was burning in spontaneous combustion carried itself all over the hollow, seeping into her very being. Ben Ray Hayes arrived when the afternoon shadows were beginning to get lost in the red light of falling sun. His tears had made gulleys through the charcoal-colored dust on his face, tracks of anguish she recognized immediately. Men had been dying all her life. Ben Ray's boy, Keller, was alongside, kicking pebbles in her dusty yard and trying to ignore the crazy goose who fussed at his shins. Ben Ray told her that her daddy was dead. Keller knelt to pet her cat and, glancing up, caught her eye. She felt sorry for him having to see his daddy cry like this. A week later, the boy came to her place at dawn and made love to her in the salmon light of early morning, kneading her flesh gently like a woman learning to make bread.

$\mathbf{T}$he Sandifers lived in an old place behind the football stadium that the WPA had built. It was two-story, painted white. Keller parked in the yard and spotted Scotty in the porch swing under the sharp light of the hanging bulb, the drop cord dangling beside his face. He was wearing the green baseball cap, his hallmark. He'd played baseball before the liquor took him, according to Laura. His parents were from England, dancers. Even relaxed in a swing, his body was tense like a sprinter ready to go when the gun fires. Keller hopped from his Studebaker, and as soon as he walked up the steps to the porch, Keller knew that Scotty was quite drunk.

"Well, hell's bells," Scotty said.

He turned to his hunting dogs at his side. "Babycakes gone leave us," he told them, taking a sip of beer. "Babycakes gone get married," he said, rubbing one dog's mangy hair until it rose in rambunctious disarray. He didn't speak directly to Keller but to the dog. "This is pretty boy, who babycakes is marrying."

Scotty picked up his gun, and Keller moved back on the porch toward the banister. The lights from Bessemer glowed in the distance beyond the football stadium. In summer, sunsets only generated thin colors because of the steamy haze and steel smoke from the TCI plant, but now in December, the sky was a dark bruise.

Scotty put his rifle under his arm and lit a cigaret.

"You looking forward to Sunday?" he asked Keller, his blue eyes bright under the porch light.

"Do you mind if I go on inside?" Keller asked him.

Scotty took a long draw on his cigaret, smiling a crooked smile that reminded Keller of Laura. This—the resemblance between them, the light hair, blue eyes, and compact body— disturbed him. Bad blood, his mother might say, runs in a family.

Keller gathered his courage, walked past him, and went inside, where Grace was standing by a pine tree that she'd cut for Christmas. The ceilings were high in the Sandifer home, with crown molding whose green paint was peeling to reveal a gaudy gold. The place had once belonged to a rich family. The rooms were spacious. Big windows let in plenty of light. Arched entrances led to the parlor, where Scotty's hunting gear, guns, and tools stood by the fireplace. During the Depression, the place had been a grocery store, and Grace felt at times that neighbors were prowling the family room for canned goods or searching the parlor for sugar.

In the kitchen, Grace struck a match and lit the stove. Keller and Laura stood next to her. It was cold. Keller didn't understand how Scotty could stay on the porch. Maybe being drunk kept you warm. He didn't know; he'd never been drunk. Grace began heating up creamed potatoes and chicken livers that she'd cooked earlier. Keller's gut churned with hunger. Beside Grace's stove, on an old piece of wood, sat Scotty's stuffed pheasant, its red and turquoise feathers bright. Grace occasionally reached over and stroked it as if it were a living being—a cat or a lost, stray pup. Keller had witnessed this before. She might be shelling peas or reading a book, and she'd reach over to touch the dead bird. A rainy day might find her carrying it to the porch, where she'd hold it in her lap and watch the sky. Storms excited her, according to Laura. Grace was known to read too many astronomy books and had a peculiar kind of religion where she didn't take medicine or attend worship. Her overinvolvement with the universe was striking. On certain days, she'd leave the filling station under the care of anybody who came along, even a perfect stranger, so that she could ride over to Bessemer on the pretense of delivering tires for retreading.

"Would you mind keeping the station for me," she'd asked Keller more than once, "while I go to Bessemer for a minute?" Hours later, she'd return with a distant, abstract look in her wandering hazel eye. Keller knew it wasn't an affair. He suspected she'd been at the library all afternoon, reading about stars. He certainly didn't blame Grace for looking into the possibilities of life elsewhere.

The screen door opened, and Scotty came in to the family room. He sipped his beer and moved to the indoor shed parlor. Their house was wide—from kitchen to dining room to family room to parlor, like a huge corridor of space, causing their voices to echo.

Picking up another rifle, Scotty aimed at Keller.

"I don't want no trouble, Scotty," Grace said.

"Well hell's bells, Dancer, I don't either," he said. He squatted beside a toolbox, his baseball cap askew. "Just getting ready for the big hunt," he said.

"Which hunt is *that?*" Laura asked, her hooded eyes growing menacing with challenge. Keller put his hands in his jacket pockets, wishing they'd all just shut up.

"Aw, babycakes," Scotty said. "Don't pull my leg. You know what."

"Scotty, you want to eat?" Grace asked, her hazel eye looking beyond him. The fried chicken livers and creamed potatoes were on one big platter, and she set it down.

"You want to eat with us, hon?" Grace asked Keller.

"No, ma'am."

Opening the old secretary, she fished for something in a cubbyhole and handed him the newspaper clipping announcing the wedding. In the photograph, Laura was wearing her cardigan and baseball-charm necklace. The clipping gave the wedding plans, only the date was now wrong.

Laura took the clipping from her mother and tore it up, dropping bits of paper by Scotty's toolbox. From where he knelt, Scotty looked up at her, moving his eyes up to her workpants, chest, and eyes—like a man taking in a woman.

Laura rolled up the sleeves of her shirt, took off her belt, and rolled it up in her hands. Scotty took a sip of beer, still squatting near the toolbox. "Babycakes got a temper, pretty boy, you know that, don't you?" Scotty asked.

Laura kicked his toolbox over, spilling a wrench, nails, screwdriver, and fishing hooks. Keller backed up toward the door. Grace was moving the food platters over the tabletop like a hostess searching for the best layout.

"I'm leaving," Keller told her.

"You move one foot and I'm killing you," Scotty told him, but kept his eyes on Laura.

Keller put a hand on the table. His heart was going.

Laura curled the belt over her wrist. Her jaw was set. Keller had never seen her like this. He wanted to go home.

"Really," he said to Grace. "Really, I'll just be going, all right?"

Grace's wandering eye scanned the room.

"Scotty, get up," Grace said. "Laura go on upstairs now."

"Pretty boy, you make one move toward that door, and you're dead," Scotty said.

Laura kicked the wrench. It spun under the secretary. "You're an animal," Laura said to Scotty, backing up toward Keller. Just as she reached for Keller's hand, Scotty leapt up from the floor and shoved him against the stucco wall. He didn't hit him, he just held him there pinned against the wall.

"Now," he said, "you don't make a move. Dancer," he said to
Grace, "you just finish putting supper on the table. Babycakes,
you sit in your chair like a good girl. And you, pretty boy, you
just move right over there to that guest chair. Dancer, set a place
for pretty boy right beside babycakes."

Scotty backed away, took off his baseball cap, then knelt to
retrieve the wrench from under the secretary and placed it on
the dinner table by his fork. Keller sat beside Laura. Grace
spooned creamed potatoes and chicken livers onto Scotty's plate,
then Laura's, then Keller's.

"Want some milk, honey?" she asked Keller, wiping her
hands on her apron. Her good eye was solid as a blue marble.

"Yes, ma'am," he said. Laura began eating. How could she
have an appetite, he wondered, then understood that it was
sheer defiance, perfected over the years.

Grace put four glasses of milk on the table, sat down, and
started eating. Scotty sipped beer from the amber bottle and
leisurely smoked a cigaret, flicking ashes into a jar lid. He leaned
forward, studying Laura.

"All right, pretty boy," he said.

Keller took a bite of chicken livers and avoided his eyes.

"Now, let's talk about babycakes," Scotty went on, turning
the wrench over on the table.

Grace got up and returned to the table with a salt shaker.
"Need any, hon?" she asked Keller.

"No, ma'am."

"All right," Scotty said, smushing his cigaret butt into the jar
lid and leaning forward, slapping his green cap on the table, his
eyes remarkably bright for a drunk man.

"Now, you take babycakes here. A good kid, wouldn't you
say, Grace? A damn good kid. Look at that face."

Laura was eating, oblivious to Scotty. But Keller saw the rash
crawling up her neck, all the way to where the tips of her hair
brushed her ears. The rash took her skin whenever she was
angry or aroused. It happened whenever he kissed her.

"Now, pretty boy, you tell me just what it is that you like
about her."

Keller put his fork down.

"Come on, now, we're all family. Don't be bashful."

"The planets are lining up," Grace said, looking out the window.

"And what does that have to do with the price of rice?" Scotty asked her, taking his fork and moving the food around on his plate. Outside, his hunting dogs barked.

"You can see Polaris," Grace went on, staring wistfully through the window at the stars.

Scotty moved his potatoes to one side of his plate without looking down at what he was doing, staring instead at Grace.

"The moon's such a jealous creature. Takes up the sky with its light."

"You're crazier than a nigger on a Saturday night," he said.

Grace sighed. Her wandering eye lit on Keller.

The semi-dark room grew suddenly brighter. Keller looked out the window and saw that the lights at the football stadium had been turned on. "Who's playing?" he asked nobody in particular. Nobody responded. "Nice night for a game," he said.

"Now, pretty boy, that's what I call smart. That's downright *inti*lectual," Scotty said, waving his fork. You ought to go to college. You ought to go down to Tuscaloosa and learn to be a scientist, don't you think so, Grace?"

Scotty leaned over the table.

"Boy, I crushed your cigarets a while ago when I hugged you," Scotty said, looking Keller squarely in the eyes. "That wasn't manly of me, and I offer you this in apology, not your brand I realize," he said, handing Keller a Pall Mall.

Keller took the cigaret and accepted Scotty's lit match.

He smoked, relieved not to have to eat.

Scotty pushed the jar lid over to him. "You always smoked Luckies?" Scotty asked him.

"Yes, sir."

"Hmmm," Scotty said, surveying his Pall Mall.

They smoked in silence. Cars were beginning to park alongside the stadium road. The stadium lights lit the night sky, causing the stars to disappear. The Sandifer house was quiet. Laura reached under the table and took Keller's free hand. He wished she wouldn't do this.

"Now, pretty boy," Scotty said, shaking his head. "There's one thing I got to ask you. Now, babycakes, don't you take this wrong," he said, pointing his cigaret at Laura. He took a big draw and blew smoke up, musing. "You've witnessed here, this evening, babycake's temper. Just a tad of it." Scotty stood, picked up the wrench and held it in Keller's face. "Babycakes is on fire, boy. You know that?"

Keller didn't say anything and pulled his hand from Laura's.

"Babycakes reminds me of a wild horse."

Grace got up from the table, shoved her chair under it, and left the room.

"Babycakes got that boy's haircut. You like that, don't you, pretty boy?"

Laura wiped her lips with the back of her hand. Keller saw that the rash had taken her face. She got up, her eyes raw. She never cried. It amazed him.

"Yes, sir." Scotty chuckled. "Clark Gable here likes that."

"Shut up, Daddy," Laura said, batting at his hands.

"Don't bite the hand that feeds you, babycakes," he said to her, still looking at Keller. "Babycakes don't have good sense, pretty boy. You gone have to teach her a thing or two since you so smart."

"Stop it!" Laura screamed.

Scotty turned his chair around, straddling it like a cowboy, ignoring her.

"You like those workclothes, too, don't you?" Scotty asked him.

Keller got up.

"Don't get all upset, boy. It's nothing to feel sorry over. You can't help it you like girls who act like boys. There's even a name for pretty boys like you, ain't there?"

Keller felt the adrenaline pumping. He turned his chair over and grabbed his jacket from the couch.

"Don't move another inch, pretty boy, or you're dead," Scotty said evenly.

"Kill me," Keller yelled at him. "Go on. Shoot. Shoot me," he said, and went out the door.

Scotty overtook him on the porch, wrestled him to the ground, and struggled to hold him down. It was then that Keller realized the impotence of a drunk man and gingerly tossed him aside, into the bushes beside the porch.

Keller ran to the Studebaker, jumped in, and revved the engine. He saw Scotty running toward the car, and before he could shift into reverse, Scotty had jumped on the hood. Keller backed up, ignoring Scotty's hands beating against the windshield. He took the back alley to avoid the stadium traffic, and Scotty leapt from the Studebaker. Through his rearview mirror, Keller saw him land on his stomach, then hop up like a sprinter.

Keller drove home under the crescent moon, making the Studebaker rise to fast speed, allowing the cold night wind to get his face. He was wearing a blue wool cap. When he turned off Warrior Road into his neighborhood, he saw Scotty's truck behind him. He immediately accelerated, fearing the worst. Did Scotty have a gun? Braking, Keller screeched into his own yard, causing dust to fly. But instead of parking alongside, Scotty's truck drove past and, at the end of the road where the stone wall lined the creek, slowed to a snail's pace by Bolivia's house.

Scotty didn't like Bolivia's cats. Scenting the telltale hunting dogs whose mustiness permeated his jeans and hands, they generally arched their backs in feline disgust. They'd crawl territorially into Bolivia's bony lap, where they slept with ears up, listening for danger.

Bolivia felt that Scotty was undoubtedly the hardest of her visitors to satisfy. Because he wanted something other than her body, his visits were lengthy and laden with a sadness she understood but couldn't remedy. What she appreciated most in men was the simplicity of their needs and desire. Scotty was complicated.

She had thrown an old Indian-print tapestry over the raggedy sofa this particular evening. The junkman had given her the colorful piece of material. Scotty ran his fingers over the design but didn't comment on it. His usual pattern was to talk, brooding over his daughter while he drank moonshine whiskey from the metal cup Bolivia collected clacker in. Bending forward on her sofa so that the green baseball cap hid his eyes, he'd smoke his Pall Malls, brushing the calico cat aside with his boot.

She'd been baking teacakes for his daughter's wedding reception when he arrived, wearing overalls and his filling-station workshirt that had *Sandifer* stitched in red thread over the pocket. His ears were pink from the cold.

"Come in, Mr. Sandifer," she said.

If it'd been any other man and if she hadn't been so pregnant, she would have removed her yellow apron, opening the bedroom door. But instead, since it was Scotty, she emptied the clacker from the metal cup, poured him some whiskey, and prepared for a series of rambling ruminations over a world beyond his grasp—Hitler's maneuverings, the cost of benzol gasoline, baseball, and his daughter.

He searched the room for a saucer to flick his ashes into. "Here," she said, handing him a jar lid. Still wearing her apron, as if she were his wife and not his confidante, she pulled the rocker up. The apron was tied under her breasts to accommodate her belly. The baby's head pressed down on her.

Scotty took the jar lid and flicked ashes. His hands were shaking, and his clothes were dirty.

"You been rolling in the dirt?" she asked.

He didn't answer. It was clear he was upset over something. He smoked silently.

"Can I have a cigaret?" she asked.

He smiled crookedly. He had thin, severe lips. He probably bit like a snake during lovemaking. She'd never met his wife. Since she didn't have a car, there had never been a reason to visit the gas station. What kind of woman loved a man like Scotty Sandifer?

"Have all you want, sugar," he said, tossing her the pack. "Thanks."

He smoked for a few minutes and finally eased into a semblance of feeling at home on her sofa. "I guess you heard my daughter's marrying your neighbor."

"Yes," she said, picking up the calico. The gray tabby and solid black were by the fireplace, gazing suspiciously at Scotty, their ears moving like radar devices.

"What do you think of that family?" he asked, brushing ashes against the jar lid set haphazardly on the tapestry.

"Nice folks," she said.

"You think that boy's worth a dime?"

"Sure," she said, recalling his naive, cradling hands.

"I think he's a useless son of a bitch."

"Maybe that's because he's marrying your daughter?"

His thin lips crept into a grimace. "So you think that's why I think he's a useless son of a bitch?"

"Of course," she said.

He rose, his face flushing in anger. Pacing beside the fireplace, he flicked his cigaret into the hot coals.

"Can you get some more wood from the back?" she asked, "while I put some things up?"

She went to the kitchen and put the bowl of teacake dough into the icebox. Scotty went out the back door to the woodpile.

He returned and tossed a log to the fire, stoking it with his boot, causing a thin orange flame to rise. He lit another Pall Mall, put his hands on his skinny hips. The fur on the cats' backs rose, and they left the hearth in disgust over Scotty's proximity to their favorite resting place. "Oh, Franklin D.," she said, picking up the gray tabby.

Scotty turned to her. "What's that?" he asked.

"This is Franklin D.," she said, stroking the tabby's bristly fur.

"And this is Eleanor, I suppose," he said, gently nudging the black cat with his boot.

Bolivia smiled. "No, *this* is Eleanor," she said, gesturing to the calico. "They're married."

Scotty's smile broke. The blue of his eyes was like water— deep and subject to change. He was drunk. Pointing his cigaret at Bolivia in accusatory fashion, he asked her the same question. "You think that boy's worth a dime?"

"Yes, Mr. Sandifer, I do."

She rocked back and forth, brushing the hooked rug with her bare feet.

"He's a son of a bitch," Scotty repeated.

"Yes, I understand." The snapping of the fresh pine log made the flames leap. Bolivia studied the changing patterns of light. Scotty tossed her the Pall Malls.

"You understand what?" he asked her.

"That you're losing your daughter."

He stood beside the fire. His jaw was moving as if he were chewing tobacco. "I ain't talking about my daughter. I'm talking about that useless son of a bitch."

"Who is marrying your daughter," she reminded.

"I've a mind to kill him."

Bolivia nodded. "And then she'll be yours? You think she'll love you then?"

He squinted, staring at her. "What's all this bullshit of yours, baby? We ain't talking about love. We're talking about killing, you hear me?"

"Killing's sometimes part of love, I reckon. But you're not going to kill anybody, Mr. Sandifer. You're just passing through the fire, that's all."

He looked at her.

"She's your baby, and she's leaving you. And there's not one thing you can do, so you might as well quit drinking yourself crazy over it."

"Let me tell you one thing, baby. Now, let's get this clear," he said. "You talking like I'm in on this thing or something. You talking like I'm part of some love affair," he said, almost choking on the words. His hands trembled. "This thing don't involve me."

Bolivia reached over to touch his leg. "Sit down, Mr. Sandifer. You need to just sit down and be quiet."

He sat on the sofa. He was shaking like a leaf.

Bolivia got up from the rocker and sat beside him, taking his hands. They were cold, chapped, and small. "Nobody ever really takes a girl from her daddy. You need to know that. You need to believe that."

He looked at her like she was crazy.

"We ain't talking about me and her. We're talking about *him* and her."

"You're too mad to know what you're talking about," she said.

She went back to the rocker.

"You ever thought about giving up liquor?" she asked him, stroking Eleanor, who'd once again given up making friends with Scotty.

He laughed.

"Well?" she pressed.

He looked at her. "You ever thought about giving up men?"

"I have given them up," she said.

He looked at her belly, then back at the fire.

"Whose baby you carrying?"

She felt the sick feeling—reality—rise in her, but squelched it as she'd learned to do. If he knew the truth, he'd kill everybody in sight, including her.

"I can't quit drinking, baby," he said. "You had a reason to quit men. There's no reason for me to quit drinking."

She looked at how the muscles in his arms rose through the material of his shirt, tensing, never at peace. "What's your wife's name?" she asked.

"Grace."

"Is she pretty?"

Scotty stared at her. She thought it was the first time he'd ever looked her squarely in the eyes. She let him in, offering her entire being vulnerably but not seductively.

He didn't answer her question.

"Is Grace her real name?"

"Yes."

"Grace," Bolivia repeated. "That's a Bible name, isn't it?"

Scotty took off his baseball cap, making his sandy curls come alive. He'd taken off his boots. His socks were the color of moss.

"Yeah, sugar, grace is biblical."

"Could you get me a Bible?" she asked.

"I don't have one," he said. "Sorry."

Bolivia tossed her cigaret into the flames and bent forward in the rocker, resting her chin in her hands, elbows on knees, so that she was particularly close to Scotty. "Have you ever heard of foot washing?" she asked him.

"Well," he said. "If I'm not mistaken, some beautiful woman was in love with Jesus and washed his feet, and all the men raised holy hell about it."

Bolivia felt goosebumps running all over her flesh.

"I believe she was a whore," Scotty said. He shook his head. "That might not be right, though. Why're you asking, baby?"

"Tess asked me to come to a foot washing at her church on Sunday," she said, wondering if Tess knew this part about the whore. The idea of a colored church carrying on a ritual based on the act of a whore was unusual, but even more unusual was the idea of a white woman like Tess Hayes going into a colored church at all, even if it was to make money singing.

"Do you know Tess?" Bolivia asked.

"Tess who?"

"Keller's mother."

Scotty rose, getting his boots from the hearth. "No," he said.

Bolivia looked at his socks. "You never met her?" she asked incredulously.

"Oh, I know her," he said irritably. "I just don't make it a practice of talking with her."

"You ought to," Bolivia said. "She's like an angel."

"Foot washing." Scotty chuckled.

"Strange to think of going to a foot washing the morning your son's getting married," she said, and the instant she said it, she felt her stomach turn. "I mean the morning after the day your son gets..."

But it was too late. Scotty had turned to her, his eyes mad and bright.

She put her hand to her mouth.

Scotty threw another log on the fire. For an instant, the entire room came alive in amber light. The shadow of Scotty's compact body was silhouetted against the wall. Bolivia stroked the calico's neck, wondering how long Scotty might linger here, keeping her from the unbaked teacakes. But when the fire had grown to a strong, crackling blaze, he put his boots and jacket on, readjusted the baseball cap, and turned to her.

"Fire's going good now, sugar. Ought to keep you warm till bedtime."

His eyes were kinder, and Bolivia wondered if he'd really put it together that the wedding day had been changed. Gathering her up like a bunch of kindling, he cradled her. His chest was hard like stones.

Scotty drove past the Hayeses' place, cautiously braking his mud-colored truck so as to study the house. The square yard, holding a sweetgum tree and fenced dried cornstalks and a woodpile, was unbelievably tiny, the house only a rectangular carbon copy of all the houses around it. He didn't know Ben Ray, the father, personally. He was a miner. Scotty knew how the black coal dust settled along the windowsill of a miner's house. He hated it.

Now, the liquor having worn thin, he felt the emptiness and vulnerability of leaving drunken bliss. Sobriety was like home-sickness. He didn't relish coming off a good drunk. But at the high point of a night's drinking, he transcended the misery of being on the wrong planet. Last fall, he'd gone a day without a drink when he was in bed sick with croup. Grace had given him paregoric to quell the cough, and the euphoria lasted all the way to twilight, which was when he generally got the homesick feeling that caused him to drink. The next morning, he'd awak-ened with no hangover, feeling a bliss so earnest that the sight of a bluebird on Grace's clothesline made him want to cry.

Now, as he drove on past the Hayeses' place, he looked up at the stars, pondering things. The girl Bolivia was different. She wasn't a drunk, but he still felt kin to her. He turned onto Warrior Road but didn't stop at the dark filling station for liquor. He felt an aching for Grace, for her sturdy body in the warm, blue cotton nightshirt that comforted him.

When he got there, though, he found Laura asleep on the sofa in the family room, wearing one of his filling-station shirts that hit her at mid-thigh. Her legs moved. Wondering tenderly what might be chasing her in dreams, he considered throwing a blanket over her or carrying her upstairs, but she wasn't his. Had she ever been? He knelt beside her, resisted the urge to touch the light hair that crisscrossed her brow. Her hands made fists. Even in sleep she was ready to keep him at bay. The idea that she might lay open those palms for a man was unthinkable. She was a baby, a petal.

He banked the fire and kicked his boots into the parlor, where his hunting gear and guns were scattered like toys on the bare hardwood floor. And instead of seeking Grace's loyal flesh, he got beer from the icebox and sat under a yellow sliver of moon, in the cold, with his dogs.

Tess slept with the shades up. Tonight, there was a crescent moon—gold and splendid. A solitary star rested in its bowl. The bed was pushed up against the window. Tess raised herself up on her elbows so she could see the road.

She tried to pray. But God wasn't listening. She figured he was tending to affairs in Europe, where the war was raging. She didn't understand who Hitler was. Roosevelt was like what she recalled of her father—calm, sensible, and big. But these were all foreign affairs. Her baby getting married Sunday was another matter. She knew he was up. The scent of fresh cigaret smoke crept under her closed door. Ben Ray was snoring lightly. She ran her fingers over the brown-bearded edges of his lips. Desire disturbed her now because it wasn't localized like it used to be when she was younger. Rather, it sat in her brain like a puzzled animal.

Gathering her pea-green bathrobe from the sewing machine, where she'd tossed it earlier, she quietly opened the bedroom door, and passing the table where she'd earlier fed Bolivia and Ben Ray, she noticed that Bolivia had left her egg basket.

In the family room, Keller sat on the sofa. His feet were propped on the crate they kept beside the hearth for holding firewood. He was wearing Ben Ray's big wool plaid shirt—red, charcoal, and white squares—over his own clothes.

"Hi, Mom," he said.

"You cold?" she asked. His arms were crossed hard against his chest, drawing Ben Ray's shirt into a wrinkled mass.

"No, ma'am."

"Hungry?"

He smiled. "Sit down," he said, gesturing to the old gray-cushioned mess they called a chair. Drawing hard on his cigaret, he stared at the fire's blue-and-orange light, his Clark Gable face handsome. He didn't look like anybody else in the near or distant family.

Tess nestled her cold feet up under her bathrobe. She fingered the cameo ring that a preacher had given her one Christmas back in Kentucky when her rendition of "Jesu, Joy of Man's Desiring" had brought three dozen miners to the altar, where they'd knelt and cried. She hadn't yet considered this year's holiday. It was three weeks away—unspeakably sad because Keller wouldn't be waking here.

"Will you pack?" she asked him.

"Pack?" He blew a smoke ring.

"Pack your clothes. You know, to move."

He shrugged.

Tess stared at the fire. Nobody knew how to get married. It was life's strangest moment. She knew that the compass that pointed him toward getting married would go haywire overnight. Not that he'd begin lusting after women and things he couldn't have; just that he'd lose his bearings, wondering where to go from there.

"I don't have much to pack," Keller said, tossing his cigaret butt into the fire, where it was instantly lost. Tess studied her cameo—the woman's stoic ivory face.

"You will stay at Lila Green's place for a while?"

"Right," he said.

"And then?"

"Mom, don't worry," he said, leaning forward, stretching his arms and yawning, his brown hair threatening to fall over his eyes.

"I'm not worried, Keller."

He smiled. "You've been great," he said.

She wanted to pursue this. Great? So far? During the wedding plans, meager as they were? All his life, great? She sat quietly to see if he'd say more. He didn't.

And so she again felt she ought to offer him something tangible, like food. "Sure you're not hungry?"

"I snacked," he said.

His brown eyes studied Tess curiously. She waited.

"Why did you invite Bolivia to dinner?" he asked.

Tess smiled and unraveled her legs from under her bathrobe, propping them instead on the crate that Keller was no longer using as a footrest.

"I like her," she replied.

Keller crumpled the empty pack and tossed it to the fire. Leaning forward, he set the ashtray on the crate beside Tess's bare feet.

"What did y'all eat for dinner?" he asked.

"Beans."

"Did she talk?"

Tess looked at him. "Of course she talked."

"About?"

Tess tried to recall. She shrugged. "Just neighborly kinds of things," she said. She hesitated, then added: "I invited her to the wedding. Is that all right?"

"Why did you do that?"

"I don't know," she said and looked at him. Something crossed his face. She recognized it as irritation.

"You think it was wrong to invite her?" she asked.

He rose from the sofa and stood by the fireplace, staring at the embers.

"You want to be friends with her or something?" he pressed.

"Yes, I guess I do. Is that odd?"

"She's a whore," he said.

"She's also a person. She's going to be a mother, Keller."

He didn't say anything. "You don't know, do you," she began, then hesitated, looking down at her cameo ring, "who the father is?"

He turned abruptly from the fire. "How would I know that?"

She shrugged. "I was just curious. Men talk."

"Not as much as women. It could be anybody's, couldn't it?" he went on.

"I suppose so."

Tess looked at his trousers. They were wrinkled, and she remembered the other thing she needed to ask him. "The suit you'll wear at the wedding," she began. "Have you picked it up yet?" He and Ben Ray were borrowing suits from the preacher and his son, who had extra ones. The fits were remarkably identical. God's hand, Tess was certain, was working together with her prayers. He might be tending to the war in Europe, but his partner—the Holy Ghost—was busy tailoring here in Sweet-gum Flat.

"No," Keller said, banking the fire with the heavy iron poker. "But don't worry, I will in the morning. First thing," he said.

"Did you eat with the Sandifers?" she asked him.

"I tried to. Scotty was on the warpath."

"Drunk?"

"Drunk."

"What happened?"

He rolled up his shirtsleeves and looked at the floor. "He was pretty crazy," he said, staring at his boots. "Pretty damn crazy."

"Like what? What did he do?"

Keller looked at her, searching her face as if deciphering what she might be able to absorb. "He came at me."

Tess felt her heart going. She stood up. "What do you mean, came at you?"

"Sit down, Mom." He waved his hand in the direction of her chair.

She sat down.

"He didn't hit me or anything. He just came at me, you know, got up in my face."

"Did he *threaten* you?"

Keller laughed.

"Well, did he?"

"Yes, he threatened me."

"What did he say?"

"Well, he said he'd kill me if I made a move toward the door."

Tess got up and reached for a cigaret even though she didn't smoke. "Keller, I'm going to shoot the bastard! I'm going to hire somebody to kill him, do you hear me? I'm going to hire somebody. I know a lot of people. I know people in *Birmingham*. Now, you know there are plenty of people in Birmingham who'd kill for money."

He laughed again. "Are you going to smoke that cigaret?"

She was holding it like a dart.

"This is not funny," she said, waving the cigaret in his face. "You'll understand this when you have a baby. When some lousy son-of-a-bitching maniac threatens your child, you don't just stand back and watch. Now, I'm serious, baby!" she yelled.

"Mom, please," he said. "You're going to wake Dad up. And it's nothing, O.K.? He's just a sorry drunk, that's all."

"I know that. But he's also mean as a snake. He's going to ruin the wedding, you know that, don't you? He'll find out it's been moved. He's clever."

Keller waved it away. "He won't bother anybody on Sunday. He'll be too weary to move after his usual Saturday night. He's not so bad," Keller said and yawned again, then tapped his pack of Luckies, searching for the last cigaret that had lodged itself against the far corner.

He lit it.

"I'm never going to be able to sleep now," she said.

"Scotty followed me home," he told her. "I think he stopped at Bolivia's place."

"Oh?" Tess said, her skin crawling with the pleasure of gossip.

"Yep."

She readjusted her bathrobe and sat on the edge of the chair. "Well, what do you make of that?" she asked as demurely as possible.

He grinned. "Got your mind off things, didn't it?"

Keller," she said as an idea hit her. "He's not the father, is he?"

"Go to bed, Mom. Get some sleep. You've been great."

"Sure you don't want anything to eat? There's milk. Want some hot milk and sugar?"

"Go to bed, Mom," he said. "You've been great," he repeated and patted her on the shoulder like a father might. She knew, this time, that he meant great in the bigger sense, the grander scheme. She knew it was all that'd be said on the subject, that he was indeed leaving her, that it was sad only for her and not for him.

On Sunday, Bolivia rose at dawn, fixed toast, and tossed bread crusts to the chickadees and juncos in her yard. In winter, the birds were recklessly brave, disregarding her cats. This morning, she fed the leftover beans to the calico and gave the others some bones from the neighbor's trash. She didn't mind rummaging through garbage. It was maternal and instinctual. The cats were depending on her. Now, chasing the crazy goose and scurrying hens, she gathered eggs. The eastern sky was beginning to grow a chalky shade of pink. A rooster crowed. Sunrise was coming. In the alley, women were making first trips to the outhouses before cooking breakfast and going to worship.

She went inside. In her bedroom, she studied her face in the filmy mirror. Her skin was lighter than most Melungeon women, carrying more olive-yellow than cocoa. Tess had flinched when she told Bolivia they were going to a *colored* church. Bolivia knew this was because Tess wasn't quite sure if Bolivia was herself colored.

This morning, she pushed the slop jar under the bed. Her dress lay over the quilt stand. It had belonged to her mother and was solid ivory with yellow, red, and turquoise threads sewn in the bodice. The hem was frayed. Reaching her ankles and shaped like a tent, it fit her bulging body. She dressed. Shoes were going to be a problem. Her flat brown pumps with buckling soles were all she had. Wrapping a shawl over her arms, she went to the porch to wait for Tess.

Bolivia stared at the stone wall where passionflower and honeysuckle grew in summer. Behind it, the creek trickled toward Warrior River. Tess arrived shortly in her family's Studebaker. Leaning over, she opened the passenger-side door for Bolivia. Tess was wearing one of her snow-white dresses. A ginger-colored clasp shaped like a duck secured her long hair in a honey mass over her left ear.

"Hello, sweetie," Tess said to Bolivia, backing the car straight down the road, as if moving in reverse were the natural way to drive. All the way up the snaking hill toward the chapel, she hummed a melody Bolivia vaguely recognized. Bolivia had walked this dusty road hundreds of times to meet various men. In summer, vines and briars threatened to entangle anyone on foot. Buttercups grew amidst the gnarled branches of hardwood trees. Sweetgum balls pricked bare feet. Bolivia craved the passion of this winding road during the warm season. It wasn't that she longed for the hungry men; it was the road itself and the thick heat she wanted just now.

Suddenly, with no warning, Tess rolled down the car window and started singing. Her voice rose—crisp, sweet, yet strong.

"Just practicing," she said to Bolivia, as she smiled, and parked the car beside a maple.

Tess led her in.

Light crisscrossed the tiny foyer, falling in yellow sheets from the windows on either side. Brown men and women sat on the benches alongside the walls, staring at one another.

"This is where we wash feet," Tess explained to Bolivia, readjusting the duck-shaped clasp in her hair. "Come on with me, first," she whispered.

Bolivia followed her up the aisle to the crude wooden cross at the altar, where a figurine of Jesus, half-naked, partially draped in bright skimpy robes, stood on a table beside an offering plate. Tess set her mandolin case down and removed the instrument.

"Now," she said, taking Bolivia's arm gently. "We can go back and do the feet." She led Bolivia back down the aisle. "You ever been here?" she asked.

"A time or two," Bolivia said, averting her eyes upward to the white ceiling.

"They've been waiting for me," Tess whispered, gesturing to the men and women who sat on the benches, wearing the fine-looking clothes that Negroes wore on Sundays. The women smelled of strong fragrances and chewing gum. Some of the older men were humming, nodding their heads as if in a trance. "They love me. They think I'm a healer," she whispered.

When they arrived back in the foyer near the church door, the men rose in unison and went into the sanctuary. A few women stood up and crossed the narrow anteroom to the benches alongside the other wall, sat, and faced the women opposite them.

"The women wash the women; the men the men," Tess whispered and sat Bolivia down at the end of one row of benches. And, setting her mandolin on the floor, she sat directly opposite Bolivia.

A woman on the far end, wearing a rose dress, reached under the bench and pulled a towel from a small wooden trunk. Sprinkling it with liquid from a vial—perfume, Bolivia assumed, the woman passed it up to Tess, who knelt to retrieve a small bucket from under her end of the pew. Pushing her mandolin to one side, she went over to Bolivia and knelt in front of her.

"Take off your shoes, honey," she said softly. "You're just getting your feet washed."

Tess smiled up at Bolivia, whose brown legs were shaking under the frayed hem of her old dress. She felt just like she did when a doctor was tending her. The woman in the rose dress began reading something from the Bible. Bolivia glanced down at her. Her mind was racing with the words—something about Jesus laying aside his garments, taking a towel, and pouring water into a basin. Somebody named Peter got into an argument with Jesus over it, saying that he'd never allow Jesus to wash his feet. She listened hard, but Tess's hands were distracting. Tess rubbed her heels as if polishing stones, on and on, until Bolivia herself came to believe that her worn feet were worth something.

The woman in the rose dress stood up and said, "The servant is not greater than the Lord. If you don't let me wash you, you have no part of me."

Bolivia kept waiting for the part that Scotty had mentioned about the woman washing Jesus's feet, but there was no word of it. Was there another foot-washing story? When Tess was done, she gave Bolivia the towel, sat back down opposite her, and whispered, "Your turn."

Bolivia knelt, and, taking Tess's feet into her hands, touched the skin of another woman for the first time since her mother died.

Afterward, since they weren't staying for the service, they walked back into the sharp morning light. The graveyard beside the chapel was a sprinkling of markers that eased over the east slope of the hill. There were a few lingering remnants of this year's unseasonably warm fall. Red leaves dangled from the big maple tree by the rusty cast-iron bell that nobody ever rang. Bolivia knelt to pick some wild aster and yellow sweet clover.

"My mother cooked with this," she told Tess, crushing the already-dried blossoms. "Smell it."

"Vanilla," Tess said, holding Bolivia's hand as she inhaled the flowers' scent.

They walked past the markers, headed back to the car parked under the red maple, and climbed in. Bolivia glanced up as they began winding down the hill, where summer's tangled undergrowth had died almost completely. When they reached the valley below, Tess stopped the car near the superintendent's home. Bolivia looked at her questioningly. Tess looked straight ahead, gripping the steering wheel. In the pasture behind the superintendent's brick home, a few cows grazed languidly. Tess kept her eyes fixed on the animals.

"I've got to ask you something," she said, reaching up momentarily to adjust the clasp in her hair. She turned to face Bolivia, her green eyes burning like incense. "Have you ever made love to Scotty Sandifer?"

Bolivia looked at her own hands, limp in her lap. They looked soot-stained rather than cocoa. No woman had ever asked her anything like that. The ice was broken, and she felt herself drowning in silent shame.

"The reason I'm asking," Tess began—but Bolivia kept her eyes cast to her lap. "Look at me!" Tess snapped, and Bolivia jumped inwardly and looked up. Tess's eyes were bright, translucent. "—is because I've thought before that he must be a grand lover," she said and smiled.

It was an invitation, Bolivia understood. Tess wanted something she had—knowledge. But in the case of Scotty Sandifer, there was simply nothing to tell. Unable yet to face Tess, Bolivia turned to the window and looked in the direction of the commissary.

"I never had him," she said softly.

"He's never come to your place?" Tess asked.

"Yes, he comes over," Bolivia said, and glanced furtively at her. Tess had the clasp between her teeth, peering into the mirror attached to the car's interior roof.

"And?" Tess pursued.

"He talks."

Tess turned to her, still holding the clasp in her teeth, her eyes searching Bolivia's face. Bolivia knew what she was supposed to say. "He's kissed me," she offered.

Tess's shoulders dropped, causing her snow-white dress to fall against her sturdy chest.

"What," Tess asked, looking languidly, questioningly, at Bolivia's lips, "was that like?" And then before Bolivia could answer, she broke into laughter. "Let me guess," she sang, cranking up the Studebaker once again. "Mean!" she yelled, rolling the windows down, so that the crisp wind bit them both.

Bolivia looked at her.

They wound on along the road, over the railroad tracks, past the creek, the stone wall, Bolivia's place, until they were in front of the Hayeses' home. A wreath garnished with aster, bits of scarlet leaves, nuts, and berries hung precariously on the fencepost. "A little something for the birds," Tess said.

"You made it?" Bolivia asked, getting out of the car.

"Yes."

Tess threw open the door to the house and went in. Bolivia was struck anew with the eggshell walls, rainbow clay pots, the miracle of interior light. Plus, a sprinkle of Christmas ornaments adorned the dinner table where they'd eaten together Friday evening. Ben Ray was dressed in navy-blue pants and red suspenders. Bent over the hearth, he was polishing his boots. A fire was going.

Ben Ray looked up, his brown eyes a question. Bolivia hesitated at the door, knowing she didn't belong here in this home during this hour. Above the mantel, a photograph of Keller carried a reminder of who she was and the multiplicity of reasons she should leave. Tess flung her shawl on the crate beside the sofa.

"Bolivia made teacakes," she told Ben Ray. Glancing up from his boots once more, he smiled at Bolivia. She fingered her skirt, then let her eyes fall to the colorful threads at the bodice. Tess began singing "I'll be loving you, always." Dancing all over the room, without a partner, she was, to Bolivia, the portrait of a drunk. Yet she'd had no liquor. Keller appeared in the doorway from what Bolivia guessed was his bedroom. Upon seeing Bolivia, his Clark Gable face lost its grace and he averted his brown eyes.

He didn't speak.

"Bolivia's here," his mother sang from the kitchen, where she'd gone.

"Hi," Bolivia said quietly.

He nodded politely, then walked over to his father.

Ben Ray rose from polishing his boots, surveying Keller. He adjusted Keller's tie. "Nervous?" he asked.

"No," Keller said. "Just ready to get this all done."

Ben Ray looked at his watch. "I think I should take you on over to Lila Green's place, then come back and get your mother and Bolivia and the food," he said.

"We'll get a ride with Brother O'Flynn," Tess called.

Bolivia walked over to the dinner table, fingering the Christmas ornaments. There were teal-blue balls with flakes of ivory snow, a yellow canister with gingerbread boys painted along the border, a crystal angel who had a broken wing. Where did Tess get the money to buy these treasures, and where did she buy them? In Birmingham? Bolivia had never even been to Bessemer, much less Birmingham.

When Ben Ray drove the Studebaker past Scotty Sandifer's filling station, Keller noticed that Scotty's truck was parked beside the benzol pump. Because it was Sunday, the station was closed. Keller strained to see inside, wondering if Scotty might have slept there. A cot was kept behind the counter—for what, Keller had never quite fully understood, but he supposed it was for nights when Grace Sandifer grew fed up with Scotty and kicked him out of the house.

Keller quickly dismissed the idea. Surely Scotty was hunting this December morning, or laying up in bed recovering from last night. They drove on past fields of dried cornstalks and occasional lingering patches of turnip greens until they came to the catfish farm that marked the beginning of a neighborhood. Warrior Road narrowed. A canopy of pin oaks, which in summer provided a green umbrella of foliage, now formed a sinister yet fascinating pattern of dark branches against the blue winter sky.

Keller stared up, trying to feel something other than emptiness. Why had his mother chosen this particular weekend to invite Bolivia in like some long-lost cousin? Tess's unpredictability
was no secret, but he'd always chalked it up to her having to deal
with so many preachers. Church itself was enough to make anybody crazy, and Keller knew his mother's brand of spirituality
was, at best, unwieldy. She had no use for ritual or legalistic fer-
vor. Women were strange. They made God a kind of lover, pro-
jecting all their pain and madness in his direction until,
collectively, their passion created a too-modern being who knew
and understood all their thwarted desires. Keller didn't know
where Laura stood in these matters. They'd never talked about
God. Since she was so hell-bent on a fierce independence of spirit,
he assumed she didn't have a man in the sky.

Lila Green's place rose in the distance—a quiet white house
with latticework and a gazebo in the big yard, where hickory
leaves had fallen and lay like a yellow welcome mat. Not only
was this the house where he'd get married; it was also to be his
own address for the foreseeable future. Keller, however, didn't
feel welcome. If it was anybody but Laura, he'd have told Ben
Ray to turn and drive on toward the Warrior River and then
perhaps on to Laurel, Hattiesburg, and New Orleans, where
together they'd board a steamer and travel the Mississippi.

Ben Ray turned the car in to Lila Green's side yard, and just
as he did, Scotty's truck pulled in behind them, screeching to a
halt that caused Lila's hickory leaves to rise in a burst of yellow.

Ben Ray stroked his beard. Keller studied his father's brown
eyes.

"Son of a bitch," Ben Ray said, popping his coal-stained
knuckles. "Son of a sorry bitch."

Keller and Ben Ray got out of the car.

Scotty remained in his truck, his green baseball cap pulled
over his eyes, the kid in the dugout. Keller went over to him,
kicking leaves, hands jammed in pockets.

"Hello, Mr. Sandifer," Keller said, jamming his hands deeper
into his pockets, so deep he felt the texture of his own hairy legs

under the wedding pants. The truck window was rolled down. Scotty was shelling peanuts into a brown paper sack, his stubby fingers and bit nails clawing the nuts free.

"Nice day for hunting, ain't it?" he asked Keller, his eyes grabbing Keller in a chill of intimacy.

Keller looked at the ground.

"Yes, sir," he said.

"Want to hit quail over in Praco?" Scotty asked.

"No, sir. Not today."

"And why's that?" Scotty asked, his snake-thin lips curling to grimace.

"Getting married," Keller answered foolishly.

"Marrying who?" Scotty asked, taking another peanut in hand and crushing the shell easily, as if it were a mere ripe berry.

Keller looked away, realizing that Scotty had drawn him into the identical conversation they'd had at the station Friday afternoon. On the porch, Grace Sandifer stood in a blue dress, like a poised soldier in command of her surroundings.

Keller turned from the truck. Laura leaned from behind Lila Green's front door, poking her head out, waving to Keller. Grace quickly shooed her back in, but Keller had seen that she was wearing only a flimsy slip, causing the day, the reason for his being here, to suddenly shift back into focus. He walked away from Scotty's truck and joined his father.

"Hello, Grace," Ben Ray called from the yard, as if nothing out of the ordinary had happened or would happen on their children's wedding day.

When they mounted the steps to Lila Green's neat, symmetrical porch, Grace drew Ben Ray up in a friendly hug, and they stood in an embrace that caused Keller to crawl with uneasiness. He was afraid they might cry or something. And then the preacher, Brother O'Flynn, pulled in to the yard. Grace's wandering eye surveyed the car.

"Tess and Brother O'Flynn," Ben Ray affirmed, backing up against the porch banister.

Grace's stationary eye joined the roving one in a fixed stare.

"Who's with her?" she asked Keller.

"Bolivia Ivey."

Keller watched Grace, anticipating her usual quick recovery from hearing unusual information. "Yes," she said and turned deftly to Ben Ray. "Her father was killed in the No. 3 accident, wasn't he?"

"Right," Ben Ray affirmed, staring appreciatively at Tess, whose white dress rose in the wind. She was carrying a tinseled canister of cookies. Bolivia followed a few steps behind, toting a tray of food—like a slave girl, Keller thought, which, for all he knew, might be his mother's intentions for that relationship. Tess mounted the steps to the porch, her face alive with the flushed joy of a woman stylishly late for a party.

"Grace," she said breathlessly, and turned to hand the canister to Bolivia—ah, yes, Keller thought, the slave girl. She embraced Grace warmly, then turned to Bolivia.

"Do you know Bolivia Ivey?" she asked Grace.

Bolivia smiled like a dark mystic.

"I brought her along," Tess said.

"Yes," Grace said, studying Bolivia with unhidden interest. All the women were eaten up with curiosity, Keller knew. "Yes, good," she said.

Over in the side yard, Scotty's truck abruptly sputtered. He gunned it. For a moment, Keller believed he was leaving, but he only moved the vehicle to a less conspicuous spot. It was clear that he had no intention of going hunting.

Brother O'Flynn, who'd loaned Ben Ray the wedding suit and Keller his son's Sunday best, took Keller's hand in preacherly fashion. But Brother O'Flynn was missing two fingers, and shaking his hand was, Keller thought, like holding frogs in your palm. The man was Irish, ruddy-complected, and of good cheer. He didn't seem perplexed in the least that the neighborhood whore had ridden in his car alongside the mother of the groom. Miner preachers were a special breed, Keller knew.

"I brought Bolivia to take care of Scotty," Tess said, and Keller's spine crawled with disbelief, but Bolivia miraculously rose to the occasion.

"Scotty's a friend," she said to Grace. "A *friend*," she emphasized, gazing at Grace in a piercing way. "I don't think he'll interfere," she said.

Grace stared at her.

"Scotty won't cause trouble," Bolivia went on.

Keller watched Grace's wandering eye travel over Bolivia's face. "You don't think so?" Grace asked curiously.

"No, ma'am," Bolivia replied.

Grace smiled, studying Bolivia's face as if she'd never laid eyes on anything quite like her. Keller wondered if they had ever met.

"You know Scotty, then?" Grace asked.

"Yes," Bolivia repeated.

Grace glanced over at Ben Ray. Ben Ray looked away.

"He loves you very much," Bolivia told her.

Grace's eyes narrowed. "Do you study the stars?" she asked.

"No, ma'am."

"Hmmm," she said, standing up straighter, smoothing her blue dress. "We'll have to talk sometime," she said. She turned to go back inside, stopped, and faced Bolivia once more. "How," she began, letting her wandering eye go its way, "do you *take care of* Scotty?"

Bolivia looked at her.

"Tess said you were here to take care of Scotty," Grace said.

Bolivia shrugged, looking over to the yard, where Scotty was shelling peanuts. "Sometimes you just have to say 'no' to him."

Keller reached for a cigaret. All of life had gone absolutely insane.

"Sometimes," Bolivia said and stared Grace in the face, "sometimes you have to chain him up. When a person acts like a dog, you leash him up."

The smile kept leaving and returning to Grace's face.

"And so you intend to leash him up today?"

"Yes, ma'am."

Grace looked at Ben Ray, then at Tess, then at the preacher.

"Scotty's a boy," Bolivia said.

Grace motioned for Bolivia to sit in the porch swing.

"You're going to have that baby by Christmas," Grace noted. Bolivia nodded, letting her feet dangle from the swing. She was watching Scotty like a hawk.

"You got him figured out, huh?" Grace pursued.

"Yes, ma'am."

"We ought to talk sometime," Grace declared and turned to go inside.

Keller stuck his hands in his pockets. He wanted to run.

Brother O'Flynn laid a hand on Bolivia's head as if to bless.

"Jesus Christ!" Keller said to Ben Ray a few minutes later as they smoked Chesterfields on the back sleeping porch, where Laura had said they'd sleep come next spring.

Ben Ray flicked ashes on the red-tiled floor of Lila's sleeping porch. A laundry heater was going, but Keller shivered nonetheless, growing sick with anxiety and uncertainty. It was bad enough getting married, but having Scotty Sandifer and Bolivia Ivey there was just too much.

"Mother's crazy," Keller said, pointing an accusatory finger at Ben Ray. "I mean, she's a lunatic," he said with finality, as if an ultimate lifelong verdict were being delivered to the man responsible for allowing this.

Ben Ray smiled, flicking more ashes and then shuffling them into a tiny pile with his boot. "She's thirty-seven," he said.

"So what? What the hell does that mean?" Keller asked, staring at the land beyond Lila's estate.

"Women begin to want strange things," Ben Ray said gently.

"Like what?" Keller said, weary of new ideas. The discovery of all of Laura's potential complexity was a tedious thought, something he didn't intend to witness. He was sure idiosyncratic maneuverings were peculiar to his mother.

"They get antsy," Ben Ray said.

"So Mom's antsy. What does that have to do with her bringing a whore to my wedding?"

Ben Ray laughed, opened the screen door, and tossed his

cigaret butt to Lila's side yard, where a prim garden held the remnants of flowers whose names Keller didn't know. "Just don't let it worry you."

"Grace Sandifer must think this is a little *weird*, don't you think?"

Ben Ray smiled.

"I mean, all that about Bolivia taking care of Scotty. It would be different if she was a nurse or a preacher's wife or something, but we all know who she is."

Ben Ray's red suspenders were tight over his broad shoulders, crimping the starched shirt. "I'll tell you one thing," he said, his brown eyes widening, "you don't need to worry about Grace Sandifer. She's as strange as the day is long. Didn't you see how all three of them—Bolivia, your mother, and Grace—stared at one another like gypsies?"

Ben Ray lit another cigaret.

"I mean, when women're trying to have a wedding or a funeral or a baby born, they'll do whatever it takes to carry it off."

In the side yard, Bolivia stood by Scotty's truck, the hem of her Indian tent dress blowing in the wind. Her baby made a maddening orb, causing the material to cling like sheepskin to her basketball belly. Keller asked Ben Ray for a cigaret.

They smoked in silence as the guests began to arrive.

The piano, china cabinet, secretary, and satiny sofa all stood against the wall. The fireplace where the vows were to be spoken was a mess of plants, candles, and pale orange carnations. Lila had pinned one to Keller's shirt a few minutes earlier. Keller stood beside Ben Ray, waiting for Laura to come from the bedroom. Lila's walls were lined with paintings of birds—a flamingo in a pond, eagles, hawks, and quail like the ones Keller had shot in Praco with Scotty.

Over by the mint-colored curtains, in matching rattan chairs, sat Grace and Tess. Behind them were miles of candles. Margo Benton went to the piano and began playing a hymn. Tess rose to sing. "I come to the garden alone while the dew is still on the roses, and the voice I hear falling on my ear, the son of God discloses." When she came to the chorus, "And he walks with me, and he talks with me and he tells me I am his own," Laura emerged from the bedroom.

Keller could tell that Laura felt encumbered by the dress. Somebody had stuck odd-shaped leaves in her hair. She had the air of a petulant prince. Her arms were gold in the candlelight. Brother O'Flynn read from his Bible. Keller tried not to let his eyes wander, but through Lila's sheer mint curtains he saw a watercolor view of the side yard, where Scotty and Bolivia were standing under the hickory tree. Scotty had taken his hunting dogs from the truck, and the beagle raised a leg to the magnolia, spraying a stream that Keller couldn't see. Scotty threw a bottle in the direction of Warrior Road. Keller believed it hit a neighbor's car, but he didn't hear it hit.

What Keller heard was Brother O'Flynn asking, "Who gives this woman to be married?" and Grace replying, "Her father and I." He knew the vows were approaching. Ben Ray stood beside Keller. Keller wondered if his father was also watching the side yard, where Scotty was now moving back toward his truck. He got his rifle and began loading it. His dogs pranced and bayed, ready for orders. Scotty surveyed Lila's house, then aimed at the sheer mint curtains where Keller stood, watching.

Brother O'Flynn was asking him a question. He was asking if he'd take Laura to be his wife, to love and cherish, in sickness and health, till death. He told Brother O'Flynn that he would. Ben Ray handed Keller the ring. Laura's fingers were bent as if ready to grasp a wrench, and the ring wouldn't slide. It was fixed midway on her finger, the knuckle roadblocking its passage.

She smiled at Keller, and he knew why he loved her, why he was marrying her, why it would work. She was more than a woman. She was also a man, a comrade, a wisecracker with substance.

Brother O'Flynn ignored the ring's incomplete journey down the finger and went on with the ceremony. During the prayer, Keller turned his head back to the sheer mint curtains. In the yard, Scotty stood with his rifle directed at the living-room window. He cocked it, and when he did, Bolivia grabbed him in a clumsy tackle, her big belly knocking against his sprinter's frame. He fell forward in the yellow leaves. Keller suddenly remembered the way Bolivia made love—her thin arms over her head like a bony halo. He winced inwardly at what he'd done to her.

Outside, Scotty tried to stand but struggled like a seasick sailor on a rocking shipdeck. He was drunk.

Keller tried to close his eyes because the preacher was praying, but he didn't dare. Ben Ray squeezed his hand. Keller glanced over at his father, who was wide-eyed, watching the scene through the curtains. If they could just get through this prayer, Keller thought, Scotty could come crashing through Lila's sleeping porch, overturn the punch bowl, toss the carnations into the candles, set the whole damn place on fire, cut off the preacher's other fingers and have at it with Keller. He'd love it. He'd love to fight the bastard. And as long as Scotty was drunk, it'd be no match. Laura could floor him—and would. She would crush her diamond-studded knuckle into his blue eyes.

The prayer went on and on. Brother O'Flynn was praying for the damn president, for Hitler's demise, for the flag, for a resolution of Europe's war, for Tess and Ben Ray and Grace and Scotty and the church and the neighborhood and the men of the No. 3 mine and the steel plant and the farmers and the lilies of the field and God knows what else he'd come up with. Scotty charged forward, his sneakers tangling up with each other in the pine straw. Beyond him, some men were walking across the barren field, where a plow was overturned. The men were moving in the direction of Lila's home, perhaps to investigate the ruckus, but they'd never get there in time. Bolivia threw her body to the earth in an effort to trip Scotty up. It worked. Like a scrambling mountain lion, she wrestled him. Scotty's dogs began chewing the hem of her dress.

Keller's heart raced. Why was she doing this for him? Why was she risking this for him? He ached with regret. He hated himself. He wondered how much longer he could go without telling somebody the truth that he knew, that only he and Bolivia knew, and that he scarcely could utter to himself.

Scotty had managed to slip from under Bolivia's straddling

body and was gathering up his rifle and prying the dogs loose from the hem of Bolivia's dress. It was over—the fight and the vows. Bolivia lay still, exhausted, in the yellow hickory leaves. Her belly rose over her body like Keller's world, what it'd become, the crux of all of life's predicaments, the hope and failure of all he wanted.

Lila's back bedroom was musty, saturated with the smell of lingering Old Spice and fish oil. Laura's grandfather had died in this very bed only a year earlier, and Keller sensed his ghost threatening to rise like vapor from the drafty floors. Laura stood by the vanity. Like a spool of thread unraveling, she peeled the wedding dress from her body, leaving it heaped like a snowpile on the heart-of-pine floor. She stood naked, arms crossed, just like he'd seen her do when diagnosing a bad engine or injured tire.

Keller studied her body. Its angularity was startling. She didn't move. Finally, he lifted the quilt and she slipped in beside him. They lay under the cover. He felt for her hand. She'd already removed the wedding ring, placing it beside his wallet on the bureau.

"You can smoke," she said.

"I don't want to smoke now."

She rose from the blankets to raise the shade. Moonlight took her face. Sprigs of the dried hydrangea that had crowned her head in a regal arc were sprinkled over her hair.

He reached up, leaning forward to make sure her nipples were real. They were tiny like the eyes of a baby. She raised an eyebrow. He kissed her, pulled her down and under his body. It was all he'd predicted—the boylike boniness of her spine, the muscular legs, the grip of her hands.

When it was over, she kissed the palms of his hands.

His heart was racing, and he felt like he might cry.

"What are you thinking?" she asked him, raising herself up to study his face.

"Nothing."

He was afraid he'd hurt her, yet she was so aloof it scared him. She seemed suddenly older and wiser than he as she surveyed his face like a mother might.

"Please," he said and put his face near hers.

"Please what? Are you all right?" she asked him curiously. She seemed entirely at ease. Hadn't they just experienced the same storm? He looked out the window. A few stubborn rust-colored sweetgum leaves clung to the treetops, refusing to believe winter's arrival. A star glowed with strange colors. He tried to decipher the impression, wondering if it might be Mars.

"I don't have any cigarets," he told her.

"Did you see Daddy during the wedding?" she asked. "Was he there? Somebody told me they saw him."

He explored her eyes. "I saw him," he said.

"Where was he?"

"Outside."

"I heard that Bolivia Ivey was with him."

He shuddered inwardly. "That's right."

"What was she doing?"

"What do you mean, what was she doing?" he asked.

She propped herself up in the bed, pulling the quilts higher. "I mean, was she here for a reason?"

"My mother brought her."

Laura's eyes widened, and a smile formed on her face. Keller studied her mouth, wondering where he was going to buy cigarets on a Sunday night.

"Why did she bring her?" Laura pursued.

"My mother's crazy."

"She's really not," Laura said. "She's a singer."

He looked at her, wondering what that had to do with anything.

"Listen," she said, drawing the quilt up to her chin. "I'm sorry about what Daddy did to you the other night."

He shrugged.

"He's crazy," she said. "He'll always be crazy."

"He's a drunk," Keller said.

"But he's never going to love us," she said.

He searched her for traces of grief but saw none.

"Are you afraid of him?" she pressed.

"Only when he's drinking. Are you?"

"I hate him," she whispered, looking out the window at the sky.

He nodded.

"No, not hate," she said. "I feel nothing for him, nothing at all."

"I need a cigaret," he said. "Let's go for a drive."

Ben Ray had left him the Studebaker.

She smiled. "Those Luckies are calling," she said and was up in a flash, throwing on her filling-station garb, lacing her boots like a good soldier. He had the distinct feeling that she'd be able to take anything life threw at her.

Ben Ray met them at the door, wearing his coal-stained overalls and heavy coat as if leaving for the mines. His face was set firm in a way that drew Keller into mild alarm.

"Everything all right?" Keller asked.

Laura leaned against the wood banister, her legs crossed.

"Yes," Ben Ray said and smiled, finally, at Laura. "Hi, sugar," he said.

Keller reached for his father's coat pocket. "I need a smoke," he said.

Ben Ray opened the door wide, gesturing them inside. "I should have known only a nicotine fit'd send a boy home on his wedding night." It was meant lightly, but Ben Ray's face was stony.

"Where's Mom?" Keller asked, feeling the comfort of his parents' surroundings—the crate beside the sofa, his mother's clay pots and piano, his father's Chesterfields.

"She's asleep," Ben Ray replied.

"Don't wake her," Keller instructed.

Laura sat beside him on the sofa. She started to prop her boots on the crate, then thinking better of it, leaned forward instead, clasping her hands in front of her, taking in the room anew, though she'd been here on many occasions for dinner.

Ben Ray took off his heavy coat but didn't sit. Instead, he stood like a soldier, staring into the fire, silent.

Keller felt a distinct barrier. Something was wrong.

"You weren't going to work, were you?" Keller asked.

Ben Ray stroked his beard. His brown eyes were fixed on the fire, his hands jammed into his overall pockets. "Nice wedding," he said to Laura.

"The ring wouldn't go down my finger," she said, shaking her hair rambunctiously in an effort to free the bits of leaves and dried hydrangea that the crown had left.

"Nobody knew," Ben Ray told her.

She smiled and popped her knuckles.

Keller studied his father. A new fear began to strangle his earlier joy over the sight of Laura lacing up her combat boots, and that was the realization that Bolivia might have told Tess the truth about the baby, and Ben Ray was caught in the middle.

Finally, Ben Ray sighed and looked rather sternly at Keller.

"Japan bombed Pearl Harbor this afternoon," he said and lit a cigaret, tossing the match into the fire.

Keller felt immediate relief. He had no idea what this meant; he only knew it didn't have anything to do with his life. Ben Ray sat in the gray ragged mess of a chair beside the crate, leaned forward, and studied Keller and Laura wistfully. "During your wedding," he said.

"What's Pearl Harbor?" Laura asked.

"Hawaii," Ben Ray said.

Keller stared at the fire. He understood that this wasn't good. But no matter how bad it was, it wasn't as bad as his parents' finding out about the baby. As long as they didn't know about Bolivia's baby.

"There was a Japanese air attack on Hawaii—that's us, you know," he said, looking first at Keller, then at Laura, then at the fire. "They blew up a battleship and destroyer in Pearl Harbor."

Keller didn't say anything.

"No doubt, Roosevelt'll declare war on Japan in the morning," he went on.

Keller nodded, feigning interest.

"It's something to think about," Ben Ray said.

Laura rose and stood near the fire, warming her hands behind her. Ben Ray smiled tenderly at her. Keller knew he was appreciating her attire—the filling-station clothes on her wedding night.

"But," Ben Ray said, stretching his arms forward and yawning, "it's too soon to say what this will all mean in the long haul." He got up. "You kids want coffee?"

"No thanks," Keller said. He hesitated. "But I could use a pack of cigarets."

Ben Ray walked to the dinner table. He reached into Tess's coral sweater, retrieving a pack.

"What's Mom doing with cigarets?"

Ben Ray smiled. "She says the junkman gave them to her. What's that fellow's name?"

"Charles," Laura told him.

Keller took the pack, lit one, and smoked it while his father stoked the fire. It rose, making patterns that danced off the wood.

Charles, the junkman, lived behind his brother's place in a white frame house surrounded by five acres of land. Since his brother was superintendent of the mine, Charles often did repairs on company houses. At one time, before he bought his flatbed truck, he hauled tools in his mule-drawn wagon. He was, by trade, a carpenter, though he considered himself an entrepreneur. In summer, when the neighborhood children were free to roam the hollow collecting old plowshares, leaky buckets, railroad spikes, copper wire, and their mamas' discarded pots and pans, Charles traded scrap iron. In winter, he hauled coal and iron in his flatbed to company families in order to supplement his warm-weather job.

This morning, he fixed coffee in his kitchen, which contained not much more than a crate table and strings of dried peppers hanging like ornaments from wall to wall. His cat had just given birth a few weeks earlier, and she sat by the laundry heater nursing her black babies. Charles looked out the window. His brother had stormed in yesterday afternoon to tell him that Pearl Harbor had been bombed.

Charles wanted to see the neighbors. He loved the neighbors like he loved land, news, and the turquoise male peacock that lived among his geese in the pen beside his compost heap. But more than anything, he loved Bolivia. He loved the sight of her, the bony arms hanging like injured arrows alongside her Indian body. He didn't understand why he loved her. Early on, he'd made love with her relentlessly, as if trying to fathom a depth, or overturning soil in an effort to harvest the best spring crop. When it had become clear that she was carrying a child, he'd hoped he was the father and therefore bound to her genetically, spiritually, and, he hoped nuptially if she'd agree to give up her independence. But she'd insisted that the seed was planted by the Hayes boy, who had married Scotty Sandifer's daughter yesterday. He didn't question her. But the idea of her knowing who the father was, considering the number of men she'd slept with, was absurd.

He understood, though, that Bolivia *knew* certain things because she was connected to a kind of magic probably rooted in her Indian heritage—if she was indeed Indian. She called herself a Melungeon, and hinted that her people were part Portuguese. She'd told him that she was born on Newman's Ridge in the Blackwater Valley of Tennessee. "The northwestern slope," she'd added, while her dark eyes gazed deep into his face as if this particular piece of geography carried a special, murky significance. She often did this. She'd seize on a bit of her history and her eyes would come alive. Her mother carried a basket all day along the ridge, gathering persimmons, wild fruits, nuts, and vegetables, she'd said. All her mother's people were artists, weavers, and painters. They lived in mud-daubed cabins, and the woodsmoke curled above the rooftops like ghosts' fingers. In 1932, they'd moved to Wilder, Tennessee—a busy, coal-mining village in the midst of mountain wilderness sprinkled with tiny

farms. Her mother had died that Christmas during a long strike
where a small monthly allowance from UMW allowed only a
ration of lard and meal. Children were dying like houseflies
from measles, pellagra, and pneumonia. And it was pellagra that
killed her mother. She'd told him that an emergency relief
group had provided coffee, beans, sugar, cornmeal, and meat to
her father the day her mother died and that on Christmas Eve,
parents wrapped their children up in blankets and carried them
to the relief station that supplied candy, apples, and a toy.

Charles poured the dregs of his coffee into the sink, threw on
a jacket, and went outside. Stretched east to west was his cornfield, the dried-up stalks drooping in brown misery. It'd been a
bad year, with scant rainfall and an early frost. He surveyed his
brother's land—which, Charles understood, was his for all practical purposes, since he farmed, harvested, and plowed it. He
also fed the horses, slopped the pigs, milked the cow, and re-
paired broken items. In his yard, behind the fenced peacock and
geese, was a woodshed where he kept scrap iron before taking
it to its ultimate destination to be made into steel. His weighing
scales were kept in the shed, too. The sight of children coming
over his land carrying their mothers' discarded aluminum pots
and pans was good. He felt that, in his business, everybody
profited. Even children got a taste of the marketplace, the power
of making money, and he considered himself an instrument of
goodwill.

Throwing open the bird pen, Charles let the peacock wander
free from the prison of squawking geese. The light of morning
sun lit the bird's turquoise feathers, causing him to shimmer in
natural splendor. In the distance, the land rose and fell in brown
waves. Charles liked winter.

Since his house was situated in a patch of cultivated land, atop
the hill, he had a panoramic view of a good bit of the camp,
including his brother's home, the post office, the schoolhouse,
and Bolivia's entire street, that led to the stone wall, railroad
tracks, and stream. For this reason, he could see men arrive at
and leave her place. Since she'd been pregnant, however, nobody

slept with her—her idea. Despite the fact that this included him, and he missed the mystery of her body, the relief over knowing other men weren't there made it worth the sacrifice.

Inside the barn, he fed the horses, milked the cow, then tossed dried corn to the birds in the pen. The pigs would be fed at dusk, after Charles had gathered the day's food discards from his brother's wife. He went back into his house, crushed some dried peppers, and put them in a jar to give to Grace Sandifer. She liked cooking with red pepper. He liked Grace. Everybody liked Grace. And he was certain that if war talk was under way, it'd be taking place at the Sandifer filling station. Grabbing a pack of Luckies, he jumped in his truck parked under the sweetgum tree and headed toward Warrior Road.

The red brick station stood like a tiny mansion in the distance. Approaching it, he braked early, hoping to avoid making the inevitable cloud of dust and exhaust. Charles parked the truck beside the benzol pump.

He went inside and, reaching into his jacket pocket, retrieved the jar of dried red pepper. He handed it to Grace, who sat behind the counter. Her good eye registered.

"Thank you, love," she said.

She took his hand into hers. Grace's hands were like sandpaper.

"Get yourself a Nehi," she said.

"I hear you had a wedding yesterday," Charles said, reaching into the icy drink box.

"That's right," Grace said, handing him a Hershey bar. "You need any merchandise today?" Meaning, of course, cigarets or condoms.

"No'm. You need wood?"

"Not this week," she said, opening the cash register and fingering the coins. Grace loved to count money. She wasn't miserly, he knew; she just liked the feel of metal. He understood it well.

"I guess you know," Grace said, thrusting the *Birmingham Age-Herald* in front of him. The headline read JAPAN OPENS WAR ON

U.S., HAWAII AND PHILIPPINES BOMBED. "You need to read this," she said, pointing to a commentary by John Temple Graves that began, "Let us thank God on this Monday morning of fate that the military madmen of Japan do not understand the United States of America."

"Has Roosevelt declared war yet?" he asked her, picking up a toothpick from the counter.

"Not as I know of," Grace said, adjusting the radio knob to bring in a clearer sound.

"Scotty here?" he asked.

"Out back," she said.

He went out the door and walked to the rear of the station.

Scotty was tossing clay pigeons in the air but wasn't shooting them. In fact, he didn't have his rifle handy. Sitting on a bench with a lumber company logo painted on the back and wearing his green baseball cap pulled low over his eyes, he bore the mark of a loner. At the sight of Charles, he tossed the baseball cap aside and his eyes brightened.

"Want a beer?" he asked, and stood, pulling his jeans up in an effort to make them cling to his skinny hips. Charles had often thought that Scotty Sandifer was the kind of man who'd one day just blow away in the wind.

"Too early," Charles replied, but shook Scotty's hand.

Scotty went to his truck and got his rifle.

"Want to shoot?" he asked.

Charles didn't know where Scotty got the clay pigeon disks—a costly luxury. But Scotty was well liked among men and worked one day a week at the steel plant.

Charles took Scotty's rifle, aimed squarely, and fired when Scotty tossed the disk.

A hit.

Scotty whistled and guzzled a drink of beer.

The sky was blue overhead. Scotty lit a cigaret and handed it to Charles. They smoked silently, leaning against the brick station as they watched some crows fly over the nearby field and disappear in the thin layer of smoke on the horizon near the Fairfield steel plant.

Charles rubbed his boots into the dark, moist earth—a mixture of soil, gasoline, and slag. "Well, what's Roosevelt doing? Think he'll declare today?"

"He better," Scotty replied. He walked over to an old Ford parked by the oil pit. "We ought to disembowel this baby," he said to Charles. "How much you think's in it, body and all?"

Charles's heart rose. He shook his head. "There's no telling," he said.

"What year is this anyhow?" Scotty asked, tapping the engine.

"Thirty-two, maybe?" Charles replied.

"Well, it ain't worth shit."

"Whose is it?"

Scotty looked over at him. "Frank Graham's."

Charles nodded, trying to recall if he'd ever seen the car parked behind the commissary.

"My daughter's husband works for Graham, you know," Scotty said, shivering, even though it wasn't particularly cold in the morning sun. He zipped his jacket up.

Charles didn't say anything.

"You know the Hayes boy, don't you?"

Charles took a long draw on his cigaret and stared at the Ford. Part of it was rusted, the color of peanut husks. He didn't know what was going on with the Sandifers and the Hayeses, but he assumed there was bad blood.

"I know his mama," Charles said. "She can sing the horns off a billy goat. I hear they pay her over in Birmingham in some of them big churches to do revivals."

"Mark my word," Scotty said, "that woman's got some money." Scotty pulled his cap lower, shading his eyes.

"Japs," Scotty said under his breath. "Can you believe they did this?"

Charles heard a car screech into the station. The dust flew. Even from behind the brick building, they got the residual.

"It's Laura," Grace called from inside the station.

Scotty didn't say a word. He got into his truck. A few bottles of beer fell from the cab. He cranked it and screeched recklessly from the station, almost grazing the side of the building. Behind his pickup, dust rose like an evening gown.

Charles went back inside.

Grace was holding a cedar tree. Beside her stood Laura, dressed as usual like a boy, holding the hand of the Hayes boy she'd married yesterday.

"We've got a Christmas tree for the station!" Grace exclaimed.

Charles tried to get in on the banter, but Keller Hayes's presence made his skin crawl.

He rode back through the neighborhood, stopping first at the commissary. Frank Graham was standing on a ladder, stocking shelves with cornmeal and sugar, wearing his customary brown sack apron. A broom was propped against the laundry heater, which wasn't working right and never had worked right. The place was always cold. The sprawling U-shaped space was too big to heat. Winters had been milder in more recent years; but still, in January nobody tarried here, and Graham himself spent most days in the room adjacent to the old store, where he had a fireplace and a wife with arthritic legs. Charles eyed the new bolt of gingham over in dry goods, thinking of Bolivia, but instead bought her some peppermints from the big jar beside the cigars.

Graham, on seeing Charles, scurried from the ladder and wiped his dusty hands on his apron. "What's going to happen?" he asked, rubbing a thumb over his eyelid, a habit that drove Charles crazy. Graham, Charles felt, was one of those antsy Irish types with freckly skin who wear the pained expression of a guy who's just sat on a pin.

"You mean the bombing?" Charles said, handing Graham a penny for the candy.

"What else?" Graham said impatiently, grabbing a cigar from the box beside the peppermints. "Whatever else could I mean?" he said impishly. Charles smiled, leaning over the counter. Out the window, he caught a glimpse of Keller Hayes, obviously returning to work after having delivered the cedar tree to the filling station.

"You got a newspaper?" Charles asked.

"No. You?"

"No. I saw one over at Sandifer's place. Where's your radio?" he asked, watching Keller Hayes hauling cedars from a truck to the back. "What's he doing?" Charles asked.

"We're selling Christmas trees this year."

"Now, who the hell's going to buy a tree when they can go cut one?"

"I figure your brother'll be in the market."

Charles chuckled, understanding that Graham's trees would appeal to men who liked other men to do their work.

"We're in this war. You know that, don't you? Just waiting for the president to say so," Graham said, chewing his cigar and brushing loose brown sugar from the countertop.

Keller walked in.

"Clark Gable here is going to be mincemeat," Graham said under his breath, using his cigar to point at Keller. "All these kids are. It's sad. It's awful sad," he said. "Got a light?"

Charles gave him matches. He lit the cigar.

"How many cedars you find?" he called to Keller.

The boy's hands were cut—tiny splintery gashes. Charles offered him a Lucky.

"Thanks," he said.

Keller struck a match and looked up at his boss, as he lit it. "They're all cedars," he said.

"Where'd you find 'em?"

"Over near Praco."

"How'd you know where Praco was?" Charles asked, looking at the bleeding hands.

"I was born there," Keller replied, studying the shelves Graham had stocked. He looked at Charles. "I've hit quail there, too," he added.

"Emma wants one in the store," Graham said to Keller. "How about getting the tallest and haul it on in," he instructed. Keller walked behind the counter and out the back door. "Boy's a hard worker," he said, chewing on his cigar. "Hard worker. He'll make a good soldier. Kid's got no idea we're in a war. Kid don't understand a thing," he said.

Charles rode back home. After doing some of his chores, he sat at his kitchen table, smoking and waiting, staring at the newborn kittens beside the heater. Finally he saw her coming over the hill, crossing the stream not by bridge but, in her usual fashion, stepping over mossy rocks, taking the arduous route to his place. She was wearing a calico dress she'd cut the belly from, leaving a gaping hole. By wearing an apron tied under her breasts, she draped the bulging heap of baby. Today's apron was bright orange, a new one.

Bending forward, she walked up the hill to Charles's yard. The bright orange apron tied over her belly gave the impression of a pumpkin. Her ragged shawl flapped in the slight wind.

"You're cold," he proclaimed, drawing her to his body.

"I want a Bible," she said, her arrow-thin arms dangling idly. Her eyes were unwavering.

"Where'd you get this?" he asked, fingering the orange apron.

"Tess Hayes."

"How was the wedding?"

He let her go and, turning his body from the wind, lit a cigaret. The geese squawked at Bolivia, their necks reaching up in acrobatic urgency as the yellow beaks let loose the awful noise. Charles went to the shed, returning with their breakfast of dried corn kernels.

"The wedding was fine," she said. She took his hand. "Do your chores," she instructed. He'd put off the barn jobs because she liked to watch that part.

In the barn, he pulled up a stool and slid under the cow's fawn-colored frame. She was slow to let down, and his hands got raw with cold. Finally, the white liquid hit against the pail. When he glanced up at Bolivia, he saw that her arms were crossed over her chest.

"Do you think I'll have milk?" she asked him.

"Most mothers do," he said, looking up at the cow's underside.

"Why do you want a Bible?" he asked her and then added, "Light me another cigaret."

She reached into his jacket pocket and got the pack of Luckies. "I want to read about foot washing," she told him.

He looked over. She was drawing hard, savoring the nicotine. "I've got a Bible inside," he said. "You can have it."

She leaned over, holding the cigaret between thumb and index finger, and gave him a draw, then walked toward the other end of the barn, keeping the cigaret for herself. He liked to watch her smoke.

"You know we're going to be in the war now," he said to her.

She didn't respond.

Broken planks of wood allowed a bit of sunlight in, causing the barn to come alive with yellow rays. Bolivia put her hands in the light. Since she'd moved on into her pregnancy, she'd become even more spooky, Charles felt. She'd often get mesmerized by spiders spinning webs or the rustling of rats at night, holding her head at an angle, listening to distant music. He didn't like it. Before the pregnancy, she'd been, despite her eerie Indian way, at least accessible in conversation. Now she was in a hundred places.

"I saw Keller this morning," he said.

She bristled, snapping her hands out of the shaft of light.

Charles looked over at her.

"Where?" she asked.

"He was at the station. With his wife," he added. "Then he was at the commissary. He'd been cutting cedars."

"Do you think his wife is pretty?" Bolivia asked him.

"Are you jealous of her?"

The cow's stream of milk dribbled, then ceased its flow. Charles wiped his hands, pulled the bucket, and rested his hand on the fawn-colored rump, watching Bolivia's face.

"Why should I be jealous?" she asked.

Charles lifted the bucket. "He's married to her."

"I don't love him," she said, but even as she said it she looked down at the hay, and Charles knew she was lying.

"Let's go in," he said. "We got to get some things settled."

Inside, Charles made hot tea. Bolivia got cups and saucers from the pantry. It was his mother's china and carried a print of what looked to Charles like grapes and ash leaves.

He poured, then turned on the radio, hoping for news from Roosevelt, but got a "Lum and Abner" instead.

Bolivia got sugar from his cabinet, sat back down, and began undoing a braid.

Charles folded his arms over his chest.

"I think you need to start thinking about what's going to happen."

She looked up and smiled. But the smile fell quickly from her face like a falling star, over her sadness, her parents' death, the hard past.

"Does the boy know for certain that it's his?"

She shrugged. She unloosed the other braid and began combing her fingers through the long, dark hair. It was the texture of a paintbrush.

"Well?" he pressed.

"I think so," she answered quietly. The radio static grew. Charles rose to turn the knob. His kitchen windows grew moist with steam from the tea water.

Bolivia rose. "I need to go to the bathroom," she said. Her unbraided hair fell over the orange apron and calico dress. Her eyes were void of any feeling. The screen door slammed shut behind her as she walked down the path to the outhouse. Charles went to his bedroom, where a mess of blankets crossed his mattress and makeshift curtains fell from the window, making the room look like a war-torn fabric mill—not to mention the pile of dirty wash beside the cedar chest that'd belonged to his mother. Opening it, he retrieved his mother's Bible—it had a thin blue ribbon marking Luke 2. When Bolivia came back inside, he gave it to her.

"You might start with this story of a pregnant virgin," he

said. "Did an angel tell you not to worry over who the baby's father is?"

She looked up at him. Her eyes were like a closed door.

"What good is it to worry?" she asked him.

"How do you know for sure it belongs to Keller?"

She sat in a chair and rested her arms on the table. He sat across from her.

"He didn't have anything with him that morning."

"And everybody else you saw last spring did?"

"Yes."

She twisted a strand of hair in her fingers, staring at the Bible.

"Are you giving this to me?" she asked him, running her fingers over the blue ribbon that marked Luke 2.

"You aren't being practical," he told her.

She looked at him.

"The boy's married," he went on.

"I know," she said and the shadow of a grin crossed her face. "I was there, Charles, when he got married."

"I wonder what everybody thinks about you and this baby."

She looked at him quizzically.

"Well, don't you wonder?" he pressed.

"It's my business," she said quietly and took the ribbon from the Bible.

He got up and shook her shoulders. "But it's my business, too, can't you see that?"

She didn't say anything. She looked at his lips.

He got up. "It's my business because everybody thinks it's my kid," he said.

"You wish it was yours?"

"Of course I wish it was mine. I love you," he shouted.

"Can I have the Bible?" she asked him.

"You were just with him once?" he asked, kicking crumbs of food into corners with his boots.

"Yes," she said and put her hands over her belly.

"Did you like him?"

She looked down.

He didn't know what he wanted from her. His head hurt.

"You're not going to answer that, are you?" he asked.

She shook her head.

"Why not?"

She didn't respond.

"Because you don't like to tell the truth, right? Is he too good to talk about?" he asked and leaned against the sink.

She looked at him. Her eyes were empty.

"So, how do you know it's his?"

"I told you. He didn't have anything with him."

"Boy's too dumb to buy rubbers. His mother-in-law peddles them, you know." He paused. "So maybe he just didn't know better, you think?"

She nodded.

"You do. You think so?"

She looked at him.

"Maybe he was a virgin, then?" Charles went on.

"Yes," she said. And it wasn't something he'd prepared for.

He studied her, taking in her brown fingers, orange apron, and loose hair.

"How do you know he was a virgin?" he asked, disgusted and hurting with her honesty, wondering how far he might take her.

"His hands."

"What about his hands?" he asked, watching her face.

"Boys don't know what to do with their hands," she said and looked him in the eyes. "They lay their hands flat like this," she said and put her palm down over her leg. "They just don't know"—she paused, looking for the words—"how to let their hands go," she said, cupping her palm, "like this."

"They're uneasy," he said.

"Yes," she said and smiled.

He wanted to hit her.

"They're scared the first time," he went on.

"Weren't you?"

"I can't remember."

"Yes, you can."

"I can't," he lied. He did remember who and when, but it was more than twenty years ago, and that in itself was enough to silence him from talking about it.

She rose and moved toward him until the baby's mound brushed against him. "Do you believe I love you?" she asked.

"No," he replied. But he didn't resist her arms and, in fact, held her a long time. She was like a child, his child.

"Can I have the Bible?" she asked again.

"Yeah, you can have the Bible."

"Tell me where all the good stories are," she said, looking up at him. Charles nodded. His grandfather had been a Methodist preacher, a circuit rider, who lived during summers with Charles's family. Charles had once made the mistake of telling her that he knew certain passages by heart. He didn't want to do this. He wanted first to make her talk more about Keller Hayes, then he wanted to make love to her hard.

She turned the thin pages of the Bible, handling them carefully as if afraid she might tear them.

"You want some lunch?" he asked her.

She shook her head.

"I'm going home for a while," she said. "Come get me later."

He stood at the window and watched her walk down past the peacock and geese, clutching the Bible. Reaching over, he turned on the radio. Through the static, he heard that war had been declared.

II

Tess rose before dawn to pack Ben Ray's lunch, taking care to make extra ham sandwiches. When she wrapped her robe tighter and threw open the screen door to go to the alley outhouse, the icy air bit her. A wave of cold had washed in. Fog hid the salmon morning color. She couldn't see her neighbor's house, her own house. Unable to get her bearings enough to locate the outhouses, Tess squatted in her yard, where a few lingering weeds tickled her muscled thighs. A junco flew right by her face and vanished.

A train whistle blew.

Making her way back to Ben Ray's woodpile, she gathered kindling and pine. Inside, she touched her giraffe and elephant figurines on the kitchen shelves and put the black pot on the stove, ready to prepare beans for dinner. This evening she would take the bus to Birmingham to sing evening mass at St. Paul's

Cathedral. The priest was a friend who'd given her reams of new sheet music—songs she'd never heard. He'd told her about a new composer named George Gershwin and promised her that his music would take her breath away. She knew this was meant to entice her to sing at his church, rather than accept the invitation to the wealthy Presbyterian on Highland Avenue with stained-glass windows of a red-and-turquoise Jesus and yellow lambs, symbols she didn't understand.

In the bedroom, Ben Ray snored under the quilt, causing it to rise and fall rhythmically. Tess dropped the pea-green robe from her shoulders and slid into the warm sheets that smelled of tobacco. Wrapping her legs over Ben Ray's body, she kissed his beard and eyelids.

"It's cold," she whispered, staring ahead out the window that rose over their bedposts. "It's Christmas Eve," she said, looking at the gray sky. "You can't see a thing. You can't see your hand in front of your face."

Ben Ray opened one eye. He pulled her down to him.

"What time is it?" he asked.

"Not enough for love," she said.

He held her hard against his body, then got up.

When he left for work, she stood on the wooden steps that led from the front stoop into the yard, where the neighbor's chickens scurried in the frozen mud. Generally, if she chose to watch, she could see his overalls and denim workshirt trail all the way past Bolivia's house, over the bridged stream, past the stone wall. For a long time, she would watch him carrying his dinner bucket of sandwiches and sour pickles, bending forward up Pinegar Hill in the direction of the mine. Today, he turned to wave, and even before his body had left their yard, it vanished into fog.

Tess went back inside and brushed her hair by the chifforobe mirror.

She'd been resisting the urge to go by Bolivia's place. Keller's being gone had sent her into the blues, not unlike the depression following her miscarriages. What she wanted was to run her hands over Bolivia's big brown belly. She kept having dreams of being pregnant with the baby herself, of losing it.

She walked over to the sewing machine and picked up the angel ornament given to her by a church in Birmingham. The idea hit her to carry it over to Bolivia. She dressed and packed up a basket of nuts and fruit to take, too. She slammed the door behind her.

The fog was mystical. Roads, yards, and garden plots were erased. You were left to rely on the internal compass, the seduction of possibilities. Possibilities, she felt, was what was missing from her life. Going to Bolivia's place gave her a taste of possibility. Of what, she didn't know. It was as if Bolivia's baby had become a nucleus, drawing her like a magnet into its orbit, or was it just Bolivia herself? There were questions she wanted to ask her—how many men, how many times, under what sky, in which season, was it good, and why do you do it, but most of all, *who is the father?*

When she knocked, Charles opened the door. There was no sign of Bolivia behind him.

"Is she in labor?" Tess asked breathlessly.

Charles smiled, opening the door wide to let her in. "No," he said. "She's in the alley. She pees every half hour," he said, offering Tess the rocker that held a black cat. He shooed the cat.

"Here," Tess said, handing Charles the basket of fruit and nuts. She took her coat from her shoulders and draped it over the back of the rocker. "You always pee a lot at the end," she told him. And suddenly it dawned on her that, of course, Charles was the father. The realization left her embarrassed. She felt her face grow red-hot.

Tess looked the room over. A cedar was decorated with pine-cones and strings of bottlecaps and bits of painted newspaper.

"I did that," Charles said, glancing up from lighting his cigaret.

"Ah," Tess said. "Nice. Looks Christmasy."

Charles smiled. He was as big as a horse. She wondered how he kept from crushing Bolivia's ribcage when they made love.

The screen door in back creaked, then slammed shut. Bolivia walked into the room, wearing the orange apron Tess had given her over a broomstick-pleated dress. Tess clutched her pocketbook, which held the brass angel.

"Hi," Bolivia said quietly.

Tess rose.

Bolivia sidled up. "It's cold," she said, looking into Tess's eyes as if asking a question. Her cheeks were bright.

"Yes, isn't the fog wonderful?"

"It's like smoke," Bolivia replied.

Charles flicked ashes into the fire. He was wearing a camel coat with a fur collar. He looked like a dog meant to pull a sled over the North Pole. Tess wondered if he'd marry Bolivia when the baby came.

"I brought you a little something," she said, reaching into her pocketbook. Inside the purple lining, the brass angel was wrapped in one of Ben Ray's handkerchiefs. She gave it to Bolivia.

Bolivia ran her thumb over the angel's wings and didn't say anything.

"I like it," she said finally, as she reached for Charles's cigaret, took a long draw, then exhaled smoke in a delicate stream. "I like it very much," she said, cupping it in her hand.

"It's for the tree," Tess said.

"Oh, I can't do that," Bolivia responded. "The cats will knock it down. They've already destroyed all the balls we made."

"Whatever." Tess shrugged.

"I'll put it on my shelf in the kitchen where you keep your toys," she said.

"It's really nice, kid," Charles said to Tess.

Charles was probably her age, but he always called her *kid*.

Tess reached for Bolivia's middle. "I've been dreaming about this," she said, running her hand over the baby's mound. "Don't you love the way your skin feels?" she said, wishing she could touch her flesh.

"What do you mean?" Bolivia put her hand over Tess's, guiding it to a hard knot. "That's the feet," Bolivia whispered and smiled. "What do you mean about the way my skin feels?"

"Like it's going to burst," Tess replied.

Bolivia lifted the apron up.

"Not a single mark," Tess said, admiring the brown skin. "What?"

"No stretch marks. That's probably because you're dark."

Bolivia looked at her.

"Sometimes in the dreams, I feel the baby turning in water," Tess told her.

Bolivia let the apron fall back down.

"I must be crazy," Tess said to Charles, laughing. "I keep dreaming the baby is mine."

Charles stared at his boots.

"The other night, I dreamed you cut your finger," she said to Bolivia, remembering. "I turned on the faucet and milk streamed out. My finger started bleeding, too. Our blood got all mixed up in the sink. Ugh"—she shuddered, glancing over at Charles—"that's awful, isn't it?"

Charles didn't look at her. He and Bolivia were silent.

"I'm sorry," she said, fearing she'd been rude, talking to a pregnant woman about blood.

"We're hauling coal this morning," Charles said and stood up. "Want to come along?"

Tess considered.

"Yes," Bolivia said. "We can talk while he hauls."

Tess remembered the questions she wanted to ask.

"Oh, all right, why not?" she said. "But I've got to sing in Birmingham tonight." She didn't add that she wanted Bolivia to come along. Now that she'd reasoned that Charles was the father of the baby, Bolivia no longer seemed like a stray, and she knew Charles wouldn't want the mother of his child riding a bus to Birmingham in the dead of winter.

Charles's truck rolled along Warrior Road in the direction of the Sandifer station. His headlights cut the fog like yellow moonbeams. He was taking Grace a free bit of coal for her Christmas present before making his usual deliveries. At the coalyard, the women had stayed in the truck, and when he returned from loading they were laughing.

Tess was draped in a wool shawl. Charles considered her attractive but not in the usual way. Her hair, the color of a lion's, blew all over the place. Her eyes were like green marbles. Charles had heard her sing. When she and Ben Ray had first moved in, there was a rumor that they were gypsies and that she had the ability to heal injured bodies and make things disappear. But he knew now that she was only a singer. He knew, too, that Scotty Sandifer was right—she had a nest egg of cash buried somewhere. And now he felt sorry for her because Bolivia was carrying her grandchild and she didn't even suspect. It made him sick.

When they pulled in to the station, Tess exclaimed, "Keller's here!" and leapt from the truckcab. The Hayeses' Studebaker was parked beside the oak. Bolivia didn't move. Charles hopped down and got the sack of coal from the back of the truck to give to Grace, but Grace wasn't there.

Laura, her daughter, was leaning over the counter, chewing a bit of straw. Her slight boy's hips and short, blond hair gave her a sauciness that, Charles felt, translated into seduction.

"Mother's gone to Bessemer," she said huskily, looking him in the eyes. To Charles, the raspy voice made her sound like she was perpetually coming down with a case of laryngitis.

"She's always gone to Bessemer." He chuckled. "What do you think women do in Bessemer anyhow?" he asked.

She raised an eyebrow and shrugged.

"Well, I brought her some coal," he said, setting the bag on the cement floor of the station. "It ain't much, but Merry Christmas."

"Thanks," Laura said, and straddled her stool. "How is Bolivia?" she asked.

He flinched at the thought of what was in store for Laura once the baby was born. Wouldn't it bear the mark of her husband? Or would Bolivia's Melungeon genes override any of the boy's features?

"She's fine," he replied.

He caught her eye. A flash of recognition crossed her face—a mixture of embarrassment and amusement, as if she were just taking inventory of his situation: a pregnant girlfriend who could be carrying any man's baby.

"Need any Luckies?" she asked, recovering quickly enough, and he smiled, touched that she knew his brand.

"No, kid."

Laura's eyes widened and grew bright. "Tess," she called, on seeing her mother-in-law at the door to the station. Getting a comb from her shirt pocket, she wet her fingers and dabbed the blond bangs to make them lie flat. They tended toward a cowlick.

She sauntered over to Tess. A towel hung from the rear pocket of her workpants.

The women embraced in a quick, obligatory gesture. The minute it was over, Tess glanced back to the truck, as if checking, Charles thought, to see if Bolivia was watching. Laura looked beyond Tess, out the window. Bolivia sat in the cab, her eyes downcast.

"Bolivia," Tess explained. "Bolivia Ivey," she said, as if awkwardly introducing her.

Laura looked at Charles.

"Where's Keller?" Tess asked brightly.

"He's out greasing a car," Laura told her, gesturing to the oil pit behind the station. "Graham gave him the day off, so he's helping me." She was still looking out at the truck where Bolivia sat.

Tess said she liked the cedar tree in the station's far corner. It was decorated with strings of popcorn. Charles stood beside the air compressor.

Laura hopped up, rear-first, onto the drink box.

Tess took the stool behind the counter and opened the newspaper. The headline read ALLIED WAR COUNCIL CONVENED, JAP FORCES LAND BELOW MANILA. Below were other war stories. The weather forecast underneath called for a cold and sunny day after the fog lifted. Charles looked over Tess's shoulder at the war stories. He began reading, "German forces reported nearing annihilation in Leningrad area," but Laura got down from the drink box and pointed to a local piece about the steel plant's open hearth and blast furnaces turning out more in 1941 than ever dreamed, in an effort to meet the war's demands.

"Demands," she said to him. "War's demands."

It was as if she were posing a question. Her blue eyes were those of a child. Charles felt for her, for all she didn't know, for all she'd learn in time.

"Your daddy here, kid?" he asked, tossing his empty bottle into the trash bin by the door. The women moved to warm their hands by the laundry heater.

"No, sir. He's working today," she replied—meaning, Charles knew, at the steel plant.

"Christmas Eve," he said, shaking his head. "They ought to give a man a break."

"Not on your life," Laura said, zipping her jacket.

Charles walked out to the truck. The fog hid the big cornfield behind the station, but a few pine trees gave a hint of green in the distance, causing the gray morning to break slightly.

"You all right?" he asked Bolivia. She nodded, searching his face with the question her eyes always held but never asked. "We'll be going directly," Charles said. "You want to come on in and warm up, have a Hershey and Nehi?"

She shook her head.

"I'm going to say hello to Keller, and then we'll go," he told her, watching her eyes to see if they responded, but they only held the same dark question and no hint of either uneasiness or desire over the mention of Keller's name.

It was cold. He pulled his fur-lined collar up to warm his neck and walked down into the oil pit, where Keller held a grease gun in his hand.

The boy turned. "Hey, Charles."

"Morning."

"Cold enough for you?" Keller asked, squirting the dark liquid into the holes in the car's underside.

"Looking for a white Christmas?" Charles said.

"Not during your lifetime," he said and looked over and smiled. "Mine either," he added.

"How old are you now?" Charles asked.

"Nineteen."

Keller screwed the caps back on and wiped his brow with a handkerchief. His face was smudged with grease.

Charles looked at the metal toolbox beside Keller to see how rusty it was, if it was getting near time to scrap. The black paint was chipped, but it wasn't old yet. "Where you living now, you and Laura?"

"With her aunt over on the crest."

"Miss Lila?"

"Right."

"She taught me in fifth grade," Charles said.

"She taught everybody."

"Need any wood or coal?" Charles asked him.

"No, sir, not as I know of."

"You keeping up with this war?" he asked.

Keller looked at him and smiled. "Little as possible," he said.

But don't you know your life is hanging on the line? he wanted to ask, but, of course, didn't. "It's not good, is it," Charles asked, feeling him out more, "this war we're in now?"

"Sure isn't."

"You reckon we're in for a long haul?"

"Yes, sir, looks that way."

Charles ran a nail over the toolbox, and a bit of black paint flaked. "Let me know when this box is ready to scrap," he said.

"Yes, sir, sure will."

The boy's eyes were dark like Bolivia's. Charles's stomach turned with the idea of the baby's raisin eyes. "Best move on," Charles said. "By the way, your mama's inside," he added. "She's delivering coal with Bolivia and me."

Keller's suave face lost its color, but Charles didn't know if this was because of the mention of Bolivia's name or his mother's name or the fact they were riding together in Charles's flatbed truck. He turned to walk back up into the gray light, but when he did, headlights broke the fog—two shrouded orbs of light coming straight for the oil pit. Charles didn't move. It was Scotty Sandifer's pickup. Scotty screeched to an abrupt halt, jumped from the cab, and scrambled down into the pit, where Keller stood frozen with the black toolbox. Charles stood aside, letting Scotty come down in. It was, after all, his station and his oil pit. Scotty took off his green baseball cap and ran his fingers over his sandy curls.

"There's been an accident over at the No. 3," he said to Keller.

All three men reached for a cigaret.

"Is it Dad?" Keller asked, leaving his hand over his Luckies, over his heart.

Scotty squatted down, removed his cap, and put his head in his hands. "We don't know. They're all trapped. It wasn't an explosion. Just a wall fell."

Keller's knees gave. He backed up against the wall of the pit. Charles reached for him, an instinctual parental grab, and Keller leaned against him, letting his face fall into the fur collar of Charles's coat. Charles felt the boy's breath, warm and sweet.

Normally, on Christmas Eve, when friends came over to the station for fruitcake and the warmth of the potbellied heater, Scotty began drinking at noon, whiskey rather than beer. But this morning, he was driving Tess Hayes to the No. 3 mine. When he'd crawled from the oil pit and gone in and told the women, Tess had turned pale and put her hand to her face. He'd led her to his truck. And now in his rearview mirror, he saw Charles's flatbed carrying Keller and Bolivia, leaving Laura to tend the station. The fog was lifting, allowing pale light to wash over Warrior Road.

"How did you find out?" Tess asked him, clutching a hand-kerchief. He glanced over at her. She was absolutely still, the way women are when there's trouble.

"Somebody called us at the plant," he said.

"I forgot you work," she said flatly. He looked at her again.

She turned. "I'm sorry. You know what I mean," she said, and her eyes engaged his. He knew she knew her husband might be dead. It had always struck him how preoccupied people were with unnecessary details when tragedy was at hand as, even now, she'd begun picking lint from her winter coat. The new light of midmorning caught in her crazy hair, and he realized that it was her hair that had always made him distrust her.

"You say you're sure it wasn't an explosion?" she implored. "Just a wall fell?"

"That's right," Scotty said and lit a Pall Mall. He offered her one.

"I don't smoke," she said.

"It can't be so awful as the one last spring," he said, thinking of how the men had described Bolivia Ivey's daddy as having been smushed like a pancake against a wall. A trapper boy had lost all his limbs. Scotty shifted gears as he began the ascent up Pinegar Hill to the mine. Frost clung to the pine straw and lichen along the ravine.

Scotty's rifle hung behind them on the rack inside the cab. When they passed the graveyard near the entrance to the mine, Tess stopped picking lint from her coat.

"What do you know?" she said softly.

"I know it can't be as bad as what happened last spring," he repeated, trying to offer her something.

"How do you know some may be alive?"

"I came up here when I heard about it. The ones who got out say they's plenty of men back behind the rock. I asked if Ben Ray might be one of them, and they said yes. Then I went to find you," he said, and Tess started crying.

A crowd was gathering. Behind him, Charles's flatbed was lost in a stream of headlights coming up Pinegar Hill, as if the funeral procession were already under way. Ahead, the barbed-wire fence was cut in half, leaving a gaping hole for onlookers clustered at the foot of the scrap hill or beside the flatcars or even atop the bathhouse, where they were bundled in thick jackets, blankets, and scarves, silent and stoic. Scotty remembered when his father worked in the tiny mine up near Lizard Ridge, where charcoal-stained Shetland ponies pulled loaded cars from the coal face to wood hoppers. He later moved to the Dolomite mine and was killed there when four trip cars broke loose and raced like mad down the slope. Arcs from the cable ignited the dust and caused the mine's mouth to roar fire so intense that the tipple burned. The day was, in Scotty's memory, laden with fright more than grief. The power of the mine was terrifying. So was his father. He drank, and Scotty was afraid of him.

As he helped Tess from his truck, Scotty tried to guide her through the mud to the bathhouse, but she resisted being led and made her own way. He noticed the scent of liquor from somebody's breath and wanted a drink. He wanted a normal day's day of drinking and a traditional Christmas Eve fight with Grace. But he knew this day was going to be long and messy and that it would be hours of standing here in the cold with Tess Hayes waiting for dead miners. He wasn't going to have a drink until sunset. It was a jarring thought. There were days when he did make it till dark. Then there was always the needling idea that most men didn't have to drink every day. He wanted, in some way, to be like them. So he sometimes decided he'd try to go all day without a drink. The idea began to plant itself that he might go all day *this day* without a drink. He knew from experience, though, that he wasn't likely to make it. He stomped his cigaret into the layer of slag that coated the frozen mud. Cars unloaded women and children until eventually they were spread all the way back to the graveyard. He looked for Charles's flatbed truck but didn't see it.

Keller moved his body as close as possible to the door of Charles's cab, but despite the struggle, his left elbow kept brushing Bolivia's belly. It was as if an animal were asleep under her big coat. Occasionally it moved, so definite that Keller shivered involuntarily and Bolivia looked over at him. His fear was growing right along with the baby. And now there was this—his daddy. He tried to swallow a sob, and the effect was the gag of impending vomit. Charles and Bolivia reached over to touch him, and at their touch, he started crying. Traffic jammed Pinegar Hill. Horns were blowing. People were cursing so loud their voices carried through the closed windows of the truck. The fog that had lifted along Warrior Road was gathering again as they went higher up the hill, so thick that it spooked him anew, just as it had this morning when he woke with a start and reached for the solace of Laura.

Charles jumped from the cab to investigate the stalled stream of miners' cars. When he closed the door, Bolivia took Keller's hand inside hers and rubbed it. He'd forgotten that her hands were soft, a surprise considering her leathery ginger skin strung tight to the bones. She cradled his hand as if it were a fresh glob of dough, and he didn't stop her. He looked at her. She was crying, and he remembered that she *knew*, of course she knew what it was like to have your father crushed under a mine wall. But she hadn't had the luxury of making the ascent up Pinegar Hill with hope in her heart. News of her daddy's death was hand-delivered by Ben Ray with no warning, no promise, only a hard, indelible fact. And out of that fact, the baby was conceived.

With more care than he'd ever known, with a tenderness he didn't know he had, Keller reached for her belly and felt the baby respond to his hand moving.

She put her hand over his. "It kicks a lot in the morning," she told him.

"Does it hurt?" he whispered.

"No," she whispered back.

"What does it feel like?"

"A cat," she said.

He moved his hand higher.

"That's the legs," she told him.

"Legs?"

"Yes, it's turned."

He looked at her. Her dark eyes were sparkling.

"What do you mean *turned*?" he asked her.

"A baby turns when it gets close to being born. Its head is down here," she said. "Between my legs, like the rest of this town," she whispered and they both laughed.

Keller put his head down over her stomach. She ran her fingers all through his hair. He closed his eyes. When he opened them, he saw Charles's face at the window. He didn't care. He didn't care about anything at all. If his daddy was dead, he didn't want to live, either.

Charles got in.

Keller kept his head in Bolivia's lap, listening, feeling his baby kicking his ear.

"He knows," Bolivia said.

Keller didn't respond. He closed his eyes.

"Charles knows," she repeated and kept her fingers moving in his hair.

Keller turned his head a bit so as to gaze into Charles's eyes. They were gentle like Ben Ray's.

Charles took off his gloves and blew on his big hands.

"Does your mama or daddy know, you reckon?" Charles asked.

"No," Keller said.

"Charles wants to raise this baby," Bolivia told him.

"Good," Keller said and closed his eyes again. He felt like he was dreaming or drunk.

Charles put the truck back in gear and Keller raised his head. Up ahead, the tipple rose. When the bathhouse came into view, he saw that people were up on the roof. Beside the scrap hill, he saw his mother standing alongside Scotty Sandifer, who held her elbow, and he started crying again.

Scotty and Charles left Keller with the women and headed for a small gray building, the office of the mine superintendent, Charles's brother. The shade was up at the clacker window, which on normal days would signify that advances were being doled out to the men in line. There were two pay stations, two holes in the window: one for blacks, one for whites. Charles threw open the screen door, with Scotty at his heels.

The office was jammed with miners, crying women, and a photographer. Ranger, Charles's brother, was on the telephone. He was wearing a blue cap. "On Christmas Eve," he said when he saw Charles. His face was gray as cobwebs. Charles knew that his brother was genuinely stricken, and he was overcome with compassion over the inevitable blame that might be cast on Ranger even though everybody who worked for him liked him. In general, the higher up you were in the coal business, the greater the snipes from below. But in Ranger's case, the snipes came from the upper echelon, who suspected that Ranger was still one of the boys who supported the union movement. Overhead, a fan blew in an effort to circulate heat from the potbellied stove beside the big safe. Its drop cord dangled right above Ranger's cap. A woman backed into the Graphotype machine and fell, knocking metal plates all over the floor.

"Get the women out of here," Ranger said quietly to Charles.

Charles understood that it wasn't just their stricken faces that were making Ranger nervous. It was the lingering superstition that allowing women even close to the mouth of a mine would cause disasters. Charles had heard a story of a miner's wife in Kentucky who disguised herself and rode a mantrip all the way in to find her husband, who'd left his dinner bucket at home. When she was discovered, the story went, over a hundred men quit for the day, fearing for their lives.

"And tell that blueblood photographer to go on back to Birmingham and stuff his stocking," Ranger said. He had no use for reporters or for Birmingham.

Charles moved toward the woman who'd fallen over the Graphotype machine. He offered her his hand and led her gently to the door. "What's your husband's name?" he said softly, knowing that it was irrelevant but wanting to give her something. But even as she spoke it, he wasn't hearing. He was looking out the window toward the mine, where a group of black-faced men were clustered. He wheeled back to Ranger.

"Who's that?" he shouted. "They're already out!"

"All the front main got out," a man yelled back at Charles. Charles recognized him as a shot firer.

"Is Ben Ray Hayes with them?" Charles asked, opening the screen door for the woman at his side. She walked off, the hem of her long, shabby dress trailing on the ground behind her. Scotty Sandifer followed after her, offering, Charles guessed, whatever solace he had in him. He then returned to the office and began leading women from the room one by one, holding them by the elbows and taking them out into the cold.

"Ben Ray Hayes ain't out," the shot firer told him.

"We're going in as soon as I call Birmingham," Ranger told Charles. "I don't think we need the coroner," he said, with what Charles felt was undue optimism. "There's an ambulance over there," Ranger added.

"Any bodies yet?" Charles asked the shot firer.

"Don't know."

Charles eyed the scattered metal plates on the floor, wondering if they were still being used. They'd make good scrap. He leaned against the oak desk he'd built for Ranger. An oil lamp sat on it. The photographer got a notepad from his tweed jacket.

"Does this mine belong to Woodward Coal and Iron?" he asked Scotty.

Scotty blew smoke in his face.

"You work here?"

Scotty didn't answer.

To Charles he said, "You're the superintendent's brother?"

Charles nodded.

"Is it true that he is the neighborhood Santa Claus?"

Charles laughed at the budding attempt at a human-interest story.

Ranger rose from his desk and headed for the door. Charles and Scotty followed. Since there had been no explosion, there was no mob, no hysteria, only a cluster of women wrapped in heavy coats and holding the hands of their children, having received the news by word of mouth. Charles caught sight of Tess and Bolivia and Keller, standing in the muddy slush beside the scrap hill, staring ahead at the mouth of the mine. Men were jammed in, making sure there was no blackdamp before entering. There was certainly none coming from the entrance as Charles had witnessed at explosions. Ranger took the hands of women as he passed them, just like a preacher does on Sundays, and then, on coming to the mine, stared into the black abyss.

Charles lit a cigaret. A cold mist was falling.

Scotty stood beside him.

A woman next to Charles, wearing a scarf wrapped mummy-style all over her face so that only her eyes showed, said to him, "Are there bodies yet?"

"You got people down there?" he asked her.

"My son-in-law. He's a brattice man," she said. "Aren't you Ranger Avery's brother?"

"Right," Charles said, looking away.

"Why don't he tell those people in Birmingham they're going to rot in hell?" she pressed.

He looked at her.

"They's been a inspector up here more than once this year. Ventilation is sorry, they's dust and dirt and loose roof on the haulage roads. Why don't they *do* something?" she said, and began unwinding the scarf from her face.

"You're wrong about the ventilation," he said. "This mine has some of the best in the country," he told her.

The crowd was growing. So was the noise, and with it came a cluster of men toward the mouth.

"You going in?" a section foreman asked Charles.

Ranger turned back to Charles. "Go back to the office," he told him. "Gather the women up—the ones who got men in here—and see to it they're warm and got fresh coffee. I shouldn't've made them leave the office. Make sure the photographer doesn't take their pictures. Then come on back down. We'll wait for you."

Bolivia stared at the tipple. She'd never been up here before. Her daddy was buried down the road at the cemetery, but the day they buried him she had not noticed the tipple in the near distance or even the scrap hill. She knew that the sulphur stench came from a scrap hill, but she'd never seen it until now. The baby's head pushed harder against her body until she felt that her skin was going to rip open and the baby would spill out against the hard frozen mud. She'd seen kittens being born and dogs, too—the way the mother broke the sac and drank the water up. She wondered if she could will the baby to wait a few more days until all this was over, but early this morning she'd noticed that the pain was coming in waves rather than isolated moments. She missed her mother. Her mother had told her, "I was in labor with you for four days." Perhaps the same would be true for her. Her mother had told her that she was born on a spring evening. She'd been out gathering nuts and berries along the ridge when her water broke, coating her brown legs with a liquid that felt like warm milk. Earlier that day, she'd punctured her foot with a nail and had rubbed it with kerosene, or "coal oil," as she called it.

Her mother had a cure for everything—swamp root for kidney ailments, quinine for chills and fever, and turpentine for cuts. Her cut foot, she said, hurt more than Bolivia's head forcing its way down the path to light. Her mother could predict things before they happened. Bolivia knew she had it too, because this was something that mothers passed on to daughters through their blood. She knew she had it, but she didn't choose to let it grow and flourish. She didn't want to know the future. Life was bad enough as it was.

Bolivia stood beside Tess, trying to make the idea come alive that Ben Ray wasn't dead, but she could not quite construe it. What concerned her most was Keller. Her mother had told her, "Once you have a baby with a man, the man's life is yours. You know the roads he'll travel. You can predict his every move." Bolivia didn't believe her; she only missed her. Yet when she'd touched Keller's skin in the truck, her hands tingled and a rainbow of light came to her.

Tess turned to Bolivia. "Are you too cold?" she asked softly and reached for the baby's shape.

"I need to sit down," Bolivia told her.

"Yes, yes," Tess said. "You need to get back in the truck. You really need to go home. This is no place for you," she said, and then quickly put her hand to her mouth. "Oh," she said.

Bolivia looked at her.

Tess's sturdy shoulders fell. "I just remembered your father."

As they walked to the car, Tess held Bolivia's elbow. It wasn't easy getting up into Charles's cab. They sat beside one another, quiet and cold. Bolivia watched the cars coming up Pinegar Hill, their headlights glowing in the morning fog. Women poured from the cabs of trucks, huddling close, and moving in the direction of the mine. In the distance, she saw that the railroad trestle that ran over the ravine was busy with people taking a shortcut.

"I miss my mother," she said to Tess.

Tess turned to her, then wrapped her arms around her and drew her close. "I know you do, sweetie," she said.

Bolivia buried her face in Tess's heavy coat and sturdy body. She didn't want to be let go. This, she supposed, was what most women felt in the arms of a man.

"Don't worry," Tess said. "I'm going to birth your baby."

Bolivia didn't say anything. Would Tess deliver the baby if she knew the truth?

Mercy.

She raised her head. "What did you say?"

Tess was staring out the window. She didn't respond.

"Did you say something?" Bolivia asked her again.

"I said I'm going to birth your baby."

"After that, I mean. What did you say after that?"

Tess kept staring out the window. "Here comes Keller and Charles," she said. She put her hands on her cheeks. "Oh, I don't want to know anything. I don't want to know anything yet."

Bolivia looked at the sky. A patch of blue, the size of a hand, was showing. Mercy, she said to herself, and her mother's voice replied back, *Mercy.*

Charles motioned for Tess to roll the window down.

"We don't know anything yet," he said.

Keller's hands were jammed hard into his pockets. He was shivering.

"Somebody needs to take Bolivia home," Tess said.

Keller felt Charles's eyes on his back. "Do you mind?" Charles mumbled to him. "I need to stay here. And Ranger says for the wives to just stay in his office," he said to Tess.

Keller helped Tess from the cab, grateful that she wasn't hysterical like some of the women who'd just arrived. Charles gave him the keys. Keller got in and cranked the truck. His hands were freezing. It took an eternity to battle the traffic back down Pinegar Hill to Bolivia's place. When they got there, he parked beside her yard, where overturned clay planters lay in the frozen remains of a turnip patch. The goose who'd nipped his shins the morning he'd come to see Bolivia squawked from under the porch but didn't attack. He hesitated, knowing he ought to leave. Bolivia opened the door wide, though, and he went inside. He hadn't been here since the morning he came to see her nine months ago. That morning, he hadn't noticed the string of dried red peppers across the room or the Indian-looking thing spread over the sofa. He went to the back, gathered some firewood, and started a fire going. Gradually the room warmed up. She stood beside the stove, rocking a pot of milk over the heat.

"You like hot cocoa," she said, more of a statement than a question.

He nodded. The reality of what had happened to Ben Ray flooded him as if he were just hearing the news of the cave-in, and he sat down in the rocker, staring at his mud-caked boots.

Bolivia handed him a mug of steaming hot chocolate. He studied the cedar tree trimmed with decorations.

"Where'd you get that?" he asked her.

"Charles."

She sat on the sofa with the bright tapestry, her bony hands folded in her lap. She was wearing an orange apron that he believed had been his mother's. Cats rubbed against her legs—a calico, a tabby, a mixture he didn't know. The black one leapt up and curled itself over the baby's mound.

"She loves the cats," she said. "She kicks at them every time."

Keller looked at her. "She?" he questioned.

"The baby's a girl," Bolivia told him.

"How do you know?"

She stroked the cat. "There are black cats up in Tennessee with one eye," she told him. He sipped his cocoa and tried to avoid her eyes. "There was a three-year-old boy who was run over and killed by a train, and afterward a one-eyed black cat ran all around the boy."

"Who told you that? That's all bullshit."

"My mother," she said. "And there was one that ran along the trestle near Wilder, warning people of bad news."

He looked at her. "What's Wilder?"

"It's where I was born."

He realized that he knew nothing about her.

"And"—she leaned forward, pushing the cat from her lap—"when they had that big explosion after the strike when I was little, a one-eyed black cat was found in the mine, crawling all over the bodies, sniffing and purring and carrying on. But if you give a black newborn kit to somebody you love, it will bring good luck. Your daddy's still alive," she said and rose from the sofa, holding her hands over the baby. Her riverwater eyes were fixed with points of light.

"How do you know?" he demanded, putting his mug on a crate and grabbing her arms from the rocker. She stood over him.

"I hope he is," she said, her voice weakening.

"But you said it like you meant it, like you knew," he pled.

"I felt like he was alive."

"But what do you mean, you *felt* like it? Do you still *feel* like it?"

"I shouldn't say, because I may be wrong."

She stood in front of him. He held her thin arms and she gently pulled his head forward until it rested against the baby. He felt like his life was skidding recklessly off the side of the road. But she stroked his hair just as she had in the car, and he was hypnotized once more by the sound of the baby.

She tilted his face upward. Hers was radiant.

"Are you a witch?" he asked her.

"I'm a Melungeon."

He looked up at her. He'd heard this before, but he didn't understand what it meant. Somebody had told him it meant a nigger hillbilly.

"My mother was a medicine woman," she went on.

He didn't know what the hell she was talking about. He didn't want to know. He put his head against her again, listening to the water, wondering why it made him believe that Ben Ray was alive and that the rest of all this was just a bad dream.

"Men do walk out of tombs," she told him.

"What does that mean?" he asked and felt the baby squirm. "Did you feel that?" he asked her. "Did you feel it move?"

"Of course," she said and gently touched his lips with her fingers.

"Men can be dead and arise," she told him.

"You've been reading the Bible," he said and stopped her fingers from moving over his lips because he was beginning to want to kiss her.

"Charles found me a Bible," she said, and knelt down to be eye level with him, as he was still sitting in the rocker, leaning forward, his muddy boots digging into her blue-and-green hooked rug. "Those women at that tomb seeing an angel, then seeing a dead man walking in the flesh. And did you know that Jesus loved a whore?"

"Yes," he said.

A square of sunlight came through the ripped place in the dingy sheets draped over her front window. It danced on the strung bottlecaps that dangled from her cedar holiday tree. He'd heard no carols this year. The war, he reasoned. He studied her face curiously, touched her braids as she knelt by his chair, idly untied the red yarn, and put it in the pocket of his blue jeans. She nodded as if she understood that it would somehow bring him good luck. The neighborhood was particularly quiet, and Keller realized that everybody was either trapped in the mine or praying.

The morning he'd come to see her last spring was warm, and a paper moon hung seductively low, giving an illusion of lingering night. He'd risen with Ben Ray and walked with him as far as Pinegar Hill, his father's dinner bucket brushing Keller's legs as they moved along. They parted ways at the railroad tracks, and Keller went on to work at the commissary. Graham wasn't there yet. Keller went inside to the back of the store, where a wooden loft and triangular window—his favorite place—overlooked the west side of Sweetgum Flat. There in spring, fields would begin to bear traces of green corn seedlings, and the smell of manure mixed with sweetshrub gave off a natural, sordid blending of something terribly alluring, the way he felt women must smell and taste after you'd already done it once and were beginning to do it again. He'd stood there in the loft at the commissary, staring at the cornfields, with Bolivia's face seared in the darkest part of him. The worst part was knowing that it was her shock, the way her face had caved in as Ben Ray delivered the news that her daddy was dead, the dark eyes drawing inward, the impact of fresh grief that aroused him for reasons he didn't understand. And the idea drove him crazy, had driven him crazy day after day since the incident until finally, that morning, he could bear it no longer and walked down the alley past all the outhouses, bearing up the acrid odor of all the waste in his world. He hadn't gone to her front door. He was too scared. He tapped lightly on the back door with a mess of cats swarming at his feet, a goose nipping his shins. She was wearing a flimsy nightgown. Her house smelled like bacon grease. She didn't say a word, just let him in, first to her kitchen, then to her sitting room, then to her bed, then to her.

It was semi-dark in her room, because sheets draped the windows.

The room was spare, with one table that held a metal cup. He sat on the edge of the bed. She lay down. "Do you like to take it off?" she asked, gesturing to her nightgown. She was dark, almost colored, and this made his heart race.

He knelt beside the bed. "No, don't take it off," he said. He had a fleeting, foolish idea that he should have brought her a flower. "I'm sorry," he whispered.

"For what?" she whispered back, though nobody was listening.

"For your daddy," he said quietly.

Her eyes grew moist and she reached for him and pulled him down to her. Keeping his boots on the floor, he buried his face in her long, brown hair. He hadn't intended to be in her bed when he told her he was sorry.

"Where's your mother?" he whispered.

"She's dead."

He put his arm around her. He was beside her, yet his feet were still on the floor. He was afraid to move them. As long as his feet were touching the floor, he was safe.

"I'm sorry," he whispered. He'd held girls like this before, in the backseat of cars.

She lay in the crook of his arm and put a hand on his chest. He knew she felt his heart pounding, knew that she knew that no matter how good his intentions had been for coming to see her, he was now just a man.

"It's nice of you to come," she whispered. He made himself look at her—the dark, wild eyes. "Do you want anything?" she asked, and he felt himself weakening.

"I just came to say I'm sorry," he said. "I'm sorry," he repeated, but now he knew he was sorry for something other than the fact that she was an orphan.

He was sorry that he wanted her.

It was midmorning. The sheets over the windows caused the light to stay a fixed pale-yellow. Fabric colors looked stained—her gown, the sheets, his own white shirt that rose and fell with his breath. She ran her fingers in a space between the buttons, feeling the patch of hair on his chest. He wanted her to unbutton his shirt, but she didn't.

"Can you keep living here without your daddy?" he asked. "Maybe."

He looked at her face. "Do you need money?"

"I make a living," she said.

He searched her eyes. They were those of a woman, not a girl. "Do you miss him?" he asked her.

She put her arms around him. He felt her crying, but she didn't look up, just moved against his body. He put his hands in her hair. She didn't make a sound, just lay beside him, moving in his arms. He couldn't get her close enough. He kept drawing her body up to his, running his hands over her back, until he suddenly realized she'd grown still—an eerie stillness he recognized as unexpected arousal. His hands froze along her spine.

"How old are you?" she whispered.

"Nineteen."

"A boy," she said, looking wistfully at him. "A virgin."

He nodded.

She lifted the nightgown over her head, rolled over to her back, and put her arms over her head. He'd heard that whores didn't feel anything. But her face was alive with desire.

"It's all right," she comforted. "It's all right, baby."

He closed his eyes.

"Take off your boots," she said.

He sat up, leaned over, and unlaced them.

"You want to leave your shirt on?" she whispered.

He nodded, wondering if her door was locked.

"It's all right," she said.

"No," he relented. "I want to take it off."

When he did, he saw her take in his chest. It was tanned from working shirtless in his mother's garden, planting spring seed. She shook her head, staring in wonder, and he knew she liked what she saw.

"The door?" he asked lamely.

"I locked it."

He lay down beside her, in his jeans.

She was naked.

Taking off his jeans, he laid his wallet on the table beside her bed. She looked at him quizzically—a brief moment that only later did he understand was her unspoken question of a condom. In that moment, though, it didn't register. It didn't matter. She pulled him down to her with an urgency that caused him to quicken. He struggled to make it last as long as possible, but he knew he was drowning.

Now, she was kneeling beside the rocker, holding the baby as if it were already born, a separate entity wrapped in an orange apron that had belonged to his mother, her eyes still sparkling as if a part of her brain were illuminated, and her eyes were only peepholes to the light.

"There's nothing to forgive you for," she said.

"I will always love you for what you did at the wedding," he told her. "For fighting Scotty back."

"Yes, you'll always love me," she said. "But not for reasons that you think."

He looked at her.

"It's time for you to go," she said and brushed his chapped lips once more with her fingers. "Your wife will give you children," she said. "Boys," she added and smiled, an ordinary smile, the way regular girls smile, and he felt a flood of relief. He stood up and took his mug to her kitchen. Her backyard was filled with blackbirds, a host so dense that the entire earth was the color of coal. They all rose in unison and disappeared over the ridge beyond the last outhouse. Beside her sink was the canister that had held teacakes for his wedding.

"I am praying for your daddy," she told him as he put on his coat to leave.

He told her, "Merry Christmas," and headed back up Pinegar Hill to the mine, his gut churning with renewed anguish over what he might learn when he got there.

Fearing a congested parking situation, he parked Charles's truck by the cemetery that lay just south of the mine area. Leaves covered most of the markers. He zipped his coat up and put his hands in the pockets of his blue jeans. Tall amber weeds blew in the wind. He walked on up the hill toward the mine, and the sulphur scent got stronger. A guard stood near the entrance to the bathhouse and superintendent's office, but as Keller got closer he recognized the man as the blacksmith.

"You got immediate kin here?" he asked Keller. His face was sooty.

"Yes, sir. My daddy."

The blacksmith's face lit up. "Ben Ray Hayes's boy, ain't you?"

"Yes, sir. Is he out?"

The blacksmith put a big hand on Keller's shoulder. "No, he's not. There's a group who just went down to investigate. Now, you know there wasn't no explosion, don't you?"

"Yes, sir."

"That's a good thing," the blacksmith affirmed.

"Yes, sir. You got any cigarets, sir?" Keller asked, patting his own empty pocket.

The blacksmith gave him a crushed pack of Camels. "Take the rest," he said. "Does your mama know about this?" he asked, lighting a match for Keller and shielding the flame from the wind.

"Yes, sir. She's up here somewhere," Keller said, staring beyond the blacksmith to the superintendent's gray office, the tipple, and the scrap hill. He dug his boots into the mud and slag, inhaled the savory nicotine until his lungs burned with satisfaction, then flicked the cigaret with his thumb.

"The women are in the office," the blacksmith said, and went into a coughing fit—a sound that Keller knew all too well.

"Thanks," he said and walked over to the office.

He found women and children on the floor. Most of the children had their heads in their mothers' laps, but a few boys were crawling under the Graphotype machine, playing with the metal plates scattered on the floor. Keller had never been inside the office; he'd only stood at the payroll window with Ben Ray when he was a boy alongside the other white men, staring curiously at the colored men on the other side of the partition, wondering why they had to stand in a separate line and why they were bigger and darker.

Tess was holding another woman's baby, but when she saw Keller she rose, handed the baby to its mother.

"You don't know anything yet, do you?" he asked, searching her green eyes for information.

"No," she said. "A group went in a while ago. Scotty Sandifer went too, Keller," she said as if this were significant.

He shrugged.

The office was warm and bright. The sun had broken the fog

and was coming through the venetian blinds in yellow bands, striping the big safe in the corner. On the wall was a state map with black dots signifying coal seams. They ran like dark fingers over the land, darting in and out of the Appalachian foothills of Alabama.

Tess messed with his shirt collar the way she'd done all his life, and he backed away the way he'd done all his life.

He put his cigaret out in an ashtray that said in red print BIRMINGHAM, THE MAGIC CITY. There was a skyline that showed the Tutwiler Hotel, the Comer building, and the Alabama Theatre all on the same street, geographically incorrect and disproportionate in size. He kept his eyes fixed on the ashtray. Everything was important, everything that belonged to the company that might save his father's life.

Tess sat down on the floor. He knelt on one knee beside her. "You got to sing this evening in Birmingham," he said softly and smiled. "Catholic money," he whispered, raising an eyebrow and evoking the laugh he sought from her.

The woman next to her, whom Keller recognized as the machine runner's wife, said to Tess, "Don't pass it up. You may need it more than you think." A few others nearby laughed. They were all on the floor, all sitting cross-legged.

"Y'all want some coffee?" he asked them. "Or listen, I can go to the commissary and get sweetrolls. We can, you know, use this as an opportunity to milk Graham," he said in collusive rancor.

The women laughed. One asked Keller for a cigaret, and another said, "Law, Myrtle! You don't smoke, do you?"

"Right now, I can do whatever I want," Myrtle joked.

They began to chatter, to break the deathwatch. A few rose to get coffee, and were amused by the sight of their boys scattering the company's metal plates from the Graphotype machine.

Keller went back outside. When he did, he saw a group of men coming up the hill from the mine. His heart began pounding, and he started down the hill toward them. The superintendent, Ranger Avery, was carrying a safety lantern. Charles and Scotty were on either side of him, and behind the trio was a host of miners and laymen alike, wearing their lamplit hats and overalls.

Keller looked at their faces.

When he got close enough, he moved alongside Charles. Charles turned to him. "There are a few bodies," he said. "Not your daddy's. The left section where your daddy was working is blocked." Charles's eyes lit up. "We can hear his voice, boy. We can hear your daddy's voice. All his crew is alive. We just can't get to them yet."

Keller felt his knees give, just like they had in the oil pit when Scotty told him the news of the accident. He reached for Charles, and Charles held him steady.

Charles turned to his brother, the superintendent, Ranger. "This is Ben Ray Hayes's boy," he said.

Ranger extended his hand to Keller.

Keller shook it. He hadn't spoken to the guy since the night he took his daughter to the Valentine party five years ago, but he saw him every Christmas along Warrior Road dressed as Santa Claus, tossing peppermints to kids. They walked up the hill. Keller caught Scotty Sandifer's eye, but Scotty didn't respond, didn't say a word—just spat tobacco to the earth, and Keller realized they'd all been chewing it underground since they couldn't smoke.

Keller felt for Bolivia's red yarn in his pocket. He knew now that she was a witch or an angel or something.

"Take my truck home with you," Charles said. "I'll be up here the rest of the day and probably all night, too."

Keller looked at him. "I'll be back, too," he said, "after I go see Laura."

Charles shrugged. "Whatever," he said. "Just don't worry about getting it back to me."

When they got back to the office, the women rose from the floor, and the boys quickly shoved the metal plates to one corner. All stood as if saluting a general, and the superintendent took off his light, set his hat on his desk, and because his head was bowed with compassion, they knew that there were bodies. He began searching their faces, but because he didn't know them well enough to know their names, he had to call out the names of the men whom they'd found, whose bodies were still below awaiting stretchers that hadn't arrived and the coroner who hadn't been called. And with each name, the stricken wife's face would implode upon itself as if dynamited, and the rest of the women would turn inward to her, so that the room became pockets of sorrow.

Keller took his mother aside and told her that his father's voice had been heard.

Tess, in the warmth of the sunlight and in the relief over Ben Ray being spared, decided, outside the superintendent's office, that she wanted to sing that evening as planned. She needed the money. Keller told her that he'd pick her up later in the afternoon, but Scotty, standing nearby said, "No, I want to do that."

Keller and Tess looked at him, stunned. He was chewing a weed, leaning up against the pay window—the shade was still ironically raised.

"I'll do it," Keller said, feeling his pocket but finding only the pack, now empty and crumpled, given to him earlier by the blacksmith at the gate.

"You go be with your wife," Scotty said, languidly gnawing the spindly weed. Keller couldn't tell if it was said in earnest or in spite, and he was too weary to try to decide. He shrugged and looked at his mother.

"That would be very kind, Scotty," she said, unamiable but polite. Keller took his keys and moved on down the hill. He turned back.

"But do you want me to take you home first to change clothes or anything?" he called to his mother. She shook her head. Scotty was holding her elbow like some kind of miniature soldier.

Keller ran down the hill past the cemetery to Charles's truck, on fire with the electricity of disaster and relief. He believed, in those moments of flying toward his car, that Bolivia was responsible for his father's survival, that she was a good witch who would be his guardian angel. He ran faster than he'd ever run in his life and was certain that, like in his dreams, his feet were going to escape the earth and send his body upward to the blue winter sky.

He jumped into the truck, cranked it, and sped down to Warrior Road, where the red brick filling station stood in the distance, the meeting place of his youth, the place that cradled his love and hope for order—Laura.

She was, of course, down in the oil pit, working on a car, wearing her usual green workpants with the rag hanging from her back pocket. He grabbed her from behind, and she dropped her tools.

"Is he all right?" she asked, clutching Keller's arms.

"I think so," he said, knowing as he said it that it smacked of undue optimism, but he didn't care. He felt that he could *will* Ben Ray's survival if he tried hard enough.

Laura gathered her tools.

"Finish up," he told her.

"I'm all done," she said and walked with him from the pit.

They stood beside the oak tree in the sun. Cars traveled along Warrior Road, throwing dust up and leaving dark streams of exhaust in their wake. The sun hit the top of Keller's head.

"Tell me!" Laura said. "What do you know?"

"A wall fell. Do you know Burt Snively or Red Jarrett or Buddy O'Cadlin?"

"No."

"They didn't make it," he told her and felt his courage dying. The euphoria he'd felt coming down Pinegar Hill was seeping from his skin.

"How do you know your daddy's all right?"

He sighed and ran his fingers through his hair. "They heard his voice. All his crew is trapped in a pocket."

Laura wiped her hands on her pants.

"They've got to dig through to get them."

Laura shielded her blue eyes from the winter sun, searching his face.

"What's wrong?" he asked her, sensing that she wasn't reacting. "You believe me, don't you?"

She took his hand. "Sure I do," she said, and led him inside.

What she didn't tell him was that she'd driven the car she was working on up to Sweetgum Flat a while ago. Her intent was to find him at the mine, to be with him in case the worst was true, and to brace him up. But when she passed his street, she'd seen him getting out of Charles's truck in front of Bolivia Ivey's place. She'd driven on up past the commissary, post office, and school. Then she'd gone over to the crest where they were living with her Aunt Lila, gotten some bread and peanut butter from Lila's cupboard, made a sandwich, and slowly eaten it. She'd driven back to Bolivia's forty-five minutes later, where she'd seen Charles's truck still parked. She'd felt the armor growing along her heart.

For as long as she could remember, she'd been a boy. It wasn't that she didn't like sewing or pinafores or candies. It was just that she didn't cry. She cried once when she was young. Her cat had given birth, and Scotty, particularly drunk, had told her to gather the kittens up because they were already dead and needed to be thrown into the river. Crying, she took them from their mother's tits. It was summer. She was wearing yellow pants and a T-shirt. In the car, she snuggled the sacked kittens up under her shirt.

"Daddy," she said, "they're moving."

He threw a bottle out the window and it landed alongside Warrior Road.

"Shut up. They're dead as doornails."

But she knew they weren't. They felt warm, and as they moved along her sweaty stomach she wept. When they got to the lake, Scotty tossed the sack off the bank into the river. On the way back home, he told her that if she'd kept her mouth shut and hadn't done all that crying, he might have saved the kittens.

She hadn't cried since then.

And now she was standing beside the counter, facing Keller. His brown eyes were like dark oil. Studying his face, she questioned silently what she'd be saying now—about his being at Bolivia's—if his daddy wasn't buried over in the No. 3 mine. Would she ask him what he was doing there? It was the kind of question most girls, she supposed, asked their best friend or even a host of girlfriends at the soda fountain over dopes and hotdogs. But there were no girlfriends and no sodas. Their broomstick skirts and gabardine suits were as foreign as happiness. In high school she was accepted and in fact popular in a peculiar sense. She played baseball with the neighborhood boys after school. On Friday nights she led cheers because the girls insisted. In fact, they drafted her because of the dramatic acrobatic tumbling feats she carried off: a cartwheel over a barrel with the team's logo; a handspring after the national anthem; a rollicking series of backflips over the entire football field. She loved the stadium. Since it was built directly behind the Sandifers' home, she spent her girlhood playing there after the WPA built it in the thirties. The construction of the place was one of her best memories because she lived there day in and day out, free from Scotty's wild and growing alcoholism.

But now as Keller took her hands and drew her close, she knew she probably wouldn't have said anything anyway about Bolivia, even if Ben Ray hadn't been in trouble. It was something she'd learned from Grace—that if you rock a boat, you might sink with it.

"Can you go with me over to the commissary?" he asked her.
"Where's Grace?"

"Bessemer."

"Can you just close the station?"

She looked at the clock over by the air-compressor machine.
Tapping her fingers on the green drink box, she sighed. "Sure,"
she said.

When they got to the commissary, Graham wasn't there. The
shelving ladder was up, evidence that he'd been stocking meal
and flour. Keller knocked on the door of Graham's family quarters. His wife, who had bad legs, hollered, "Who is it?" and
Keller responded. She yelled back that Graham was at the mine.
"Come in," she told Keller. Laura peered in over his shoulder.
Graham's wife was in a rocker beside the stove, knitting something purple, her legs draped in quilts. The place smelled of
turpentine and ham hocks cooking in beans.

"I'm praying for your daddy," she told Keller.

After he came back out and closed the door, he sat in the back
room on the steps leading to the loft overhead and put his face
in his hands. He was wearing a camel suede-looking jacket that
Ben Ray gave him when he graduated from high school. Laura
stood over him. He cried. Nobody cried in her family. She
watched him curiously.

She tried thinking about Ben Ray, but she couldn't stop thinking about Bolivia. What was Keller doing there? Had he ever
been with her? The thought crept up along her back, causing
her skin to flush with anger. He was *hers*.

She began cleaning her nails with a pocketknife. Keller
stopped crying.

"What's the matter?" he asked her.

She didn't look at him.

"Just thinking about your daddy," she lied, carefully sliding
the knife under her thumbnail.

Keller stood and walked up the stairs to the loft.

She snapped her pocketknife shut and followed him to where
he stood beside the triangular window, staring at the field below.

"Your daddy is taking Mom to Birmingham this afternoon," he said.

She turned to him. "What for?"

"She was supposed to sing at a church service this evening."

Laura snapped her pocketknife shut.

"Why's *he* taking her?" she asked.

Keller shrugged. "There are a lot of strange things happening," he said, and she glanced at his face. His eyes were those of a trapped animal.

"Do you think I'll have to go to war? I could get killed myself?"

She looked at the field. Nothing was growing. "I don't know anything about wars," she replied.

"Boys fight them," he said.

She wondered if Bolivia Ivey thought Keller was a good lover. She looked over at him, at his muscular arms and handsome face. Compared to all the miners, he must be wonderful to her, she thought.

She shivered.

Keller looked at her. "What is it?"

"The war," she replied.

"Daddy never fought one," he said.

"Fighting one now," she said, but she was trying to imagine Keller taking off his clothes in front of Bolivia. She felt like killing somebody.

"Come on," he said, glancing at his watch. "Let's go to the mine."

She zipped her jacket up and followed him to the car. "I've been painting the woodwork red," he told her, gesturing to the commissary's gray exterior.

"Festive," she commented.

Dusk was imminent. The balminess of the day reminded Charles of spring winds. Plus, the tragedy had all his juices going. Death's arousal was disturbing, and he understood what drove men to war and what propelled their memory back to combat. Growing up in the mines and participating in these rescue operations gave a center to his life. And he'd grown to know what to expect.

He lit a cigaret, studying his brother's face, gold in the glow from the hanging bulb as they waited for the Birmingham team to arrive along with the rescue operation from the steel plant. The volunteers were outside smoking, shuffling their boots over the earth and searching the sky as night approached. They'd be here all night; Ben Ray Hayes's voice repeated itself like magic in their minds to keep them going. The pumps were going too, keeping up a constant flow of air into the area where the men were presumed to be. Since they had their dinner buckets and water, they could sustain themselves for days. The biggest problem was that during the drilling to get through to them, another wall could fall. Charles had known this to happen plenty of times.

Charles looked out the window and saw Keller and Laura coming up the hill.

"This is Ben Ray Hayes's boy coming," he told Ranger. Ranger glanced up from the drawing of the ventilation system.

When Charles opened the door, he saw combat on the boy's face and knew he was still in shock and therefore feeling no pain whatsoever.

"This is my wife," he told Ranger, gesturing to Laura.

"I've filled his car before," she said in her hoarse voice that Charles liked. She stuck her hand forward and gave Ranger's hand a quick, firm grasp.

Ranger offered them a chair and pushed the ventilation system drawings in front of both of them. He explained what they were doing, and what they were going to do during the night as soon as the people from Birmingham arrived. He told them there was a rescue squad coming from the steel plant and that there was a backup group in Chattanooga notified and ready to come should they be needed. He drew pictures of the mine, showing where Ben Ray Hayes's crew was probably located. He spoke gently and clinically, like a surgeon with a fine bedside manner advising the family of the procedure, the odds, the prognosis, and the resolve of the operating team. Charles knew that Ranger was at his best in a crisis, that his kind was a vanishing breed of on-site supervisors who live and dwell among those who labor, that he was indeed, on this Christmas Eve, Sweetgum Flat's Santa Claus, trying to deliver oranges and nuts rather than switches.

Laura sat back in the chair, letting her boyish legs extend straight out in front of her, sighing and running her fingers through her close-cropped hair. She caught Charles's eye.

"Your daddy's coming back to help tonight," he told her, "after he gets back from Birmingham."

She smiled. "Don't count on it," she said.

"You need any coffee, kid?"

"No, sir," she said.

"Your mama doing all right today?"

Laura shrugged and popped her knuckles. "I don't know. She's been shopping in Bessemer all day."

"So she doesn't know what's happened up here?"

"No, sir."

Charles looked at his watch. Outside, the teal evening was beginning to take over what was left of a lingering sunset. Smoke from the steel plant mottled the night colors falling over Fairfield. He turned and offered Keller a cigaret, and the sight of the boy's hands lying flat on the desk made him ache for Bolivia.

Ranger pushed an ashtray forward—the one with the skyline of Birmingham in red printed on it. Ranger and Keller smoked, brushing the butts over the letters that said THE MAGIC CITY. Occasionally their ashes mingled together, their fingers almost brushed one another. Charles threw more coal in the stove and the room grew warmer. Except for the crackling of Laura's knuckles, the room was perfectly quiet.

Tess held her pocketbook in her lap along with the sheet music for "Ave Maria" and a medley of carols. Normally, a trip to Birmingham was a time of excitement, but tonight she felt only fear and a slight irritation over Scotty's insistence on driving her to the city.

"Well, you're nice to be doing this for me," she said as sincerely as possible, without looking at him.

He turned to her. She saw, peripherally, his green baseball cap.

They passed the bus stop in Fairfield, where the transfer to Birmingham was made. She looked at the roadside stand—you could buy a hotdog with mustard there, under the awning.

"Is Ben Ray alive?" she asked him, though she knew the answer.

"Yes," he replied.

"Are you sure?" she demanded.

"I heard his voice," he told her.

"Did he sound right?"

"Right?"

"You know," she said, feeling that she might cry, "like he was in one piece, like he was going to make it?"

"You got faith, don't you?" he asked.

She turned. His angular, chiseled face was set firm.

"Faith," he repeated.

"Faith in what?" she asked.

"You know. You believe, don't you?"

"Believe what?"

"In God and Jesus and that your husband's going to make it," he replied and, seeing that the light had turned green, shifted gears and moved on into Fairfield.

"Yes, that's right," she said, searching her pocketbook for some tissue in case she cried at church. She felt like a sheet of ice. She did not feel a thing other than Scotty's presence and her discomfort that he was doing her a favor. Her earlier gratitude over his taking care of her was now tempered with the dozens of injustices directed toward her son.

Feeling her nerves frayed beyond repair, she turned sharply and clutched the tissue in her hands. "*Why* did you try to spoil the wedding?" she demanded and felt the sting of tears.

He lit a cigaret and didn't say a thing. They passed decorated houses where holly wreaths clung to gateposts and candles burned brightly in frosted windows and strings of tinsel clung to cedars in people's yards. These were steel plant company houses, a sight better than miners' places.

"Well?" she demanded and kept her eyes fixed on him.

He smoked in silence, opening the window a crack to flick his ashes out.

Men always did this. She hated it when they did this, when they didn't say anything.

"I asked you a question," she said, "and you owe me an answer. I am grateful that you're carrying me to Birmingham.

It's a nice Christmasy thing to do, and I know my husband's life is in danger, and I know I shouldn't be saying these things, but *damn*."

He turned to her and smiled, obviously cheered by her cursing.

"What did he *ever* do to you? Nothing. Not a damn thing. He's a good decent boy, and your daughter's lucky as hell and I will never understand why you don't accept him and love him like we do her and why you spend your life drunk and miserable and why for the life of me you've suddenly decided to accept me as your charity case since my husband's buried under all that rock."

Scotty drove on. It wasn't until they turned onto Third Avenue and began approaching downtown that he said to her, "I haven't had a drink all day."

As if that made a hill of beans, she thought, as she tried to calm herself, breathing deeply and dabbing her tongue with the essence of peppermint that she used to prepare her voice.

"Well," she said, gathering up her poise and sheet music. "Is this some kind of *accomplishment*, that you haven't had a drink all day?"

"Yes," he said and turned to her. His eyes were fire-blue.

She turned to the window, away from him.

"St. Paul's in on Third. We're on Third, aren't we?" she said, looking at the surroundings and wishing, for a fleeting moment, that they might stop at Loveman's so she could see the windows. Families were out and about. They were standing in clusters, the daughters holding snow-white muffs and wearing blue-and-green scarves. Tess studied them curiously. They were Birmingham families, and they were out on Christmas Eve. It was enchanting—foreign and enviable.

Scotty stopped in front of the church.

"You can come in," she said, reaching for the door.

He looked at her. His face was drawn, blank. "I'll just wait here," he said.

"Whatever."

She looked at the brick façade, the tall steeple, and the court-

yard beside the church, mounted the steps, and headed first to
the priest's quarters, where she'd pick up her pay, kiss his cheek,
tell him to pray for Ben Ray, and then prepare to sing for mass.
She liked Catholics.

Scotty watched her walk up the steps. He felt for her. He
couldn't believe she'd wanted to come here to sing, but then
women had a way of prancing angrily in the face of disaster. He
knew she hated him, and he didn't blame her much. He needed
a drink. Cranking the car up, he drove past the Lyric Theatre,
where *Birth of the Blues* was playing, then checked out the
Empire and the Ritz, where Gary Cooper's face was plastered on
posters for *Sergeant York*. The only reason he ever came to
Birmingham was to take Grace to the movies, and they hadn't
done this in years. Saturday nights were too busy with liquor
and fights.

The streets were quiet.

A man stood beside his new green Chrysler with the new
fancy grillework, helping a covey of red-clad girls scurry into the
backseat. Scotty looked for the hole-in-the-wall hotdog joints
where he'd taken Grace during the early years, wondering if
they had beer. But he couldn't find them, and everything was
closed anyway. It was, after all, Christmas Eve. The park in the
heart of the city was empty. He sat in his truck by the library
and stared up at the Latin words carved over the entrance,
having no idea what they meant. He'd studied Latin in high
school, but that was a long time ago.

Overhead, the sky was dark and inky. Stars troubled him
because he didn't understand what they were or why they made
light. Things that fascinated Grace only caused him deep sadness. He felt a gnawing in his gut. He wanted a beer. "Maybe
you're just hungry?" Grace'd say in the early days whenever he
said he wanted a drink, which made him furious. She knew
better now; she'd learned. He despised the simplicity of women
and children. Hunger. If a peanut butter and jelly sandwich

could make the feeling go away, he'd eat hundreds of them. All he knew was that a few cool whiskeys made the stars friendly.

Wandering into the park, he saw an old drunk asleep under a hickory tree, his skinny legs crossed at the knee. Actually, Scotty surmised as he moved closer, he looked like a hobo who'd just been thrown from a fast-moving train. His face was bruised, or was that a birthmark? Scotty chuckled. Poor old miser. The man was out cold. A gnarled tree root provided a headrest. He slept like a baby. Scotty reached down for the brown paper sack, out of which a wine bottle's neck protruded, but he couldn't do it. Self-disgust swept him like nausea, and he turned and walked faster and faster until he'd worked up the panic of a thief escaping the law.

He got back in his truck and drove past rows of shacks painted aqua where dark men huddled in clusters smoking. He drove up Twentieth Street until he reached the star intersection of Five Points that, unlike downtown, was alive with people. He stopped at traffic light and noticed a bakery. It was open. There were people inside, peering into the rectangular glass compartments that held donuts and sweetrolls. And he knew that he was hungry. He knew, too, that Tess was hungry, that she hadn't had dinner or probably lunch either.

When he went in, the baker said, "Merry Christmas" and handed Scotty an American flag. The war. He'd almost forgotten. Right now, the war and Pearl Harbor were so secondary to the fact that he'd be up all night breaking through rocks and coal in search of survivors and that it was seven o'clock on Christmas Eve and he was sober as a judge and on the verge of tears because he suddenly realized that he was hungry rather than thirsty just as Grace had tried to tell him for years—all this caused him to stare at the American flag in his palm with distant charm as if it were a relic of some simple truth.

"What can I get you?" the baker asked.

Scotty deferred to the people beside him—a family with blond hair and jubilant faces.

"Don't worry over them. They're German. They don't want

nuttin' but strudels. We don't got strudels," the baker said good-naturedly, and the people laughed. The baker himself sounded Polish or something.

Scotty surveyed the goods. Some of the donuts were sugary curlicues with flecks of red. The sweetrolls had pecans. Almonds topped tiny cakes. He recalled, as if in a dream, that he liked nuts. When he was young, his father grew peanuts near the barn, and it was Scotty's job to harvest them in October, to gently pry the plants loose from the soil, then pick the peanuts and toss them into a big blue bowl. This was when his daddy farmed rather than mined, before he started drinking. They had pecan trees over beside the cornfield where his mother grew dahlias—big ones with bright orange faces that won blue ribbons at the fair.

The baker was sticking American flags into cupcakes.

"Well, fella," he said, "you decided?"

Scotty felt his wallet. It was full of drinking money. "I want a dozen donuts," he said. "And six of these almond things, and six sweetrolls or whatever those things are with the pecans."

"You throwin' a potty?" the baker asked.

Scotty looked at him.

"A potty," he repeated.

The German guy laughed. "He's talking about a party," he told Scotty. "He's a Yankee. He's from New Jersey."

Scotty paid for it and took the three white boxes the baker handed him. "You got coffee?" he asked.

The baker poured him a cup. "I need another," Scotty said, thinking of Tess. He knew it'd be cold by the time she finished singing, but he didn't care.

He got back in his truck and drank his coffee. It was strong and dark with chicory. He let the steam rise to warm his lips, then reached inside the white box for a donut. It tasted better than anything he'd ever eaten, buttery and flaked with sugar that he licked from his fingers. Afterward, he lit a cigaret and drove back toward the city. Streetlamps threw an apron of light in his path. He turned onto Third and braked as he got near the cathedral.

He parked beside it, studying the red-brick steeple. It looked like a man's place.

He ate a sweetroll with pecans, drained his coffee, secured Tess's cup beside the white boxes, and got out of the truck. He sauntered over to the courtyard beside the church, lit another Pall Mall, and smoked it under the stars.

A quiet city was almost friendly. Birmingham had always seemed a filthy atrocity, a place for highfalutin lawyers and the offices of mine presidents and vice-presidents who lived in mansions on the Southside and didn't give a damn. The only things he'd ever liked here were the hotdog stands and the terminal train station with the minarets that rose in poised grace against the smoky sky. This cathedral wasn't bad either. Cautiously, he walked over to the steps leading to the sanctuary and tried to see inside. And that's when he saw her, standing under a painted Mary, wearing a snow-white dress that looked for the world like a nightgown, or was it one of those robes preachers wore? He hadn't been to church in over twenty years. Bright-colored stained-glass windows glowed beside burning candles. Tess stood in the light. He couldn't take his eyes off her.

A man at the door motioned him to come in, and he quickly dodged from his field of vision, leaping to the side into a nandina bush. He stood still, feeling like a fool but alive with caffeine and sugar and what he would later understand was the vertigo of early withdrawal and the embryo of hope.

He didn't move. The man stuck his head out the door, and Scotty didn't look up. He stared at his feet in the pine straw, hoping that the man would go back and just tend to business. He remembered ushers and deacons from his boyhood—the way they liked to guard doors. As the man disappeared, Scotty heard her voice, first quiet and then rising upward in a sweet spiral, and he saw that the man had opened all four of the doors so as to let the music come out to him. The words escaped him, and then he realized it was probably Latin. It didn't matter. The song was contained in her voice. His knees weakened. He'd heard rumors that miners up in Kentucky had believed she was a healer, a saint. He picked red berries from the nandina bush and collected them like pearls in his coat pocket, listening to words he didn't understand and, in that moment, understood something. It had to do with donuts and being hungry instead of thirsty and knowing that it was in the realm of possibility to go for one day—this day, no more than this, for beyond this was a terror worse than the stars—but for one day and one night without a drink.

On the way home, she drank the cold coffee and thanked him profusely for buying it, urging him to accept some payment. She peeked into the satiny purple folds of her pocketbook, and Scotty glanced over at the bills it contained. He felt it was a justifiable night's work and vowed he'd tell Charles that she probably was rich and that was all right by him. She ate the cake things with the almonds—all six of them, and that made him happy. He liked women with appetites. He offered to stop somewhere for a hot meal, but she laughed and said nothing was going to be open at this hour on Christmas Eve. And then she grew silent, and he understood that gloom had fallen over her exuberance. There were a lot of things he wanted to ask her, but he didn't know what they were. He headed west under the stars.

As they approached Fairfield, the sky changed colors with the steel plant's night smoke. She sighed, readjusting one of the big clasps in her hair, and for a brief instant he wondered what kind of lover she might be.

"Is Ben Ray alive?" she asked him absently, as she'd done earlier.

"We heard his voice," Scotty reminded her.

"But are you sure it was him?"

"He said, 'Hayes here.'"

"How many are with him?" she persisted.

"His whole crew."

She got a piece of chewing gum from her purse, unwrapped it, and offered him a piece. He took it. Sugar was becoming quite important, the only surefire way to fend off the blues.

" 'Hayes here,' " she repeated, nervously chewing the gum. "That doesn't sound like something he'd say."

"Got to remember he'd just survived a fall. He's been around long enough to know what's up. No doubt, he's *not* himself."

She whirled. "He's the best foreman in this whole outfit. He knows exactly what he's doing."

Scotty looked at her. Women, when they got like this, were best left to lash it all out.

"Of course, he's not himself," she argued.

No need to point out that this was precisely his point. He offered her one of the donuts. "No thanks," she said and then, a few seconds later, took one.

"These are wonderful," she said.

They passed the homes that earlier were lit with candles and decorations, but they were all dark now and quiet. The traffic lights in Fairfield weren't working, and the idea that Santa Claus was coming crossed Scotty's brain. This, along with the fact he was sober, made him think of Laura and her stocking filled with oranges and nuts, but she wasn't his anymore. He felt for the nandina berries in his pocket the way you reach for a rabbit's foot or a St. Christopher's medal or whatever keeps you from harm's way.

"I heard you sing," he told her.

She turned.

"It was like nothing I've ever heard," he told her, and meant it as much as he'd ever meant anything in his life. "I'm sure you get tired of hearing people say that."

He looked at her green eyes. Her face turned inward in disarming innocence. "No, I don't get tired of hearing it. Were you *there?*" she asked incredulously.

He laughed. "I was standing in the bushes," he told her, "and a man, one of the deacons—do Catholics have deacons?— opened all the doors. It was something."

"I saw him do that! I wondered what the hell he was doing. I thought maybe he was trying to empty the place because I didn't know how to sing Latin right."

They passed the place where bus transfers were made, and

Scotty double-checked the hotdog stand just to make sure it wasn't open. He was starving. He knew he was going home before he went to help with the rescue operation; he knew he wanted Grace to feed him, and that he was going to eat more than he'd ever eaten in his life.

He hesitated. "I looked inside," he said.

She was, he could tell peripherally, looking right at him.

"There was a strange light around you," he said.

"That was," she laughed, "a spotlight."

"Not a halo," he rejoined.

"Right," she said. "I'm no angel."

When they turned onto Warrior Road, he didn't even wait for her to ask: he drove straight up Pinegar Hill toward the mine, knowing that she would want to go there and nowhere else.

Ranger was in his office. A cluster of men were gathered about, drinking coffee, wearing overalls and boots, smoking. "Evening," they said to Scotty and nodded curiously at Tess.

"What's happening?" Scotty asked.

"They're down there now," he told him.

"Who?"

"The outfit from Birmingham. Chattanooga hasn't gotten here yet," he said. Scotty studied Ranger's face. Something wasn't right. He kept eyeing Tess warily and with a degree of pity.

Scotty tried to read him but couldn't get a signal.

"Go on home," Ranger told him. "Get some sleep, and come back in the morning. We'll need some fresh people by then."

Ranger turned to Tess. "Try to sleep, ma'am. I convinced the others to do the same—the other family folk. Your boy left an hour ago. A good boy," he told her and stood to touch her arm. He then looked at Scotty. "Do me a favor, bud," he said. "Take these keys to Charles. He's down there checking on my family. It's keys to my truck. He'll either be at my place or at his behind mine—you know where we live, don't you?"

Scotty smiled. As if everybody didn't know where the super-intendent lived.

Ranger scribbled something on a piece of paper and stuck it, along with the keys, into Scotty's hand, meeting his eyes and then giving a nod toward the paper.

"Merry Christmas," Ranger said and tipped his cap.

Scotty took Tess's elbow and led her to the office door. And it wasn't until he took her into her house, lit her a fire, and closed the door behind him that he was able to read Ranger's scribbled note. It said, "Another wall fell. Lost contact with crew."

Scotty drove past Bolivia's place, braking to see if a light was on. He wanted to give her a donut. But the lights were off and there were no cats wandering up and over the washtubs or turnip patch.

Charles's place was lit up. Scotty parked beside a big tree, and the yard came alive with the squawking of geese and the wrenching call of the peacock. Charles opened the door.

"What's got into him?" Scotty asked, gesturing to the peacock.

"It's Christmas Eve," Charles replied. "He thinks you're Santa Claus."

Charles was holding a beer. Scotty felt his stomach give.

"Come on in," Charles said.

Old newspapers were strewn under the table. Painted gourds and strung dried peppers hung from the walls, on twine and copper wire.

Bolivia sat in a big chair. "Hello, Scotty," she said, her dark eyes downcast. She held yarn in her lap, and she was making something pink.

"A girl?"

"Yes," she replied. He didn't ask her how she knew it was a girl. He didn't want to know. The night was strange enough.

"Your brother sent these," Scotty said, handing Charles the keys. He eyed Bolivia. "He also gave me this," Scotty said, showing Charles the scribbled note, turning aside to keep Bolivia from seeing.

Charles scratched his head. "I know about the new fall. She knows too," he said, gesturing to Bolivia.

"I take it the families don't," Scotty said. "I had Tess Hayes with me up there. She don't know about it yet. I didn't tell her."

Charles asked Scotty to sit at the table with him. When he did, Bolivia heaved herself from the chair, dropped the pink yarn, and began making tea. She circled the men the way women do when they're at a table, and placed spoons and lemons and sugar beside their hands.

Charles told him that while they were inside trying to break the rock, a new fall occurred—just what they'd feared most—and that the wall separating the rescuers from the miners was so thick they could no longer hear their voices.

"It don't mean they're dead," Charles said, and at the stove Bolivia put her hands over her belly. She was wearing a yellow apron, and a patchwork quilt over her shoulders.

Scotty looked at Charles. "So what does it mean?"

"Just that it might not be the best way to get there now— trying to dig through, and just have the same thing happen. The Chattanooga team's due at midnight. They got that fancy gear. They's talk of just drilling straight down to the room."

"That's even worse, isn't it?" Scotty asked him. "Can't they drill right through their heads?"

Bolivia set the teapot beside the spoons and squeezed lemon juice into the men's cups.

"Thank you, sugar," Scotty said, patting her arm.

She looked straight at him.

He watched her take Charles's half-empty beer bottle and pour the liquid into the sink. Then she got a plate of deviled eggs and bread from the icebox and set it in front of him. He looked at her, and she smiled.

Charles drew him a map of the mine and told him that the people in Birmingham would make the ultimate decision about how to proceed, but that at this juncture it looked like it'd be days of work.

Scotty told him that he'd be there at the mine at daybreak. Then he ate the deviled eggs and stuffed bread in his mouth. He was so hungry. He thanked Bolivia for feeding him.

"One more thing," she told Scotty. She led him to Charles's bedroom and opened the closet. A mother cat nursing three babies blinked in the semi-dark, her amber eyes drowsy. "They oughtn't be nursing anymore," she said. "They've been drinking from a bowl for days." She picked up a black one. "It has a locket," she said, touching the white patch on its neck. "It's a boy."

Scotty looked at the kitten.

"Take it to your daughter," she said. She looked at him, her face radiant. "My baby's kicking," she said and smiled. She held the kitten in her right palm and rotated its body, surveying it.

"Take it," she said, handing over the kitten.

Scotty stepped back. "I don't like cats," he said.

"It's not *yours*," she said. "It's for your daughter."

He could hear Charles in the kitchen stacking dishes. Was he in on this? Were they using Christmas Eve as a reason to unload this unwanted litter of cats on neighbors?

"No," Scotty said, finally. "Grace don't like cats either."

"It's not for Grace," Bolivia said patiently. "It's for your daughter."

"She can't keep it. She's living with Lila Green."

"Take it," Bolivia said. "Keep it at the station."

"It'll get run over."

"Cats are too smart to get run over. Take it," she said, and let go of it once it brushed Scotty's hands. He bent to catch it, and when he did, it put its face in his palm, its wet nose burrowing in.

"Your daughter will take good care of it," Bolivia said. "You'll never regret it," she went on, and looked at him in the same way she'd done right before she poured Charles's beer down the sink, or the way he'd thought she'd looked. He was growing fearful that he wasn't going to make it. His hands were beginning to shake, and his mind was going in odd directions. He needed a drink. Bolivia bent over to kiss the cat's black fur, and when she did she also kissed Scotty's hands. She put her fingers over his lips to prevent his further protests.

"Merry Christmas," she whispered.

He went to his truck and drove home under the stars, carrying the black kitten in his lap.

When he drove past the empty football stadium and into his yard, the porch light was on. He parked beside a tree, got out, and walked toward his house.

Through the frosted windows, he saw the family at the dinner table. He knew, because it was Christmas Eve, that they were eating roast goose and ambrosia. In the back, his dogs pranced and bayed. He kicked through the leaves and leaned over to pet them, holding the cat to his chest. When the dogs caught the scent of the cat, they stood still, noses pointed to the sky, and then curiously started to sniff him out. The kitten's claws dug into his palm.

"This is a kitty cat," he said to the dogs. The setters started to whimper—a fusion of pain and pleasure. He chuckled. "Don't worry, boys. It won't get your cornbread." Every evening, at his insistence, Grace made a skillet of cornbread and tossed it to the yard for the dogs. Scotty thought it kept the animals loyal and alert.

Grace appeared at the screen door.

"What's happened?" she called. "Have they gotten any of them out?"

She moved closer, wiping her hands on her blue apron.

He looked at her good eye. "Another wall fell," he replied quietly, "but they haven't told any family people yet, so don't say anything," he said, gesturing to the window, meaning Keller.

Her hand went to her mouth. "Oh no," she said. "Are they alive?"

"Probably," he told her.

Her good eye drooped. She shook her head and then looked up at the stars. "Have mercy," she said.

Scotty ran his fingers over the black furry ball.

"What is *that*?" she asked, looking at the cat.

"What does it look like?"

"Where did you get it? Who gave it to you?"

"Bolivia Ivey."

"You were, ah, visiting her this evening, then?" she asked and glanced up, grinning.

"Yes, and I was so good she gave me a cat."

"To bring home to me," she bantered.

"And she said to give you something else, too," he rejoined.

Grace reached to pet the kitten, and it buried its head in Scotty's chest. They stood under the tree beside the dog's pen near Grace's clothesline, which hung from one tulip poplar to another. The rest of the yard was nothing more than a plot of dirt where they battled and made up under the rules they'd established: he got drunk, they had a fight, she kicked him out, he rose sober in the morning, he got sick and scared, she nursed his body with mustard poultices and fed him milkshakes of cream and chipped ice, they played Rook, then made love, and at night he got drunk.

"Bolivia said the kitten was for Laura," he said.

Grace leaned against the tree. "I wanted to ask you something about Bolivia," Grace said. She crossed her arms. "Do you let her know you?"

He looked at her. "What do you mean?"

She looked toward the stadium. "I don't know. It's just that, at the wedding, she said some things about you."

He lit a cigaret, holding the cat under his arm. "Like what?" He thought of a drink.

"That you were like a boy."

He inhaled and blew smoke to the side.

"I felt like she knew something I didn't know."

"I hadn't never been with her, Grace."

She looked at him with her good eye. "Did I say that?"

"She's a gypsy, isn't she?" he asked, looking at how Grace was hugging herself, pinned against the tree.

"I don't think she's a gypsy."

"Or some peculiar brand of nigger?" he went on.

"She calls herself something else. I think she's from Europe."

"We're all from Europe," he said. He petted the kitten. "Cute, isn't it?" he asked her.

He knew that by now Grace realized he was sober and that she would not say anything about it for fear it'd disappear. They never talked about liquor anymore—just the incurred damages.

He looked over at the football stadium, where he often sat in the empty bleachers on summer nights, drinking alone and shooting his rifle at the moon.

Grace studied the cat.

"Where would Laura keep it?" she asked.

"At the station," he said.

He could feel the kitten's body vibrating.

"I wasn't accusing you of anything," Grace said.

"I know." She didn't owe him any apologies. Her goodness was a thorn in his side. It made him hate himself. It made him want to drink.

"I'm hungry," he said. "I'm starved."

They went inside. When he walked into the room, everybody froze just like they always did. They were eating ambrosia from china bowls, and they stared suddenly at their spoons like they were foreign objects.

"No news," he lied to Keller.

Keller stared at him. "When were you there?"

"Thirty minutes ago."

Laura sat still, looking down at the oranges and coconut in her ambrosia.

"This is for you," he said to her and handed her the cat.

Laura held it in much the same way as Bolivia had, in one hand, as if studying a piece of fruit, checking for bruises. She then let it fall to her lap and cradled it there. "Thank you," she said but didn't look at him. He knew that it would be a long time before she ever looked at him again, but this evening he had given her an invitation.

Keller left her with the kitten and drove Charles's truck past the stadium, down Warrior Road, and into his own neighborhood. Sweetgum Flat was quiet. Passing the O'Cadlin place, he saw that a cluster of cars were parked in the yard. O'Cadlin had not survived the accident, and he hated to think what was going on inside. He knew that O'Cadlin's kids were always going to hate Christmas, and that they were also going to hate mines and miners. He knew O'Cadlin's wife would run out of money soon. She taught at the company school, but she'd no longer have a job, because you couldn't teach for the company if your man didn't work for it. She'd taught him in third grade. She had been hard.

He turned in to his family's yard.

Tess's wreath of leaves, nuts, and berries caught his eye. She'd hung it on the gatepost. "A little something for the birds," she'd said.

He knocked.

When she opened it, he saw that she was still dressed to sing—flushed cheeks and starry eyes, and wearing a million things in her hair. She embraced him.

"I just got back," she said, and hurried toward the kitchen. "You hungry?"

"I've eaten," he said and took his coat off. A fire was going. He rubbed his hands together and sat beside the couch on a crate that she'd painted bright yellow. He didn't know where she got paint. She was always painting something, and he knew she didn't get it at the commissary. Probably one of her preacher friends.

Her face fell when she heard he'd eaten.

"Just some fruit," she said and got apples and pears from a basket on the table.

"No thanks, Mom. Really, don't fix anything. I just had a big meal at Laura's. Did you see the kitten?"

"What kitten?"

She flopped herself into the ragged chair and began unclasping all the things from her hair, causing it to fall all over her brown dress. The firelight made her curls turn copper.

"The one Scotty brought Laura," he replied and lit a Lucky. He tossed the match into the fire and took off his boots. Tess handed him an ashtray that said GOD GRANT ME COURAGE. Beside the words were praying hands that reminded him of the miners' wives.

"Where did you get this?" he asked.

She shrugged. "I picked it up somewhere," she said and looked at her nails. He smiled, knowing she'd taken it from somewhere. She wasn't a thief; she just had a habit of walking out of situations with something in her hand.

"What kitten?" she asked again.

"Scotty brought Laura a kitten. I thought maybe you were with him when he got it."

"No," she said. "Don't you want some eggs or something? I got bacon," she said. "Coffee?"

"Mom," he warned. But he knew she was nervous, just filling space.

"All right, all right."

They didn't say anything. She studied her nails. Behind her, the buffet was lined with all her holiday ornaments and colorful clay pots and tiny animals and figurines, and the fire caused dark silhouettes of all her toys to play on the wall under the long rectangular mirror. Ben Ray's pipe sat in the tray beside the chair.

"Do you want to go back up there this evening?" he asked her.

She shook her head. "There's no need. I'd just be in the way."

"Scotty said he'd been up there tonight," Keller said.

"Yes, he took me after I sang."

Keller looked at her. "Why did he take you to Birmingham?"

"You know how people do when you're in trouble. They get real nice all of a sudden." She looked at him, her eyes bright and green. "I still hate his guts," she affirmed.

He nodded. "Keep it up," he said.

"He was very nice, though. I don't think he's been drinking today."

Keller thought of the kitten, of Laura's hands holding it like a baby. He got up and stretched his arms in front of him, then stood by the fire, staring at the blue-and-orange light.

"He built the fire," Tess said.

"You let him in?"

She shrugged. "Why not?"

He looked at his watch. "Listen," he said, "I'll pick you up as soon as I get up in the morning, and we'll go right up there. They say that the Chattanooga team is coming in on the train during the night."

"Why are they doing that?" she asked him. "It worries me. I feel like it means something, like it's worse than we think. If they can hear their voices, why are they bringing in some big outfit? Can't that rescue team from the steel plant do it? It scares me," she said and bit her lip.

"It's always like this," he reminded her. "They got to take precautions. They don't want another wall falling. There's no rush. They have their dinner buckets all full, and plenty of water."

"I made him ham sandwiches," she said. "I wish I'd made peanut butter. It'd keep better."

Keller looked at her. "Mom, please."

"But you know how ham is. You have to eat it soon if it's not on ice."

"Mom."

"You know it's true. He'll get sick. And I put in all those pickles. Who needs pickles? I should have packed something special. It's Christmas Eve," she said, and he was afraid she was going to get crazy.

"Mom," he said gently. "Dad loves ham. Ham *is* special," he made himself say.

"I did put in some biscuits and honey."

"Great."

"And lots of fruit," she said.

"Good," he said.

"Keller," she said and stood up, her face lighting up just as it did when she was getting ready to sing a revival. "He disappeared in all that fog this morning. I swear to God, I knew it wasn't right. Did you see all that fog? I couldn't even find the toilet this morning. I peed in the weeds."

He smiled.

"I did!"

He waved it away. "I believe you."

"He was like a ghost, just vanishing with his dinner bucket. Is he alive?" she asked him.

"Yes. They heard him."

"What if they hadn't? What if we were sitting here not knowing? What would we be doing?"

"Probably the same thing we're doing now. They're getting plenty of fresh air," he told her.

She moved closer to him. "When did you hear that?" she said, quickening with the urgency of new information.

"This afternoon from Ranger Avery."

"What did he say?"

"Just what I said, that they're getting good air. They say the ventilation system is one of the best."

"Do you pray?" she asked him.

"I try to," he told her, although it hit him that he hadn't prayed all day. "Bolivia's praying," he said and the minute he said it, he regretted having brought up her name.

Tess looked at him. "I took her home, you know," he said and tried to avoid his mother's eyes.

He went to his old bedroom. The only reminder that he'd lived here was a bookshelf that held his baseball glove, some copies of *True West*, a Tom Mix poster, a marble set, and his high school letter sweater, which was folded and already gathering coal dust. His bed was covered with various types of material cut in squares. Tess was making a quilt. He looked out the window to the alley of outhouses. Once, in West Virginia, he'd believed he saw Santa at midnight emerging from the john, hoisting up his big red pants. A girl in the neighboring camp had told a newspaper reporter that Santa fed his reindeer with straw that miners left in empty coal cars every Christmas Eve.

When he went back to the family room, Tess was eating an apple.

"Leave one for Santa," he told her.

She smiled. "I will, sugar."

"Do you want me to stay here tonight?" he asked.

She waved it away. "Of course not. This is your first Christmas married," she said, and when she said *married*, her voice caught and she stopped chewing as she regained her composure. She picked up the knitting that was in her lap.

"Well, you know where I am," he told her.

He put his hands in his pockets and felt for the red yarn he'd taken from Bolivia's hair. Idly, he fished it from his pockets and wound it over his fingers, unaware of what he was doing. But when he looked at Tess, he saw the red sweater she was knitting in her lap. For an instant, her eyes met his fingers. He knew that she recognized the piece of her own red yarn that she'd given to Bolivia.

"I need to take Charles his truck," he told her, grabbing his coat.

"What will you drive?"

"I'll just walk back down and get the Studebaker if that's all right," he replied.

"Of course it's all right. It's yours now," she said.

He looked at her, confused.

"I didn't mean anything by that," she told him. "I know it's your dad's, and I know he'll be driving it for many years," she said, and they hesitated, looking down, uneasy. "I just mean that you can drive it anytime. You've always driven it anyhow," she said and smiled.

"Thanks for buying it," he said.

"God's gift," she said, and he understood that she meant that church money had bought it.

Passing Bolivia's place, he saw that it was dark and that the goose wasn't on the porch. Her washtub was filled with straw, and he marveled that she might be leaving it for Santa's reindeer even though she didn't have children. But then she probably still believed it all herself.

Charles's yard was an obstacle course of scrap metal, car parts, geese, and feed bags. He parked the truck under the tree where everybody left their car when they came to trade or buy wood and coal. Charles was standing beside the barn, tossing grain under the light of a hanging lantern.

"Hey, boy," he called.

Keller walked over to where he stood. Other than the lantern's glow, the night was black. The horses whinnied and shuffled their feet in the hay. Keller handed him his keys.

"You can keep the truck as long as you need," Charles told him. "I got use of my brother's."

"No need," Keller said, "I got my dad's car."

Charles got the lantern down from its hanging place and went inside the barn. Keller followed after him. All his senses were raw. He felt like he'd had twenty cups of coffee, and the last thing in the world he wanted to do was to go home.

Charles's face was like a polar bear's in the lantern's orb of light. He was a giant. His hands were big. Keller had heard his family came from Sweden.

They walked in and out of the stalls, where Charles spoke quietly to the animals, petting their manes, giving them treats from his pockets, and readjusting the hay as if making down beds for children. The barn was cold. Keller shivered and jammed his hand in his blue jeans pocket, searching for Bolivia's red yarn to drop in the hay to avoid further complications that might arise from its presence. It had lost its earlier magic. But when he went back to Charles's place and saw her standing on the porch, he wished he hadn't tossed the yarn.

Her braids were undone.

She stood like a dark mystic under the stars.

"Did Laura like her kitten?" she asked, and he saw that she was holding a tiny calico under her arm.

He shuddered.

"How did you know about that?" he asked, shivering in the cold.

"Come on in," she said.

Charles was loading his truck with wood. Keller looked at her brown hands stroking the kitten ears.

"I need to go," he told her.

"We have a litter," she said. "You want one too?"

He looked at her eyes. They were like magnets.

"No," he replied and ran his fingers through his hair. He felt himself giving in. He wanted to touch her stomach.

"We don't need another one." He paused. "So you gave Scotty the kitten."

"Yes, your wife needed a kitten."

Jesus Christ, he thought. She didn't even know Laura.

"Well, thanks," he said finally.

"Come on in," she said. "We've got hot tea."

He didn't want to go to the Sandifers' place. He wasn't a

Sandifer. He didn't want to watch them skate and dance around Scotty's insanity. He didn't want any more ambrosia. He wanted to take Laura to Lila Green's place, where he could bury his head in her dead granddaddy's bed under the scent of Old Spice and fish oil, and kiss her boy hands. But the plan was to spend the night at Scotty and Grace's, to wake on Christmas morning in the family tradition, to eat link sausage and unwrap gifts at dawn.

He relented. "Show me the kittens," he said and took off his wool cap.

"Charles will be in directly," she said. "I'm glad you brought the truck. He's unhappy if he's not loading wood." She moved around Charles's kitchen as if it were her own, and it occurred to him that she spent a lot of time here, that she would probably be moving in when the baby came.

The baby.

He sat in the nearest chair, ducking to avoid the string of peppers and gourds. If the yard was an obstacle course, the interior of Charles's place was a haunted house. One corner was full of cobwebs, fruit, and stacks of baskets. Canning jars, gray with filmy dust, contained banana peppers and squash and some other purplish things he didn't recognize and hated to imagine eating.

"Charles have any cigarets?" he asked her. She was squatting in a corner beside three tiny yellow bowls of milk.

"This is where they eat," she said, "when they're not trying to hang on to their mama's dried-up tits."

She got a pack of cigarets from the cabinet and some matches. She lit the cigaret for him, took a long draw, then handed it to him. When she did, he reached behind her and pulled her to him so that, from where he was sitting in the chair, his ear was to her belly. It was like a wet-weather stream when it comes alive in spring after the heavy rains. The baby kicked.

"Come on," she said, and took his arm, pulling him from the chair.

"No, please," he said. "Just one more minute."

She ran her thumbs under his earlobes and let him hold her. The baby was all over the place, like a fish or a butterfly. He thought of Laura's hands folding around the kitten. He thought of the wives' hands praying, and the big night outside holding the camp and all the people. He thought of the dark mine.

Finally, he let her go.

She led him to the other room.

Charles's bedroom had the smell of a working man who lives alone. "They're in here," she said and opened the closet. The mother cat stared at them as if awakened from a pleasant dream. The kits chewed on her belly. "They think they're still supposed to nurse," Bolivia said and folded her brown hands on her belly.

"I've been reading about Mary riding a donkey to Bethlehem," she said, and he backed away from her because her eyes spooked him and so did what she was saying. She never made sense in the broader scheme of things. Everything she said was like a fragment coming from an unidentified mine of ideas.

"Anyway," she said, "I thought you'd like to see the mother of your kitten." She smiled her ordinary-girl smile, which relieved him.

"Great," he said. "Thanks for the cat."

"She's trying to unload them to unsuspecting souls on Christmas Eve." Charles's voice boomed from behind him. He jumped. Charles put a hand on his shoulder. "You don't want another one, do you?"

"No, sir."

"Or know anybody else who might?"

"No, sir."

Charles chuckled. "You know, I'm only forty-one. You don't have to call me sir."

"O.K., sir," Keller said.

Bolivia pried the kittens' mouths from their suckling place and carried them one by one to the kitchen, where she set them in front of the yellow bowls of milk. "There," she said, bending so low that her belly brushed her feet. "Drink this, and quit chewing your mother's tits."

——

Keller said he had to be going.

Charles watched him put on his coat and walked him out the door. They stood on the porch. Charles's place sat on the crest of a hill, and below was his brother's house. Acres of land surrounded by fences held the grazing animals that ate clover and whatever other forage Charles planted. In the distance was the entire neighborhood—the street where the Hayeses and Bolivia lived, the stone wall where passionflower grew, and the creek where ferns sent up curlicues of fronds in early spring near the mossy rocks and where children crossed the stream in one perfect arc. Winter was a reminder, though, that a land scraped of its green existence is nothing more than undulating earth where men cut trees and mined coal.

The night was black. Keller lingered on the porch, and Charles knew that the boy wanted information.

"I don't know anything further," Charles lied, feeling sick.

"It's not right that I'm not up there," Keller said. "They won't keep me out, will they, if I go back up there?"

Charles scratched his head and pulled his overalls up higher, linking his thumbs through the fasteners. "No, they won't kick you out. You're a man. They can't keep you from staying." Charles leaned against the banister and brushed dirt from it. "I think they're trying to just keep everybody rested this evening, because they're going to need men in the morning or during the days to come."

"Days?" Keller pressed. "You think it will take days."

Charles looked up at the ivory moon. "Probably so."

"Why? If they can hear Dad talking, then they couldn't be very far away."

"It's a delicate business," Charles told him, looking squarely into Keller's eyes. "You understand that a new wall might fall. It happens all the time during rescue. It happens all the time."

Keller shivered. Charles saw that his lips were bluish-gray from what he guessed was a mixture of cold and terror. He didn't move to go. Charles understood that Keller didn't want to leave anybody who'd talk to him, especially someone he thought was an insider who might be privy to information.

"Your daddy's a fine foreman," Charles said.

Keller's eyes lit. "He is, isn't he?"

"He sure is."

"He's the best, isn't he?"

"That's right," Charles said and offered Keller a cigaret.

"Mom's all worried she didn't pack the right things in his bucket this morning," Keller said, smiled, and flicked ashes over the rail into the dead leaves.

Charles watched his hands. How was the kid standing up under all this? His daddy buried under a wall of rock in the No. 3 mine, his baby kicking in the belly of a woman who wasn't his wife, his own life hidden from sight somewhere in the shelves of Graham's commissary, waiting, oh just waiting, to be plucked by a war he didn't seem to even acknowledge, much less understand, or perhaps he did and just didn't let it surface into conversation. Youth, Charles reasoned. Youth allowed Keller to stand here on the porch of the man who'd be raising his child, smoking a cigaret as if its pleasure was the heart of the night. Youth made him feel alive, caused every nerve in his body to sing with terror rather than collapse in despair. Graham was right—the boy would make a good soldier. All boys made good soldiers, because they were driven toward destruction, because sex and combat were the same thing. They were pilots circling their own lives, men flying over battlefields with bombs and parachutes, incapable of dying, because, even if shot down, they knew how to eject and sail to a friendly earth. Even a foot soldier like Keller, who was running zigzag through his own self-appointed minefields, was adroit and rooted in a natural tendency to sidestep the only true disaster—surrender to fear. Youth gave him an innocent courage, the belief that everything would work out in the long run, that he was incorrigible, that he wasn't going to be trapped, caught, found out, a prisoner of war. And how long this euphoria might last! Charles knew that, for him, the bliss had carried him beyond his twenties, indeed up into his late thirties, when suddenly his parachute malfunctioned—he fell desperately in love with the neighborhood whore, he wanted children, even children who belonged to another man, he sought solace in the land, he began to understand that he was going to die someday, he learned to pray, and he gave a damn about his neighbors, his brother, his immortality, sparrows and juncos and chickadees and violets and crocuses and litters of senseless kittens who didn't even know it was time to leave their mother.

Keller tossed his smoked cigaret in the direction of the compost heap.

"You think I ought to be up there tonight?" he asked Charles.

"No," Charles replied. "I think you should go home to be with your wife on Christmas Eve. There's nothing you can do until morning."

"What do you think they're doing?"

"Who?"

"Dad and his men."

Charles searched the boy's face. He looked younger than nineteen. "Singing carols," Charles said and smiled.

"Dad can't sing," Keller responded, flat and seriously.

Charles put a hand on his shoulder. "They're doing what good miners do. They're laying low, surviving."

Keller looked away.

When he turned back to Charles, his eyes were swimming. "When the baby comes," he said, "will you come get me?"

"Yes."

"Don't ever tell anybody the truth. As long as you live, don't ever tell anybody."

"I won't, boy."

Tess slipped the flimsy peach colored nightgown over her head and stood in front of the vanity, combing her hair with the ivory brush from the set Ben Ray had given her. She struggled to get the brush to penetrate the snarls, wondering how on earth she was ever going to sleep.

The clock beside her bed read twelve-thirty.

She went back to Keller's room, where the quilt scraps lay in geometrical loveliness. Sewing was a way to make your hands do something noble.

She knelt beside Keller's old bed and tried to pray.

She prayed that God would keep Ben Ray alive. She went over the tiny injustices she'd incurred: the way her mind wandered sometimes when they made love—not to other men but to unwashed dishes, the yellow part of fried eggs that'd coagulated on dinner plates, the Butterick pattern lying on her sewing machine, the idea of painting bluebirds and parasols on her new clay pots, and ultimately these days, to a baby swimming inside Bolivia Ivey.

And even now, while trying to pray, she realized that her mind was wandering just like it did during lovemaking. She got up, carrying the folds of the peach nightgown as if descending a flight of stairs. She felt like her body was on fire, and she paced every square inch of the bedroom, feeling the claustrophobia of her company home and Ben Ray's absence. It wasn't right to be away from the mine.

She went to the kitchen but didn't fix anything. She just stood beside the stove, looking at her animal figurines and harmonica like they were foreign objects that belonged to some woman with a peculiar nature. She went out back, barefoot even though it was winter, and walked in the direction of the alley outhouse. The backs of the houses on the other side of the alley were dark, and she suddenly hated the families in them who didn't have men trapped, until her eyes led her to the O'Cadlin place, where all the lights burned and she believed she heard their muffled crying.

Minutes later as she walked back from the outhouse, she understood that God was answering prayers she'd never even said. She needed something to do, and now she knew what it was. She went inside and lit the stove. Then she got the flour, sugar, and butter from the icebox and mixed it all up with some eggs to make a cake, a perfect white cake with thick frosting. She made biscuits and stuffed them with the last of the ham given to her by the preacher at the Bethlehem Methodist church, where they'd slain a pig right on the grounds, right beside the pastureland that led to the graveyard. She imagined Ben Ray eating all this Methodist ham in the dark under his hat's orb of light. She wondered if the men were passing their dinner buckets around. Were they rationing food? Were they even hungry? Did they have enough water? How much water did the bottom section of a dinner bucket really hold—wasn't it a half-gallon? And how long could they survive on that?

The blessed thought hit her that she didn't have to sleep if she didn't want to. Nobody on earth was forcing her to lie in that empty bed. After she mixed rice and beans with mayonnaise and curry to make a salad, she went to the bedroom and stood under the picture of Jesus feeding lambs. She shed her peach nightgown and put on her old beige gardening pants. She got one of Ben Ray's big dark shirts and held it to her face, trying to smell his body, and when she did she started crying. His scent was strong, desirable, and familiar. She knelt by the bed and cried a long time, letting herself go to pieces on the dusty, coal-stained floor that she swept day and night in order to try to pretend she didn't live where she lived.

When she finally got up from the floor, her hands were black, and so was her face where the tears had caused the coal dust to collect in big smudges.

She washed her face with basin water.

In the kitchen, all the food was packed up and ready to take to the O'Cadlins', come dawn. But she knew it couldn't wait. She went out back again and looked down the alley. The lights were still burning. Gathering it all up in a big burlap bag, securing the cake in a hatbox saved for this purpose—for funeral food that had to be toted—she walked down the dark alley to the O'Cadlins'. And when she knocked, a nun came to the door. She'd forgotten the O'Cadlins were Catholic.

The nun was big. Her face was salmon.

"Bless you," she said when Tess handed her the food.

"My husband's still under," Tess told her.

"His name?" the nun asked. Her eyes were godly.

"Ben Ray Hayes."

"We will pray for him, too, along with the deceased," she said, placing the food on the table beside the door, and making the sign of the cross. Tess wanted to bury her face in the nun's habit.

"Thank you," Tess said.

"Are there other things I can do for you?" she asked.

On impulse, she asked in rapid fire: "Do you think I ought to go up there to the mine? Do you think this would be wrong? Do you think they'd let a woman stay in the office during the night? Can I go?" she asked, feeling her lips and knees trembling.

The nun's salmon face grew radiant.

"Of course you can go. You can do anything God calls you to do."

"Is he calling me?" Tess asked, shaking all over.

The nun smiled. "It appears so," she said.

Pinegar Hill was darker than any place she'd ever known. She heard owls. The ravine over to the side was a big hole with no bottom in sight. She'd stopped at her house long enough to put on her coat, but some buttons were missing and she kept having to hold it together. She was worried about passing the cemetery, because she believed in ghosts, and it was nearing midnight and she was a woman approaching a mine. If a woman goes into a coal mine, some member of her family will be killed in that mine, she recalled from West Virginia mountain people's superstitions. A woman can't churn butter if she is having her period. She'd churned butter three days ago during her period, and now she was going to a mine. If you dream of a Negro, you will have a fight with a friend. If you dream of muddy water, somebody you know will die. Don't let a bird fly into your house, or somebody will die. If you sneeze while eating, somebody will die. If you find a spider before sunrise, somebody will die. Somebody will die. Somebody will die.

Adrenaline took over. She walked fast, so fast that she felt her heart growing sore. Just as she approached the apex of Pinegar Hill, she turned to face the road she'd just conquered. Sweetgum Flat, seen at a distance here at night, was only a spattering of lights where lanterns hung on gateposts to welcome Santa's arrival. The cemetery over to the right was a benign piece of land where maples and other hardwoods had shed a carpet of red and yellow leaves, a friendly gesture to the dead. When she turned back around to the familiar sulphur stench and the fence beside the scrap hill, she squinted to see what she thought she saw—her own Studebaker, Charles's flatbed truck, Scotty's pickup, and a host of other cars, some of which she recognized as belonging to people she knew, other miners. The office was lit up. She heard their voices. They were the quiet, hushed voices of people in church right as the pastor comes in but before the service has begun. She knocked on the door, and when it was opened, she saw Keller's face and Scotty's and Charles's and some men she didn't know and had never seen, and a few women. And looking out the payroll window, she saw a stream of men heading in the direction of the mine, carrying lanterns.

"What are you doing here?" she asked Keller, though she was actually addressing nobody in particular, or perhaps everybody.

"Same thing you're doing here," Jake Hatfield's wife said to her.

Keller was leaning against the Graphotype machine, blowing into his mug of coffee. He walked over to her and helped her take off her coat.

"How did you get here?" he asked her.

"I walked."

He looked at her. "Why didn't you call me?"

She shrugged. "I didn't want to bother you on Christmas Eve. Why aren't you at the Sandifers'?"

"Why aren't you in bed?" he retorted.

She looked at the floor.

"There was another fall," he told her quietly.

She felt herself get sick.

"I didn't know either until I got up here."

She clutched her coat. "What does that mean?"

"It means that they can't hear Dad anymore. But they'd left Jake Hatfield outby the fall to keep talking to them while they waited for more equipment to arrive, and now Hatfield's inby the new fall. They're on the way down to try to make contact with him."

Tess looked at Jake Hatfield's wife. She looked all right. She was wearing a scarf with reindeer. She wasn't crying. Nobody was crying. Everybody looked strong and hopeful.

"Brother O'Flynn is coming," Keller told her.

"Why's that?" she snapped.

He smiled and took a sip of coffee. "Because it's Christmas," he said and looked at his watch. It was past midnight.

"What about the air?"

Keller nodded. "It's not a solid wall," he told her. "Neither fall is. There's room, at least that's what they've told me, for good air to go in and come out; they just can't get any men through the crevices."

Tess studied his face.

"I know," he said. "I know it's critical. I know methane's always what does it in the end."

He looked out the window. The last of the safety lanterns disappeared into the mine. Tess watched him. The need to mother was strong. She looked around at the strangers.

"Who are they?" she whispered.

"They're from Birmingham. They've called in people from the Bureau of Mines, too," he told her.

"Why did they do that?" she demanded.

Keller looked at her. "Because they need help," he said flatly. She knew he was hoping she wouldn't get loud and hysterical.

"But that *bothers* me," she told him.

He lit a cigaret, then turned to a couple of men standing nearby who needed a light. *Don't light three cigarets from one match, or the third person will die*, she remembered from mountain lore.

She was nervous and scared. She felt like she was about to jump out of herself.

By morning, the crew was back with news that they'd been able to hear Jake Hatfield's voice through the new fall, and that he was uninjured, standing in a space the size of a family room, outby the first fall and inby the new fall. He had the water they'd carried in when they left him stationed there. He was still talking to Ben Ray Hayes, who was now saying his leg was hurt. He was in pain but he was holding fine. They had fifteen sandwiches between them and all eight men had three-quarters of their water supply left in the bottom of their dinner buckets. The air felt clean enough, but he was worried that the new fall had slackened the flow of good, ventilated air, and this was, of course, their main concern. He'd asked, through Hatfield, various questions about what was being done above ground and what they were using to break through. He also sent messages from the other men to their wives, via Hatfield, that the rescuers had jotted down and delivered.

The one from Ben Ray to Tess said, "I love you. Thanks for packing ham."

Keller was relieved.

In the early light of dawn, Tess sat in the superintendent's oak swivel chair, staring out the payroll window in the direction of the mine. Her green eyes were taking in the sky. For the first time, the idea of her being a widow hit him. A woman alone. His mother.

"Let me carry you home for a while," he said to her.

She turned. She was clearly numb from fatigue and turmoil. "I'll just stay," she told him.

He knew not to argue.

"Thanks," she said quietly. "And thanks for not telling me I ought to go."

When he got to the Sandifers' place, Scotty was in the yard playing with his dogs in the mist of early morning. The beagle was leapfrogging over the setters, and Scotty was tagging alongside like a boy. In his hands, he held the black kitten, letting the dogs occasionally take a curious sniff. Keller parked beside the tree. On the gatepost was a big red apple—the sign that Santa had come.

On seeing the Studebaker, Scotty stopped playing and approached, tucking the kitten under his jacket.

"Anything new?" he asked Keller.

"Yes. They made contact with Hatfield, who's still in touch with Dad's crew. They sent some messages to their wives. Dad told Mom thanks for putting ham in his lunch," Keller told him.

"Bet that made your Mom's Christmas," Scotty said, and took the kitten out and stroked his ears. Keller thought of Bolivia, and his stomach turned a bit. Scotty put a hand on Keller's shoulder and led him toward the house.

"I'm going back up after breakfast," he said. "They're going to use all the men they can get today. I think we'll have 'em out by tomorrow, don't you?"

"If the air holds," Keller said.

Scotty stopped at the screen door, where he could smell sausage cooking. He held the kitten to his face, and Keller looked away. It was disturbing—this new fascination with a cat.

"I haven't had a drink since night before last," Scotty told him and ran his thumb over the cat's white triangular patch. "A locket," Scotty said, gesturing to the white. "Bolivia calls this a locket."

When they got inside, Laura was standing in the kitchen next to Grace, wearing a nightgown and aqua bedroom slippers. When she saw Keller, she dropped the ball of biscuit dough and embraced him. He put his face in her hair and closed his eyes. When he opened them, he saw that Scotty was standing beside Grace, letting her pet the cat. Light fell over the room. The teapot sang.

A t noon, Scotty left the house and drove his pickup in the direction of the mine, with Keller following in the car. He passed the football stadium, and turned onto Warrior Road. They weren't opening the station because it was a holiday. Since he wasn't going to drink this morning, there was no need to stop by for the amber bottles he kept there in the drink box. But as he passed the station, he took a look at the red brick columns, the overturned crates, the oil pit. This morning was particularly bright and crisp. Frost sparkled in the yards of neighborhood homes. Blue sky made him want to drink, but if he made it through today, he'd have two days under his belt. He'd heard that things get strange the third day, when the pink elephants crawl out of your brain and your body sets fire to itself.

The Studebaker trailed along behind. In the rearview mirror, Scotty saw that the boy needed air in his tires.

When they got to Sweetgum Flat, Keller stopped at his mother's place. Scotty headed on up Pinegar Hill in the direction of the mine. He parked beside the torn barbed-wire fence and walked up to the superintendent's office. A group stood beside the desk, smoking.

Charles's face was black, his overalls dusty with soot, his eyes empty. He told Scotty that he'd just come back up and that the others were still there. When they'd gone down with equipment to begin breaking through the rock, they'd gotten no response from Hatfield. They'd tried to fish a microphone up, around, and through the crevice where the air was circulating, but there was still no answer.

"His voice was clear as a bell this morning, but then when we went back down, nothing, absolutely nothing."

"You reckon he's asleep?" Scotty asked, leaning against the desk and wanting a drink; it was like a mosquito in his ear—whirring lightly but incessantly.

Charles took off his cap. His otherwise light hair was coated with black dust. "I can't imagine Hatfield sleeping in the midst of this—not this early on."

Scotty avoided the inevitable question about the ventilation. Blackdamp was what killed miners and rescuers alike.

"You want to go down?" Charles asked him and, not waiting for an answer, led Scotty out the door and down the hill to the huge, arched hole framed with concrete, where steel rails reflected light rays. A crate of hard hats had been brought in for the lay rescuers. Charles filled his own and Scotty's with carbide, and they crawled into the mantrip.

"They ain't using this stuff anymore," Charles told him, gesturing to the carbide." They got electric cap lamp now, but these old carbides were all they mustered up for us impostors," he said.

A blanket of darkness overwhelmed Scotty's natural sense of balance. Vertigo swept him. Charles's voice carried above the roar and clanking of the mantrip. "This is the Pratt seam," he called to Scotty. "Seam varies from forty-two inches to seven feet."

"My dad died in here," Scotty told him.

Charles turned. "In 'twenty-two?"

"Right."

Charles told him that the mine was well ventilated by split-ting—a total of seven main splits, with secondary splits off main ones. He said there were two exhaust-fan stations, one with two main returns and the other with four main returns, and six intakes. He described the ventilation equipment and exhaust fan with electric operating drive and a gasoline engine auxil-iary drive. "This unit," Charles said, handing Scotty some to-bacco to chew, "is located at Number One air slope near the beginning of Twelfth Left, and fortunately, that's just where we're headed."

When they got near the section of the fall, the mantrip stopped and they walked on down. In the distance, the rescue operation was nothing more than a sprinkling of yellow lights in the dark and the noise of drilling and picking. Charles gave Scotty a bucket filled with crushed limestone and showed him how to dust by hand.

They worked for a long while, until Scotty's body started to ache. Every now and then, the men stopped working and called Jake Hatfield's name. And while they waited for a response, you could see their yellow lights bowing. But there was never a response, only the still darkness and the echo of their own voices. "Hatfield, *Hatfield, Hatfield.* You there, *there, there.*"

Occasionally, Charles refilled Scotty's bucket, and he kept dusting. Water was passed back and forth in a big thermos. Scotty's eyes hurt, and he wasn't sure if it was just the way your eyes felt in response to coal dust and dark. Once he glanced up from the bucket of limestone and thought he saw a purplish ghostly figure on the brattice cloth. He blinked and it went away, but the thought of his daddy didn't. Nobody had ever told him exactly how they found him or where he was in the mine.

There was water under his boots. He'd forgotten how wet they kept the mines.

After an eternity, Charles's lamplit face appeared beside Scot-ty's.

"You want to break?" he asked, as the sound of the mantrip bringing in a fresh crew interrupted the work.

"You going up?" Scotty asked him.

"I reckon," Charles replied.

But as soon as they reached the light of day, Scotty wanted to be back down. He wanted to rescue Ben Ray Hayes. He liked the dark.

Keller was there. So was Tess—looking tired—and Grace and a lot of women, all crammed into Ranger Avery's office. They'd brought casseroles and cornbread and pies. It was Christmas, and they were women bearing food.

Tess drew him to one side.

"What did Jake Hatfield say?" she asked, her green eyes alive.

Scotty took a handkerchief from his pocket and wiped his forehead. His hands were shaking. He craved a drink. He tried to ignore what his body was doing.

"I don't know," he told her. "I've been dusting."

Her face fell.

Scotty didn't know protocol, but he knew that miners were supposed to lie in the face of disaster. He'd learned this growing up in the camps. He intuitively knew he wasn't supposed to let anybody know yet that Hatfield was silent and that therefore there was no contact with Ben Ray's crew.

Grace was spreading a red-and-white checked tablecloth on Ranger's oak desk before putting out the food. Christmas dinner, he said to himself, chuckling. When he looked at the clock, though, he saw that it was three o'clock. He was looking for Keller, and when he couldn't find him he asked Grace, who was wearing an apron and licking something from her finger.

"He just went down," she said.

"To the mine?"

"Yes," she said. "He wanted to help."

Scotty hadn't seen him get off the mantrip he'd ridden back up. He knew, though, that by now the boy knew that Hatfield was silent, and he wondered who'd let him go down and why, since he was a family member. But then he was also a man and he had every right to go.

He got a plate and began scooping up helpings of casseroles and meat and bread. When he looked up, his heart rose. Laura was standing at the payroll window, holding the kitten up for him to see, smiling the smile of a daughter. He raised his fork in salute.

Ranger Avery's office was now public property, it seemed. People were eating on the floor, studying the maps on the wall as if touring a museum, idly browsing among various documents that lay next to the oak desk in a filing drawer. Charles tossed his scraps into a trash bin and went over to Ranger's cabinet. Retrieving a stack of papers, he walked toward Scotty and sat on the floor beside him.

Scotty ran his cornbread through the turnip-green pot likker and picked a drumstick to the bone.

Charles knelt on one knee. "Here it is, my man," he said to Scotty.

Scotty looked at the yellowed paper. It read: "Dolomite No. 3 Mine. November 22, 1922. 90 killed. At 2:40 p.m. the four-car trip became jammed in the rotary dump in the tipple on the surface. In trying to jerk them free, three cars came loose suddenly and ran back down the slope, breaking through a rail stopblock and wrecking at the bottom against a loaded trip. As usual, the runaway cars raised a dense cloud of dust, and this was ignited by an arc from the 3300-volt armored cable in the slope caused by damage from the runaway cars. Flame from the mouth of the slope burned the tipple, but there was little violence inby the yard. Because of the expansion into the yard, the violence was confined to the yard and slope, and only heat and gases penetrated beyond. Violence along the slope and back was heavy."

Scotty looked at the word *violence* as if he'd never seen the word. So *violence* had killed his father. So what he'd believed as a child was true. The mine was a dragon with fire shooting from its mouth.

He read on. "About 475 men were in the mine. Of these, 90 were killed and 70 injured by burns and afterdamp. Rescue workers quickly removed the injured and dead. Most of the uninjured survivors came out through No. 2 and No. 3 slopes after the air cleared."

Scotty handed the paper back to Charles.

Charles gave him a cigaret, heaving his big bear body up to get matches from a nearby miner who was eating beside the Graphotype machine.

"Look at this," Charles said, fanning the pages in front of Scotty. "Two more the same year. One at Belle Ellen and one at Acmar."

Scotty nodded. He was thinking of his father, and wanting a drink. Grace cut him slices of pecan, chocolate, and buttermilk pie.

"You doing all right?" she asked him, her wandering hazel eye surveying him at an angle. He saw it in her good eye, that she'd been monitoring his sobriety from a distance. He didn't answer. He took the plate of pie slices and looked away. Even though he wasn't drinking she was still messing with his drinking.

Charles still knelt, paper in hand. "Look at this," he said, gesturing to the print. "Just one year later, in 'twenty-three. Another here at Dolomite. Five killed. And at Piper in 'twenty-five, six killed."

Scotty looked at Charles. Charles's eyes were those of a sled dog, Scotty thought—like ice. "Most of these just had a few deaths," Charles said. And Scotty knew what Charles was thinking, because it was what he was thinking: that this disaster in progress would involve only a few. "Overton, though," Charles said, "look here. 'In 'twenty-five, fifty-three killed. Fireboss had found gas in four places on Six right that morning, and these places were supposed to have been cleared before the men entered.' Damn," Charles said.

Scotty watched Tess Hayes. He wondered if she'd remarry. A priest, perhaps? No, they couldn't marry. A solid Methodist. Maybe she'd return to West Virginia or wherever she'd traveled.

He was certain that other men had loved her in the past, if not the present.

By now, Keller was inside the mine, discovering that Jake Hatfield had fallen silent, that there was no longer a shred of assurance that Ben Ray's crew was intact. And he knew it was time to tell this to Laura.

"We like the kitten," Scotty said to Charles.

"Good, good. Want another?"

Scotty waved that away. "No, one's fine. Tell Bolivia, would you, that it was a good idea, a real good idea."

Charles sighed deeply and searched Scotty's face enigmatically. Scotty wondered what he was looking for, and he guessed it had something to do with Bolivia. The thought crossed his mind that Charles might be wondering if he was the father, but then surely Charles himself was the father.

"Listen," Scotty said, jamming his hands into his pockets. "I'm going to tell my daughter about Hatfield."

"That's up to you," he said. "You going back down?"

"Right," Scotty said. "But let me talk to her first."

Charles nodded.

Charles called Scotty back and leaned over to get near his ear. "Tell her not to talk it up just yet, all right?"

Scotty nodded. Laura could keep a secret. How many times had he heard Grace tell her, "Just don't say anything to anybody about your daddy. It's nobody's business."

He found her in his pickup, playing in the cab with the kitten, dangling a piece of red yarn. Upon seeing him, she rolled the window down. She was wearing her workclothes.

She didn't say anything, but instead handed him the kitten.

Then she looked at her hands and began picking dirt from under her nails.

Finally, she said, "What is it?" but didn't look up.

He ran his fingers along the pink underside of the kitten's ears, then held it up in one palm.

"Kitty, kitty," he said in the falsetto voice he'd heard women use to call kittens all his life.

"What?" she repeated. "What is it?"

"It's Hatfield," Scotty said, handing the kitten back to her and leaning up against the cab door.

She looked at him. Her blue eyes were, he knew, replicas of his own.

"Is he *dead?*" she asked, squinting.

"He just won't answer anybody," Scotty told her.

"So, is he dead?"

"I don't know, baby," he said.

Her eyes caught the sun, mirrored the tree branches and the tipple that'd once burned. He had not been this physically close to her in years.

"Keller's down there," she said to him.

"I know."

"He's going to find out, isn't he?"

"That's right."

She bit a nail, and he resisted the impulse to take her hand from her mouth. She'd always bitten her nails. They'd bled when she was quite young, and he recalled how the fingers looked grasping the satiny edge of her blanket as she slept.

She reached over and stroked the kitten's black fur as Scotty held it in his hand. They didn't say anything. A fast-moving cloud passed over the sun, causing a momentary darkening. "Well," she said finally. "I guess I ought to just go back to the station."

"You don't need to do that," he told her. "It's Christmas."

She sighed and looked at him, her face petulant. "I hate it up here," she said. "It's like a funeral."

"Well, you just do whatever you need to do, baby."

She looked at his face. "You're all smudgy," she said. "Have you been down in there?"

"Yes."

"Is it dark in there?"

"It's dark." He gave her the kitten. "Tell you what. Let me take you back home or wherever you want to go," he said.

She shrugged. "O.K."

He went back inside the office. Grace and Tess were gathering up dirty plates and scraping the food into a sack. "I'm going to take Laura home," he said.

"All right," Grace said, patting his arm.

"Hey Avery," he called to Charles. "Go on without me. I'm taking my daughter home. I'll come back up in a half hour or so and get somebody to fix me up with carbide."

Charles waved to him.

They drove past the cemetery and down Pinegar Hill without talking. They didn't need to talk, because of the kitten. They stroked its fur, as it sat curled between them on the vinyl cushion, purring.

At the base of the hill, Scotty braked early so as to creep past Bolivia's place. It was habit. Everybody did it. Originally, it had been to note whose car was there, which man was visiting. Then, after her daddy died, it was to check her woodpile stacked in the yard or see if her washtub was filled with pansies or if the hen had laid eggs or if the cats were assembled. And as he glanced curiously over, Laura followed suit, straining to see what she might see.

What they saw was Bolivia leaning against the side of her home no, she was *pushing* against her place, as if trying to shove the porch wall inward. She was wearing a big orange apron, which Scotty had, in recent days, come to associate with her.

"Is she O.K.?" Laura asked him.

Scotty stopped the truck and got out. When he approached her, she didn't stop what she was doing, but she smiled spookily, and Scotty felt his skin crawl.

"Mr. Sandifer," she said. "I'm not going to have this baby today."

Scotty saw that her fingers were purple from pushing so hard against her house.

"I am in labor, though," she said, her face turning inward as if she'd just tasted a sour lemon.

Scotty turned instinctively to the only other woman there, his daughter, who had leapt from the truck and was running toward them.

Keller's chest ached. His heart pumped hard. He wasn't sure if it was dust or fatigue or fear. He'd heard about Hatfield moments after penetrating the dark of the mine. Ranger Avery had ridden the mantrip down with him and had told him matter-of-factly over the rumble of the vehicle. He hadn't asked questions. He tried to conjure up Jake Hatfield's face, remembering a dark beard. But the beard he visualized was his father's, and he was afraid he'd cry if he let himself bring Ben Ray's face into total recall.

The ride down had been frightening. He'd kept blinking in an effort to bring light into the dark tunnel, but it was no use. The dark was solid. The mantrip made a horrible noise. It moved fast, making his body shake madly. He felt sick.

When the mantrip stopped, they got off and walked in the direction of yellow lights and drills. Ranger Avery gave him a bucket and instructed him to dust. Whenever the men stopped to yell Hatfield's name, Keller stood absolutely still and kept his eyes glued to Ranger's yellow-lit face. Ranger would shake his head and murmur, "Damn," then return to drilling or shoveling or building new timber supports to brace the roof.

The mantrip returned a while later, bringing Charles, whose ice-blue eyes shone under his light.

"Scotty's telling Laura about Hatfield," Charles said, his eyes widening to accommodate the dark.

"I hope nobody tells Mom."

"They're not telling any wives just yet. No need to get everybody crazy when he might just be asleep," he said and moved toward the rescue team. Keller watched him begin to assemble more white oak props. He walked over to him.

"The air," Keller began.

"Ought to still be good in there. It's fine here," he said, and Keller shivered involuntarily against the cold that the ventilation fan was hurling in.

"But if Hatfield's not breathing, then . . ."

"Hush, boy!" Charles snapped.

Keller looked at his boots, covered in the tarlike mix of water, coal, and limestone dust. He was empty. Charles put a hand on his shoulder. Keller recoiled, knowing that the feeling of someone touching him would make him cry.

"The point is to keep working," Charles told him. "If you think too much, you won't work."

Keller dusted, stopping whenever Hatfield's name was being called. It seemed that they were calling more frequently now, and he wondered if they were anywhere near breaking enough wall down to get to Hatfield. The idea of Jake Hatfield merely sleeping was impossible.

"Hatfield, *Hatfield*, *Hatfield*," Ranger Avery's voice echoed along the black walls of the mine. This time, the men didn't resume their work but clustered in groups and drank water. Some knelt, and wiped their foreheads on handkerchiefs from their overalls. A few pissed. Keller set his bucket down and looked at Charles.

"You ought to go back up for a while," Charles said.

Keller looked at his icy eyes.

"You do what I say," Charles instructed.

"Yes, sir."

"You use your own judgment about your mother, but if Hatfield's wife is there, don't talk. That's a decision for Ranger to make. The women brought in food. Eat something."

Keller rode the mantrip alone. A tunnel of light broke the dark, hurting his eyes and making him want to retreat back where the air was clammy and you didn't have to think.

Putting out his carbide, he walked back up the hill toward the superintendent's office, crushing big, brown pin oak leaves under his boots. Christmas was almost over.

Keller peered through the steel latticework of the payroll window into the office. He saw his mother, Grace Sandifer, and a few other women making a quilt. Tablecloths were folded atop Ranger's desk, and tin plates holding casseroles and the custard remains of pies were pushed under a canopy of paper. He hated the idea of walking in, fearing the maternal haranguing over his appetite. They'd force-feed him leftovers. Women were worse with leftovers than with the meal itself. But when he did enter, they simply dropped their quilt in unison and stared at him speechless, hungry for information.

"No news," he said and took off his boots.

Tess got up and walked over to him. "What's Hatfield saying?" she asked and searched his face. He was certain that already she was picking up nuances, reading his mind as she had a way of doing.

"What?" she insisted, then led him back out the door. His feet were cold, his socks damp and stained with coal. It was growing chillier as sunset advanced, and he saw her gather her shawl up and pull her hair forward to keep her ears warm.

"They can't get no response from Hatfield," he told her.

Any inclination to withhold this truth from her had evaporated the minute she'd led him out the door. That would be unthinkable and, besides, he needed her comfort. He needed her. Staring at the hole at the ankle of his sock, he was acutely aware that he loved her. They stood in the winter light and didn't say anything. They were aware of themselves, of the fact of their being there, of Ben Ray's absence, of what it might be like to walk through the rest of life as two and not three.

"You want some coffee?" she asked him.

"Yes, ma'am," he said.

"I'll get it. Don't bother to come in here. I won't say anything."

"You can tell Grace," he said. "Charles says Scotty's already told Laura. Where is she?" he asked, looking around, suddenly seized with desire to see her, tell her, hold her.

"Scotty took her home."

He looked around for his family's car.

"It's parked over by the cemetery," Tess told him. "You just do whatever you need to do."

"I'm going home for a minute. Forget the coffee. I'll get something at Lila's place," he told her, remembering with some degree of loneliness that *home* was now at Lila Green's and not at his parents'. He hugged Tess. She wasn't clinging unnecessarily but instead was particularly self-contained, poised.

"I'll be back up here directly," he told her.

She turned to go. Sunset caught her hair, turning it copper.

He saw Scotty Sandifer's truck in the distance, approaching the mine. Just as he passed the tipple, Scotty turned and parked by the torn barbed-wire fence.

Scotty leaned from the cab, a cigaret dangling from his lips. He turned the visor of his green baseball cap up, surveying Keller's face.

"I know about Hatfield," Keller affirmed.

Scotty nodded. "It don't mean anything, necessarily," he offered. "Hatfield's probably sleeping. Hatfield always was a lazy son of a bitch."

Keller smiled.

"I left Laura with Bolivia Ivey," Scotty said casually, and Keller felt his stomach turn over.

"Looks like she's going to have that baby right soon."

"What do you mean?" Keller asked, trying to keep his voice steady.

"Well, she was trying to push her house back a few feet."

"What?"

After a moment, Scotty said, "Laura wanted to stay there in case she needed anything. You might check in there."

Keller turned to look back in the direction of the mine. He had to get Charles. He had to talk to Charles. He had to get Laura out of there.

"We better tell Charles," Keller said.

Scotty didn't respond.

"It's his baby, ain't it?" Keller pressed.

"I reckon," Scotty said. "You been dusting?"

"Yes, sir."

"I was dusting too, earlier."

It dawned on him that Scotty wasn't drinking and hadn't been drinking. It also dawned on him that Scotty was no longer his adversary and that he too was trying to save Ben Ray. He ran back to the mine to tell Charles about the baby.

By the time they descended Pinegar Hill, it was dark. The sky had lost all color and was black as the mine wall. When they arrived at Bolivia's place, she was in the rocker with a cat on her bulging lap, curled up in the orange apron, asleep in the semi-dark.

Charles shook her.

"What's going on?" he asked.

Her eyes darted, taking in the visitors.

"Laura's gone," she said to Keller. "She was only here a few minutes."

"Scotty Sandifer said you were going to have the baby," Charles said in accusatory fashion.

"I am," she said.

Charles looked at Keller and ran his fingers through his curls.

His face looked charred from all the coal dust, and a blue-and-green checked handkerchief was tied around his neck. His overalls hung loose.

"Are you hurting?" Charles asked.

"Not now," she said. She got up and looked at Keller. He backed up toward the door. He wanted out. "My mother was in labor with me for three days, Charles," she said quietly, but continued to look at Keller. Something akin to desire was on her face, and he was frightened. Keller looked at Charles.

"Well, do you want us here?" Charles asked her.

Her eyes dropped to the floor as if she'd been shamed.

"I mean, do you want *me* here?" Charles said.

She turned to him. "Of course I do," she said and then she sat back in the rocker. "Your mother wants to deliver this baby," she said to Keller. "What do you think?"

Keller backed up toward the hearth, shivering. He rubbed his hands together.

"We need wood," Charles said and went into the kitchen. Keller heard the screen door slam shut. He stared at Bolivia. In the rocker, she was like a dark African girl who'd arrived fresh for work, wearing the orange apron over printed material and relics of field-hand shoes caked with mud.

"What did Laura say?" he asked her.

"Nothing."

"Nothing?"

"Nothing."

"But that's crazy," he pled, flinging his arms forward, disgusted with her serenity. "She had to have said something. How long was she here?"

"Twenty minutes," she replied.

"How do you know it was twenty minutes?"

Bolivia's face caved in, causing a shadow of misery to flood her eyes. He'd never seen her cry. He thought she was incapable of tears. She winced, and he knew it was labor.

"What is it?" he said, moving toward her, falling to his knees and clasping her hands in his. "What is it? It's labor," he an-

swered himself in a calm voice of reason that he recognized as
his father's.

The cloud passed over her face and dissipated.

"It's over?" he said.

She nodded.

"It comes in waves," he added.

"Yes."

On his knees, he grasped her legs the way a child clings to a
mother's skirt. He buried his face in her dress and inhaled the
peculiar scent of cats and talcum. He heard the screen door slam,
heard Charles's boots coming from the kitchen, heard the wood
hit the fireplace, the match strike, the crackling of pine. But he
didn't move. He didn't care that Charles saw him hiding his face
near the orange apron that belonged to his mother, listening for
the sound of his baby.

Charles stared at Keller's coal-stained fingers, wondering just
what Keller's mind was letting him believe. Despite his youth,
he was no fool. Surely, he knew Hatfield wasn't sleeping, and if
Hatfield was dead then what of the others behind the next fallen
wall? Charles stared at the boy's skin. The predicament of the
boy's father was what kept Charles from hating him, from
grabbing him and throwing him in the Warrior River. In fact,
it made Charles love him, made Charles continue to do favors
for him and let him bury his face in the lap of the woman
Charles loved. Bolivia looked over at Charles, her eyes wise. It
was as if Keller were the child and they the heartsick parents
watching their boy struggle with the inevitable.

She pushed Keller's head gently up from her lap.

"Do we need a doctor?" he asked her.

"No."

"Why not?"

"I don't know a doctor," she replied.

"Tate," he began, meaning the company doctor.

"Never spoke to him even," she said, waving it away.

Another pain jolted her upright, then made her double over so that the rocking chair bent forward.

Keller jumped up.

"We got to have a doctor!" he cried, turning to Charles.

Bolivia went into the kitchen. Her voice was shrill but firm. "I don't want no *man* delivering this baby, Keller," she called.

Keller turned to Charles. "My mother can't deliver it," he said. "She might know. She might recognize something."

Charles took his shoulder. As if Tess wasn't going to recognize the resemblance later, for years to come, as if everybody wasn't going to see it. The child would belong to all of them.

The night was black as coal. Laura sat on the red stool beside the cash register eating a Hershey bar and reading the newspaper under the dangling light bulb. The room was quiet. Warmed by the heater, she crumpled the candy wrapper and unzipped her jacket. She loved the station—the smell of gas, the noise from the air compressor, the velvety money bag with the drawstring.

This evening, she eyed the handmade ornaments on the cedar tree. Christmas was over. She knew she ought to go on over to her Aunt Lila's or back to the mine, but she didn't want to leave this place. It was hers, safe as any place could be. Scotty had to behave here; it was a public place. Here she could walk freely, without having to worry about drawing his attention. At the station, she was the Sandifer kid, homespun mechanic who carried grease guns and sold condoms and passed out Nehis under the tarpaper roof. She was the girl who could do anything a boy could. She could put up with anything. She didn't have to think about Keller or about Ben Ray dying as long as she was here. She didn't have to think about Bolivia Ivey, although tonight she couldn't help herself.

She remembered how, when she'd been there this afternoon, Bolivia's face had changed color as each labor pain raced through her. She was like a flower blooming. Laura's heart had raced.

"Do we need a doctor?" she'd asked Bolivia, trying to act like an adult, watching Scotty out the window. He was standing in the bushes, smoking.

"No doctor," Bolivia said. And then she'd told Laura that her labor might last days. She had told Laura to go on home, and Laura felt exiled from this warm place. Bolivia noticed that.

"Stay if you like," she said.

Laura had felt Keller all over Bolivia's place somehow. She almost expected to see his fingerprints on the dusty tabletops. She gazed at the Indian-looking tapestry and the strung peppers, trying to feel comfortable, to feel like she wasn't outside the friendship Bolivia had with Keller, with Scotty, with Tess, with the entire neighborhood.

"Want me to build a fire?" Laura had asked her, getting the pocketknife from her workpants in order to whittle a piece of kindling from the hearth where she sat.

While she did this, Bolivia told her, "My mother used to wash her face in a branch, a beautiful mountain stream that crossed the trail a few yards from our cabin." She went on to say that notched logs were chinked together with yellow clay and covered by a split-shingled roof. They had a stone chimney, she said, and a clay fireplace to burn cedar logs, pine knots, and locust sticks. Her mother picked wild plums, grapes, persimmons, pawpaws, teaberries, blackberries, and raspberries that they ate in season and dried for winter. She got wild honey from bee trees. "Nobody can locate a bee tree as quickly as a Melungeon," she'd said. Laura had asked her what had happened to her mother.

"She died," Bolivia had said.

Now, in the warmth of the station, Laura tried to make order from the chaotic memory, but what she couldn't get right was why she had felt better when she left that house. Her father had held her coat. His breath on her shoulder was clean. Bolivia had kissed her cheek, and Laura felt some of the pain loosen. But at the heart of the matter, there was Keller. Why had he gone there yesterday? Did he simply move firewood, fix a leaky faucet, kill a mouse, repair a fence? Perhaps it had something to do with the mine. Did she have papers or wills or deeds or promises that the mine had made to her when her daddy died? Was Keller surveying documents, collecting information, preparing a lawsuit? No, surely not. For that would mean he was expecting the worst, and nobody was doing that. Jake Hatfield. Laura turned his name over in her mind, for he was the key that might turn the future to either light or dark. If Jake Hatfield was dead, then was everybody dead? She didn't even know what blackdamp was. All she knew was that it killed miners. It was, she understood, a kind of substance like tar flying in the wind, a tornado of black ink. Or was it invisible to the naked eye, like germs and sperm and deceit?

She reached for the dropcord in order to put the light out. She was going to walk up Warrior Road to her aunt Lila's place and have a good dinner.

Laura zipped her jacket. Just as she closed the door to the station, she heard a car pull in. Keller hopped from the Studebaker and gathered her up in the cold.

His eyes were bloodshot, his face coal-stained.

"Hatfield's dead," he told her.

"I heard they lost contact, but is he *dead*?"

Keller lit a cigaret, shielding the flame and moving abruptly from the vicinity of the gas pump. "Well, we don't know he's dead, but don't you think he is? Don't you think they all are, and they just won't tell me?" he pressed. He looked like he'd been in a fight. Black stains circled his eyes. His hands shook.

"Daddy just told me they couldn't get no response from him,

but I don't think it's right to say he's dead," she said, kicking a stone from the concrete island.

Keller looked at her. She thought he might cry, and she anticipated the rivulets carving gulleys of clean skin in his dusty face.

"Bolivia's in labor," she told him.

"Oh, really?" he replied.

"I was with her for a bit this afternoon."

He ran his fingers through his hair quickly.

"Whose baby is she carrying, do you think?" she asked. "Charles's?"

"Charles's," he affirmed.

She took his hands in hers. "I don't think it's Charles's, but it's no business of mine." She had just decided to shut things off in her mind. He loved her, she knew that. She knew that next Christmas and the ones after, she would be at home with him.

"Do you mind if we go back up to the mine?" He asked her tentatively, like a kid who had just been forgiven of something. "I dropped Charles off at Bolivia's," he went on, "and I told him I'd pick him back up after I got you."

"I'm glad you got me," she told him. "I don't like to be away from you."

In the car, he reached for her hand. He held it until they got to Bolivia's house. The feel of her hand was good, a reminder of order and hope.

Cats stalked Bolivia's porch like guards, moving in and about the washtubs of plants.

"How does she get things to grow in winter?" Laura asked.

He looked at her.

"Have you ever been inside her house?" she asked him. Her eyes were big like a child's.

He hesitated. "Yes," he told her. It was an impulse, a glimpse of something bigger than himself, what he'd later call honesty.

But in the moment, it was simply a raw impulse, a lens that opened to a new field.

"When?" she asked, and he felt his heart going, felt the lens opening. There was no choice, really. Back at the station, he felt she knew something.

"Yesterday. I brought her home from the mine."

"I knew that," she said.

"How did you know?" He didn't look at her. He looked at his hands, one holding the steering wheel, the other resting on his jeaned thigh.

"I was driving by. I saw your car."

"And did you think I was *visiting* her?" he asked.

"Yes," she said and looked up at him. He was taken with how natural and easy her love was for him.

"I haven't," he began, but he stopped because the lens was open.

"Everybody has, haven't they?" she asked him.

He shrugged.

"Probably my daddy has," she went on.

He didn't look at her.

"Do you think so?" she pressed.

He shrugged, looking down at her hands.

"And your daddy, too?" she asked him.

He didn't respond, thinking of his father, how he was going to tell Ben Ray the truth once he was out. He was going to confess it all to his father, soon.

"You have friends who have?" she went on, but it was more a statement than a question. He felt her breath, warm and close. "I guess if I was a boy, I would want to."

He nodded, still looking down, afraid to look up.

"I think she is almost pretty. Do you?"

He nodded.

"But she's so skinny. I'd be afraid she'd break."

He looked up at Bolivia's porch. The car was growing cold.

"Probably, I would if I was a boy," she repeated.

He didn't look at her.

"Probably," she said, wiped the windshield, and looked up at the stars. "Do you know anything about constellations?"

He didn't answer. He knew she was changing the subject because they both were afraid of what they were talking about.

"Venus," she said absently.

"Venus," he repeated.

"Once I knew something about the Dippers," she told him. "What did you think the first time you ever saw me?"

"I thought you were a boy."

"Sometimes I think I am one," she said.

"I loved you all the same," he told her. "I mean, once I realized you weren't a boy, that made things a lot less complicated."

She laughed.

"You aren't a boy," he told her, and put a finger under her chin.

In the dark, her blue eyes were flat as buttons, easy to fathom. He ran a hand over her hair.

"I want to have a baby, Keller."

His stomach turned.

"She makes me want to have a baby," she told him.

He looked at his fingers—the way the coal dust was caked. He thought of Ben Ray.

"It's the shape of her," she went on, "like the baby is right under her skin, and if you cut her open, the baby's face would be right there staring at you."

He felt his skin crawl. Cut her open.

"I mean, how can a baby get through such a tiny opening?" she asked him. "It seems impossible, doesn't it?"

"Yes," he said.

"I bet it hurts."

"That's what I hear," he said, but he was thinking about Jake Hatfield. It was pitch dark in there! Hatfield didn't have a safety lantern or carbide like his father's crew, or did he? If he didn't, then no wonder he was sleeping. There was nothing to stay awake for. And he was probably in shock. He recalled what it was like lying in stark blackness, the terror of opening your eyes wider and wider, struggling to adjust your lenses to make something come alive, some phosphorescent frame of an object, but there were only more levels of darkness until finally, in the heat of this summer evening, you scream for your father and his feet can be heard, knocking against the bedframe, cursing lightly, padding across the pine floor, and then suddenly with lamp in hand, he appears at your door. He bends over. "It's just a nightmare, son. Go back to sleep." But it wasn't a nightmare, you want to say. I was awake. It was the dark, and it was real.

Laura took his hand and began scraping the caked dust from his palm.

"You going in to get Charles?" she asked quietly.

"Yeah," he said and bolted from the car.

Inside, Charles was lying on the tapestry that draped the sofa, snoring lightly under the string of dried peppers. Cats were tearing painted bottlecaps from the cedar holiday tree.

"Charles," Keller whispered, shaking him.

Charles's eyes opened.

"Let's go," Keller said.

Charles got up and began putting on his boots. Keller noted that Bolivia's bedroom door was shut.

"She asleep?" he asked Charles.

Charles nodded.

"Any more pains?"

"No. I've heard women call this false labor. Did you see your wife?" Charles asked.

"She's in the car."

Charles looked at him, his icy eyes narrowing. "What about coming here?" he asked. "What did she think about you coming here to get me?"

"Where's your hat?" Keller asked him.

"It's up at the mine. I left it there."

Keller opened the door. His mind was on Jake Hatfield.

All the way up Pinegar Hill, Keller talked about Jake Hatfield. He told Laura and Charles that Hatfield was in shock, that he was in a semi-coma, and he needed a drink of water—that's why he wasn't audible. He was too hoarse to call, saving his strength, afraid of stirring rats. Hatfield was a smart guy. Keller delivered his conclusions with the certainty of a reporter.

Laura kept her hands folded in her lap. Neither she nor Charles said a word.

The superintendent's office was quiet. The night had made Tess old. Her eyes were sunken and her lips were blue with cold.

"Mom," Keller said.

Laura lingered at the door, Charles at her side.

There was one other woman there, Jake Hatfield's wife, and the sight of her caused Keller to feel sick. "Mrs. Hatfield," he acknowledged, and he saw in her eyes the fright he'd squelched in himself. She knew all right, no denying that.

"Any news?" Charles asked, reaching for a cup of coffee and surveying the women's faces.

"No," Tess said. "Nobody's come up in over two hours."

Charles took Keller's elbow and led him out the back door. They stood beside the steel latticework of the payroll window, staring at the mine entrance down the hill.

"Take your mother home," Charles said. "Something's going to break by morning, and she needs some sleep under her belt."

"I'm going down there," Keller replied.

"You do what I say."

"Hell, no!"

"Boy, you ain't got a brain left in your head. Now, you do what I say."

"Hell no!"

Charles backed off.

"You and your wife spend the night at your mother's. It'll make her sleep."

Keller didn't respond. He just turned and started to leave. Over his shoulder the radio crackled with war news and suddenly he knew what it all meant.

Back home, he sat on the porch. His mother and Laura were cooking. Women had food to pass the time, to keep their hands busy during bad times. And what did men have? What did they do with their hands? Smoke cigarets, peel paint from banisters, while wondering how many more pies would it take to bring the women to the point of exhaustion, when they'd finally sit, talk, cry, make love.

Keller considered whether it was time yet to begin bargaining with God. He'd put it off because, one, it was such an embarrassing and childish ordeal, and, two, he just wasn't in a very good negotiating position.

Tess opened the front door. "Hungry?" she asked.

He closed his eyes. There would be pinto beans, rice, milk gravy. He was going to vomit.

He didn't answer her.

He felt his mother's hand on his shoulder, so light he thought it was Laura until he turned.

Tess guided him to the table, which was set as if company were coming—holly sprigs in clay pots, and glasses of chilled milk. Laura had the look of a boy who'd forgotten to wash up for dinner.

"Bolivia Ivey is in labor," Laura said to Tess. "I forgot to tell you."

Tess dropped her fork. "No," she exclaimed, her eyes widening. "Why didn't anyone tell me?"

"You didn't need anything else on you today," Keller snapped. "We were doing you a favor," he said and buttered a slice of cornbread, buttering it so hard that it began crumbling.

Tess's hands shook as she reached for the bowl of rice.

She took a few bites of beans, then turned to Laura. "How far along is she?"

Laura shrugged.

"I mean, is she *having* it?" she demanded, getting up from the table.

Keller bolted up and ushered Tess back to her chair.

"Mom," he said, leaving his hands on her shoulders. "Please, eat. Charles is with her. It's ... it's his baby," he heard himself say, the lie causing his voice to cave in.

He glanced at Laura.

"I'm going to the mine," he said and wiped his face with his napkin.

"Keller, no!" his mother screamed. "If you won't let me go see Bolivia, then you got no right to walk out this door and go to the mine."

"Oh really?" he said. "That so?"

"We need to be together," she said, and her face crumpled.

"That's right," Laura said quietly.

He looked at her.

"I don't want you to go anywhere," Laura went on. "Please."

Later that night, he made love with her in his old bedroom

under the umbrella of her blue eyes that refused to close. He'd intended to get up and return to the mine, but sleep took him.

"Keller."

He heard his name, but he couldn't rise.

Keller.

In the dream, a copperhead was in the water hole. The quarry was filled with chunks of coal. The snake was talking to himself, and Keller was laughing so hard he couldn't stand up.

"Keller!" This time his mother's voice caused him to spiral up from the dark. He sat up in bed. Laura was curled around him, nude. He pulled the quilt up to cover her boyish chest, but his mother wasn't interested in his embarrassment.

"What is it?" he asked, hopping from bed, relieved he'd slept in his shorts.

He got his bearings. Pale light illuminated his bookshelves and her sewing items. A fire was going. The pine floor was warming.

"What?" he asked her.

"It's morning," she said. "Did you sleep?"

"Yes."

"I did, too," she said. "I feel better."

He was spooked. The unnatural light of early dawn was peculiarly gray. "So, what's going on?" he asked her.

She touched his bare arm, and he recoiled.

"Mom," he said. "What?"

"There's been a nun staying over at the O'Cadlins'," she said.

He felt terror rise to his throat. "No," he said, backing away. She was about to tell him that Ben Ray was dead, and he wasn't going to let her do this.

"I don't know anything, Keller," she said softly.

He felt his knees give submissively to his relief, and he sat on the edge of the bed, reaching for his jeans that he'd tossed over the back of a rattan chair.

"The nun's been over here praying with me," Tess said. "So has Miriam."

Miriam, Miriam. He ran the name through the files in his brain, searching for who Miriam was.

"Miriam O'Cadlin," Tess said.

Keller shuddered. O'Cadlin's wife. O'Cadlin who was dead. His wife.

"And Reba Hatfield," Tess said.

Hatfield's wife. Hatfield, old sleepyhead Hatfield, Keller thought.

Tess sat beside him on the bed. "We're on our way up to the mine," she told him.

"Great," he said and hopped into his jeans, buckled his belt, and threw his shirt on. He glanced down at Laura. He shook her by the shoulders. "Hey," he whispered in her ear. "Hey, Mom and I are heading up to the mine. Fix some breakfast for yourself when you get up. Check on Bolivia," he heard himself say.

"Coffee?" Tess asked him as they passed by the kitchen door.

He searched her face; she looked happy and serene. "Do you know something?" he asked her.

"No," she said, getting her pocketbook from the old chair in the family room and smoothing her brown dress. "I don't know anything, baby," she said quietly and smiled.

"Where are the others?" he asked.

"They're at Miriam's."

"I thought you said they'd been here."

"They were," she said, "earlier."

"How early?" he asked her, surveying the sky, which was the color of moths. It looked like it might snow. He inhaled deeply, then let the steamy vapor form a puff near his face. He zipped his jacket and opened the door to the Studebaker.

"We can't all ride in here," he said. "Is the nun going?"

"Yes," she said, "the nun is going."

"That's not a good idea," he said. "I just mean, if you got a preacher on the spot, it's like you're asking for bad news," he said.

Tess flung her hair back over her winter coat.

"She's going," Tess said. "We'll walk if we can't fit in the car," she said.

"Well, let's go," he said, zipping his jacket up even higher and relacing his boots.

They walked down the road to the O'Cadlins' place, which had been painted a strong tan, like a Shetland pony. Keller recalled O'Cadlin himself out there on a ladder slapping on the thick coats. "Buttermilk," O'Cadlin had said. "We call this buttermilk, boy," he'd said good-naturedly.

When O'Cadlin's wife opened the door, he looked at her round, gray face, and instinctively embraced her. She responded in full, with the surprise of a mother accepting a boy's offering. Keller saw the nun. He didn't know what to do. Shake her hand? Bow like a subject?

Finally, he just held a salutory hand up.

She smiled.

Hatfield's wife, he thought. Where's Hatfield's wife? Old sleeping Hatfield. Hatfield's just asleep. It had become a song that he played in his head. "Old Hatfield's just asleep."

"Reba's in the alley," Miriam O'Cadlin said, meaning the toilet, and Keller looked at the nun to see if she acknowledged bodily functions. He was curious about her. Miriam O'Cadlin turned to a fancy endtable that had on it a doily and a cut-glass bowl of peppermints. "Have one," she said to Keller.

Sucking it, he surveyed the baskets of fruit and the bouquets, funeral things. Where had they taken O'Cadlin's body, and when did they bury him? He'd been so caught up in his own turmoil, he hadn't even bothered to ask where and when they were burying O'Cadlin. He wished now that he had. The O'Cadlin place was as neat as Mrs. O'Cadlin's schoolroom had been.

He looked at Miriam O'Cadlin's face.

"This is truly kind of you," he said to her, taking her elbow and leading her to the door. "That you would want to be with us," he heard himself say. It was the voice of somebody else, the voice of his father, the voice of a strong and grown man he didn't know.

Pinegar Hill rose like a sheet of sandpaper in the morning light. Over in the ravine, fog hid the buzzards and kudzu. Keller followed after the women, watching how the nun's habit blew behind her. Tess and the other two were bent forward, strong mountain women in winter coats and scarves walking in the direction of the mine.

Nobody spoke a word.

The crisp air became saturated with invisible droplets.

Tess held a hand up. "Snow?" she asked with disbelief.

The nun put her palms up high. "Rain," she replied.

Reba Hatfield and Miriam O'Cadlin adjusted each other's scarves, their eyes searching to find what the other needed. Hatfield's wife was on the edge.

Wet specks hit Keller's face.

"This is snow. Mom," he said, and lightly touched her curls. "Mom, it's snowing. I can see it in your hair."

She wasn't wearing a scarf like the others.

Turning to him, she smiled. "Yes," she said. "It's snowing."

"Mom," he said again, and she slowed so as to keep pace with him rather than the women. "Mom," he repeated, but he didn't know what he wanted to ask her.

He watched the tiny snowflakes melt in her hair as they made their way past the cemetery, the oak tree, on into the grounds of the mine. The nun crossed herself, then followed the women into the superintendent's office. Nobody was there. Maps, diagrams of the ventilation system, and half-drunk coffee cups were scattered over the desk. It was cold. Keller put some wood in the stove and walked out the back door, past the payroll window, and peered down in the direction of the mine.

A man was coming up the hill, carrying a lantern.

Keller strained to see. It was the guy who operated the mantrip. Keller walked toward him and, upon coming face to face, seized his arm. "What?" Keller asked. "What's happened?"

The man shrugged, motioning to the mine. "They're real close," he said.

"Take me down."

"I need some coffee," he hedged.

"Take me down. My daddy's in there."

"You need a mask," he said and grabbed one from a crate near the opening of the mine.

"Why so?" Keller called to him as they got in. "I didn't need one last time."

"You do now."

The world of light vanished, in the dark tunnel. The mantrip careered down the tracks, heavy, jostling Keller's gut to the point of nausea. When they arrived at the juncture where the dark was dotted with a nest of scurrying yellow lights, Keller leapt and ran, coughing against the blackdamp and the dusty air blown by the ventilation system. Something was different. The machines were louder, formidable, the coal dust heavy, the men scrambling and talking and cursing. He didn't see the silhouette of Charles's big body or Scotty's small one. He didn't see anybody he knew. He stopped short of the operation itself, where they were using equipment he didn't recognize. Had the Chattanooga team finally arrived? He saw Charles emerge from a hole, a cragged incision made in the body of the black wall. He was wearing a mask. They were all wearing masks. If they were wearing masks, then they were searching for bodies and not men, because the air was bad and nobody could live in bad air.

Charles was moving his hands wildly, and under the carbide light, Keller saw his fierce blue eyes charged with electricity. Suffocated with frustration at not being able to hear what Charles was saying, Keller moved in his direction, stepping over equipment, picks, drills, shovels, and buckets of limestone.

"What's he saying?" he asked a black man.

"Hatfield's dead," the man said.

Keller felt his body draw in.

The men began crawling into the hole, and Keller followed after them, tearing his jeans and cutting his legs. They were clustered in the pocket where Hatfield had been trapped, and

Keller saw them over Hatfield's body, shaking their heads. "Heart attack," the black man said. "Sumpin' like that. Stroke."

"Not the air?" Keller said weakly, and then he noticed that Charles wasn't wearing his mask. He watched a group trying to get a microphone through a crevice, and he saw that Charles was breathing hard, expectantly, and then Charles saw him and Charles ran to him, grabbing him by the collar of his jacket and pulling him so hard that he fell forward and hurt his hands, but Charles was like a crazed animal, pulling Keller's body over the floor of the pocket, past Hatfield's body to the wall with the crevice, and Keller saw that there were crevices everywhere and that there was a whole ceiling of air passages, and then Charles put Keller's ear up against the wall, his blue eyes on fire with passion, and Charles called, "Hayes, your boy's here." And Keller heard Ben Ray's weak voice.

"Boy? Hey, boy?"

And Keller threw his arms against the wall and screamed "Daddy" over and over until the dust filled his lungs to the point he thought he was going to choke, and Charles pulled him down to a kneeling position and clumsily wiped the tears from Keller's face with the palms of his big hands, but there was no containing the tears, and they kept falling and falling while the men worked frenzied until the hole was big enough, and Keller listened to them marvel at how thin the wall was that contained Ben Ray's crew and that if the new wall hadn't fallen, it would've been a cakewalk. Keller didn't look up until he felt somebody's hand on his shoulder, and when he glanced behind him, he saw Scotty Sandifer, chewing a mouthful of tobacco and smiling his snakish but honest smile. Keller raised a hand as if to greet him, but it fell to his lap, so great was his exhaustion.

When the crevice had become a tunnel wide enough to crawl through, they sent Scotty because of his small frame. Keller crouched low and watched him disappear. Ranger Avery yelled to him all the way, and Scotty reported his every move. "Coming through," he yelled. "Got Hayes here, and Bellamy and Stone." Keller heard Ben Ray's voice. "Got 'em all, Avery,"

Scotty called back through the microphone they'd maneuvered in. When Scotty reappeared through the rock, he told Ranger that Ben Ray had a broken leg. They discussed how to proceed, and Ranger told Charles that somebody was going to have to tell Hatfield's wife. Their eyes fell on Keller.

"No," he begged off to Charles. "Please, no," he said.

"You need to go tell your mom, too," Charles reminded him. "Take the trip back up. Go on, boy."

When Keller emerged to the light of day, he saw his mother's hair blowing in the wind. She stood by the payroll window outside the office, staring at the mine. He ran to her. She knelt as if to accept him as a toddler who was racing in her direction, and he knelt, too, when he got to her. "Alive," she said breathlessly into his ear, and he shook his head yes, and his whole body shook with hers.

"It's snowing," he said, and watched the flakes as they fell on his jacket sleeves, making the black coal dust on them bleed gray.

"Hatfield's dead."

Tess's hand flew to her mouth, and she turned abruptly and went silently into the office. That's when he knew he wasn't going to have to tell Reba Hatfield, that his mother was going to do it for him, another tender mercy in the endless tender mercies of his parents.

He followed after her, standing behind Reba Hatfield, so that when she swooned and wobbled toward the nearest chair he caught her elbow, and she thanked him sweetly as if he'd picked up a fallen handkerchief. The guilt of being spared sickened him. Kneeling with his mother in front of her, he took her fingers, kissed them, and cried.

Miriam O'Cadlin and the nun stood nearby. Keller rose and asked the nun what to do. She pointed outside. From the window, Keller saw a cluster of women emerging from a car and recognized one as Bellamy's wife. Yes, he needed to deliver their good news.

Walking toward them, he thanked God aloud.

He told the women, in one breath, that they'd been spared and that Reba Hatfield had not, then watched the confusion of euphoria and guilt register in their eyes just as it had with his mother. They took his hands as if he were a preacher. Then he said that he was going back to the mine, but when he passed the office, the nun stopped him.

Her face was round, like an apple.

"Don't leave," she instructed. "There's no other man here."

He searched her eyes.

"My dad," he said.

"Would want you where you're needed."

"Yes, ma'am."

He wasn't going to disobey a nun.

"There are other wives, aren't there?"

"Yes, ma'am."

"Should you go tell them that God has been generous?"

"Yes, ma'am," he said, watching how her habit blew behind her, gathering bits of snow at the hem.

"That God has . . ." she began, then studied him curiously, and he felt his skin crawl. "That God has blessed you, too," she said and looked even deeper into him. "Don't forget," she said, "what God has done."

"I won't."

He looked away. "I don't have a car," he said foolishly, sincerely, picturing himself trudging down Pinegar Hill.

"Run, boy."

He nodded, but when he turned for one last glance in the direction of the mine, he saw Scotty Sandifer and some others, trudging forward up the hill, and he ran from the nun toward them. Scotty told him that Ben Ray was coming first, that they'd already pulled him through the crevice, that his leg was broken.

Keller waited at the mine's dark entrance, staring into the black mouth, waiting for the mantrip. When it came, Ben Ray hopped off with two men supporting him under the arms, and Keller stood dumbstruck at the sight of his father, who'd just emerged from his tomb, in the flesh.

Ben Ray's leg was a mess, dangling at odd angles from the ankle and knee. Scotty visualized how Ben Ray would look amputated.

It was his third day without a drink. His head was light, like an empty home before the movers come. The bad part was that nobody knew just how remarkable it all was. Three days.

"Sandifer," Ranger called from where they'd laid Ben Ray on a stretcher and were giving him fresh water. Scotty watched the way Tess Hayes's hair fell over her husband's coal-stained face as she knelt to kiss him.

"What?" he asked Ranger, lighting a Pall Mall, blowing smoke into the snow. "I'll be damned," he said in wonder, just now taking note of the flakes. It never snowed in Alabama.

"You got your truck?"

"I got it," he said and grinned down at Ben Ray. Lucky son

of a bitch, he thought. Luckiest sonofabitches alive, he thought, surveying the other crew members who were milling about like confused insects in the light of day.

"Where's Tate?" he asked, meaning the company doctor.

"He left a while ago," somebody said. "Didn't know this was going to happen."

"We need to get everybody looked at. We need to get him back up here," he mumbled.

Ben Ray asked for a cigaret.

Keller handed him one.

The other crew members, not a single one appearing to be in any pain, were waiting to use the phone. Scotty saw that Reba Hatfield was gone. Somebody had gotten her a ride home before they brought Jake out.

Scotty left for the company doctor's home, cranking his truck. He found Tate at home, chopping wood with his boys in the big lot behind their spacious company home, wearing a big apron not unlike what Graham wore at the commissary when making sausage. Tate was tall, angular, and heavily bearded, and Scotty had always thought he looked like Abraham Lincoln.

Scotty nodded to him, tipping his baseball cap.

"They got Ben Ray Hayes's crew out this morning," he said, and the doctor dropped his ax, ran inside, and returned abruptly with his black bag and overcoat.

The snow had quit falling. The doctor moved in the direction of his Ford, thanking Scotty for coming with the news.

"Jake Hatfield didn't make it," he called after.

The doctor waved his hand from the window and raced up Pinegar Hill, stalling once in his haste and revving the Ford madly.

Scotty got in his truck and headed to the filling station.

Inside, Grace was behind the counter reading the newspaper. Laura was on the floor, tossing balls of tin foil into the corner where the black kitten retrieved them, leaping up in tiny arcs.

"What?" she asked, seeing something good in his face.

"They're all out," he told her.

Laura closed her eyes.

Grace put the newspaper aside. She moved from behind the counter, her wandering eye fixed on Scotty.

"Jake Hatfield didn't make it," he told her.

Grace crossed her arms and stared out the window, shaking her head. "Poor Reba," she said, but immediately turned to Laura. "Oh, baby," she said.

Laura got up and went to Grace. They stood near the drink box in a light embrace. He wanted a drink. How could he shoot skeet without a beer? How could he hunt quail over in Praco without whiskey? How could he change oil, take tires to Bessemer, leave the steel plant on payday, make love to Grace, change seasons, ride trains, chop wood, meet a stranger, see a bluebird, face himself and all the sadness?

The field beyond the station was bare, but it would turn green. On the fourth of July, there'd be fireworks, peach ice cream, and all the happiness other people knew. Cocking his rifle, he fired at the bull's-eye he'd nailed to the oak.

He felt something brush his neck and jumped. When he turned, he was face to face with the kitten that Laura held up.

"He likes you," she said. "Imagine that."

"Imagine," he said.

He stood beside her. She was standing close. He reached for the kitten. They petted his black fur, their hands close. He tickled the white locket under its chin.

"Nice, isn't it?" she said.

Scotty blew a smoke ring.

"You used to blow those for me," she said, as the wind quickly turned the circle of smoke into an ellipse before it disappeared.

"You're lucky you still got a father-in-law. Thought he was dead," he told her, rubbing the kitten's ears.

"So did I. I need to go up there," she told him. "Can you take me?"

He hesitated. "They're taking Ben Ray to the hospital," he said. "There's something else. Ben Ray's leg was broke."

She looked up.

"Broke?" she repeated.

"Crushed, baby," he said.

"Then Keller's gone to the hospital?"

"Probably."

"What do you think I should do?"

"Stay here, so if he comes by, he'll find you."

The sky was still full of clouds, but the snow had ceased. A thin blanket of white lay over the overturned crates and gnarled oak roots. Beer bottles were scattered all around the back of the station, and he thought of all the cleaning up there was to do, days and years of cleaning.

"Have you named it?" he asked Laura.

"Zip," she said.

"Zip?"

"Zip."

He didn't question her further. It sounded nice. It sounded like a good name.

"Zip," he said, and they both stroked its underside. The kitten was docile. He thought kittens were supposed to be fidgety. Laura stroked him, too. Her fingers were made like her mother's—squared off, practical, functional.

"You going to keep working here?" he asked her.

"Until I have a baby."

He looked at her. "When's that going to be?"

"Whenever I get pregnant," she said and shrugged. He couldn't imagine her pregnant.

He knew she was going to say something about Bolivia Ivey, and she did.

"Bolivia's baby is overdue," she said.

He picked up a pine needle and chewed it, staring at his boots, which were caked with coal dust and slush from this morning. He thought of Ben Ray Hayes's crushed leg.

"You think I ought to have a baby?" she pressed.

He looked at her thin frame.

"You ought to do whatever you want," he told her.

Her blue eyes engaged his, then she looked quickly at the ground.

"Wasn't there a war when you were young?"

"Yes, but it wasn't mine."

She looked at him.

"I mean I didn't fight in it."

"Will Keller be in this one?"

He looked at her. She tucked a lock of hair behind her ear.

"I imagine so, baby."

"You stopped drinking?" she asked, looking away toward the field.

He held on to the kitten, examining the insides of its ears. "I don't know," he said.

The cat's ears were translucent, so that the blue veins were visible in the light. They were paper-thin, so delicate you might crush them between your fingers if you weren't careful.

She picked up a rock and turned it over as if it were significant.

He wished he could talk to her.

"You think we need another kitten?" she asked him.

He let the kitten leap from his hands. Laura knelt to scoop him up, but he ran inside the station.

"I wish I could tell you I had quit," he told her.

She looked at the rock in her hand.

"But all I can tell you is that I'm not drinking today."

"Or yesterday," she added, taking a quick, furtive look his way.

"Or yesterday," he affirmed. "Or the day before that."

"But you can't say tomorrow," she went on, almost in a whisper.

"No, I can't say that."

"Why not?" she asked.

"It'd be like predicting the future, wouldn't it?" he offered.

"What?"

"If I told you I wasn't drinking tomorrow."

She shrugged. "Just thought you might have some kind of idea about it," she said, and began moving away from him, toward the station.

Right before she went in, he grabbed her arm.

"Just stay awhile," he said, but he didn't know what he meant.

He let his hand slide down her jacket sleeve until he was holding her wrist.

"Stay?" She looked at him and smiled crookedly. "You mean stay here, in the cold?"

He let go of her.

"I mean, stay kind of," he paused, uncertain, and took off his baseball cap to scratch his head. "Stay in today," he said, finally.

She nodded, reached up, and put her hands on his face.

When Bolivia was a girl, she'd rise early with her mother and tag alongside to the branch—the mountain stream where they'd wash their faces. In spring, raindrops caused the branch to become muddy and lose translucence, but it didn't matter. Fuzzy green plants grew along the bank. Bear lettuce, they called it. They ate it raw with salt, and picked pails of wild greens, poke sallet, cress, narrow dock, and crow's foot, while the men logged or cleared the land. On Saturday evenings, the boys fished and waded in the stream and strung croppie on a pliable willow twig.

For breakfast every morning, her mother fixed cornbread, wild honey, and coffee, which they ate in the garret above the single room. In the surrounding neighborhoods—Snake Hollow, Mulberry Gap, Blackwater Swamp, and Sycamore Creek—the men took cornmeal, pails, frying pans, guns, and oil lanterns to the mountains to dig for ginseng, which they took to market. They slept under cliffs and ledges and searched for hickory, walnuts, and chestnuts to peddle along with the ginseng. They hunted squirrel, rabbits, turkeys, and pheasants, and took partridge eggs for food. Bolivia guessed this was why she liked Scotty Sandifer—he was a hunter like her daddy had been before the mines and the company's money. Men, she felt, were made to hunt food, not coal.

She was boiling water for tea and compresses. The pain was rhythmic but tolerable. All night, she'd kept wet rags on her belly. It didn't help, but there was some comfort. Her mother had pressed warm, liquid cloths to her whenever she'd had a fever.

She'd made Charles leave at daybreak, because she wanted to be alone. She wanted to try to will the baby out, and in order to do this she needed privacy. She drank five cups of tea and honey, then squatted by the fireplace like a girl peeing in the woods. Rocking back and forth on her heels, she prayed to her mother. It was something she didn't tell anyone, not now and not ever, that her mother heard her prayers.

Two nights ago, she'd dreamed they found Ben Ray Hayes alive. It was a prophetic dream, she knew, and when Charles banged on her door, she knew he'd come to tell her.

He said they'd taken Ben Ray Hayes to the hospital, where the doctors cut off his crushed leg. She asked how Keller was doing, and Charles got the flushed look on his face that she'd come to recognize at the mention of Keller's name. She didn't know if it was rage or love.

Now, squatting beside the hearth, she felt the warm liquid gush down her legs. The nature of her pain changed as the amniotic fluid lay in a puddle on the floor, where the cats sniffed. She knew that birth was imminent. The pain told her. It was no longer localized but felt like a machine jolting her, banging her against something, over and over.

It helped to squat, to be near the earth. If it had been warm out, if it had been spring, she'd have gone to the field beyond the alley of outhouses, where clover and daffodils grew. Melungeon women liked to deliver babies in the natural way—on blankets under trees. But it wasn't early spring; it was dead winter, and her bedroom floor was stark cold. She was bleeding now. She'd forgotten that you bleed when you have a baby, though memory was now reminding her of the times she'd watched it happen. Neighbors up in Tennessee had birthed for all the womenfolk to see. Mothers brought their daughters to witness, as her mother said, "what great wonders the Creator has made known to us."

But there were no women to see her baby being born.

Tess was at the hospital, she reasoned.

She got towels and old sheets from the closet to wipe the mixture of blood and amniotic fluid from her thighs. Pulling her dress up to her waist, she crawled into bed and waited.

Charles watched her close the bedroom door. He didn't know what she wanted from him, but he didn't want to be left out of it all. He got up from the sofa and went to her room.

"Having a baby?" he asked, kneeling to kiss her.

She didn't reply. Her face turned inward—the way people look when they accidentally bite their jaw or break a tooth. He looked at her dress bunched up near the waist. She was wearing the ivory thing with red and turquoise rick-rack that had belonged to her mother.

"Here," he said, trying to lift her in order to unbutton it. "You're getting this messed up."

Her bed was soaked with diluted blood. The liquid on her brown legs was the texture of egg whites. He'd delivered cats, dogs, horses, sheep, and goats. He'd never delivered a human.

She winced, then pushed his arms.

"What?" he asked.

"I can't take it off," she screamed.

He backed away. "Then don't," he said and shrugged.

She wrestled with the pain for a moment, stiff as a board, upright in bed. Then she collapsed.

"I can't do this, Charles."

"Got to, baby," he said, exhausted from nights without sleep, blackdamp from the mine, and now this. He went to her kitchen, lit the stove, and put water on to boil.

"Charles," she called from the bedroom.

He went back.

She was in the closet, rummaging through clothes, naked. The melon of her belly was awesome, her legs storklike.

"What are you doing?" he asked, taking her wrists and trying to lead her back to bed.

"I'm packing," she said.

"For what?"

"I'm leaving."

"Get back in bed," he instructed, perplexed and slightly amused.

"No, this is it. I'm not going through with it," she said. "I'm going to Tennessee."

"You walking?" he asked, grinning at her.

"Taking the train," she said, and he saw that her eyes were those of a rabid dog. Her hair, unbraided, fell to her chest, brushing her raisin nipples.

"Catching it in Bessemer?" he pressed, but he knew this was not funny, that she was out of her mind with pain and panic. He got the flask from his coat pocket, poured her a nip in the metal cup on her table, and held it to her mouth. She refused it, standing cross-armed and stubborn.

"Please," he said gently. "Come on, baby," he coaxed and went through her drawers hunting for another nightgown.

In the end, he wrapped her papoose-style in the sheet he'd brought from home and threw a lot of wood on the fire in the other room. For a while, she rested, but when the next round of pain arrived, she started it up again, struggling for the closet, insisting that she was going to Tennessee.

"Sequatchie!" she shouted.

"What?"

"Sequatchie. It's where my mother is buried, and my grandmother, too. I'm going to find their graves. I'm going to talk to them about this matter. Nobody told me about this, do you understand?" She was in his face, screaming louder than he'd ever imagined she, or any woman, capable of screaming. "Nobody told me I'd rip in two."

"You haven't ripped in two." He took her arm, and she bit his hand.

"Not yet, Charles. Right? Not just yet."

She fell to her knees, holding his legs, as another contraction took her body. She breathed deeply, then screamed, and finally whimpered like a trapped animal. He thought of things he knew he shouldn't think—the dignity of a dog, laboring quietly, bearing up.

As soon as the contraction was over, she started up again. "I'm gone," she said. "Now you can either help me pack my bags or you can just get yourself out of this house."

Angry, he shook her. "You've lost your mind. You're out of your head. You ain't going nowhere."

"Get out of my way!"

She clawed like a cat, bit his arm, and lunged at the bureau, stubbing her toe on her bedframe, and this was when he, too, panicked and went searching for a woman.

His brother's wife wasn't home.

All the neighbors were at Reba Hatfield's, delivering funeral food, or at Miriam O'Cadlin's. And it was only as a final resort, and against his will and judgment, that he knocked on Tess Hayes's door. Certain that she was at the hospital, he waited only a second, then headed back past the gatepost and her turnip patch.

"Charles," she called, and he turned.

She was standing at her door, wearing an apron.

"Thought you'd be at the hospital," he said, running his hand through his hair. "How is he?"

"Fine," she said. "I wanted to see Bolivia."

"She says she's going to Tennessee," he said to her.

Tess took her apron from her hips.

——

Later, when they went inside, they found Bolivia naked, packing clothes.

"This is labor," Tess said. She told Charles to gather up every sheet and towel in sight, which he'd already done.

"Get in bed right this minute," she fussed at Bolivia, shooing her like you would a toddler, patting her nude rear. "Now!" she yelled.

"Don't call a doctor," Bolivia said and crawled obediently into bed.

"We aren't calling any doctors," Tess said, "but you better do everything I say or I will."

Charles watched Tess spread Bolivia's legs and peer into her body.

"She's close," she said. "She's very close. This is an awful lot of blood, isn't it?"

Charles nodded. He didn't know what was a lot and what wasn't. Animals didn't bleed much at all. While Tess tended to her, he stood on her back porch. The wind was up. The horizon was smoke-gray. Occasionally, Bolivia screamed and cursed. He was certain the neighbors heard, but nobody came to check.

Whose baby is it, you reckon?

The question was surely coming up once again in table conversation. He thought of how Keller had asked him to come get him, of how he'd promised he would, knowing he wouldn't, of how it didn't matter anymore anyway because Keller was with his father alive, and this baby was nothing more than what it'd always been. Babies were the by-product of so many contortions of human misery and love, the twisted bedsheets of a summer night's argument, a sad wintry boredom, a flawed condom, raging desire. We were born from something frightful, Charles knew.

He looked at the chicken bones she'd tossed for the cats. Her plot of land was a junkyard—cigar butts, bottlecaps, and coal dust. In summer, flies swarmed the alley of outhouses and mosquitoes sang near the creek. But here in winter, the place almost had a cool sanctity. Nothing marred the calm.

Charles loved her. He loved it all, her complicated bones and sadness.

Tess rolled rags up, securing them with shoelaces so that they became hard bundles of cloth, in an effort to conserve the supply of available material for blood absorption. She'd never seen a woman bleed so profusely during labor, and she'd witnessed a lot of births. Once, she had delivered a set of twins in Kentucky to a woman who weighed near three hundred pounds, and she'd hardly bled a drop. Tess reasoned that the bulk of fat substance provided a barrier to anything oozing from the woman's pores. In fact, come to recall, she'd hardly sweated, even though it had been a scorching summer night. It was the damnedest thing she'd ever seen in her life. Now, she thought, I'm looking at the skinniest human being alive, and she's going to hemorrhage all the water weight she's got.

"When did the water break?" she asked Bolivia, poking four fingers up as far as she could reach, noting that there was plenty of space. She was up to seven or eight fingers wide. She was close.

"A few hours ago."

"Was it leaking before?"

"No."

Bolivia's throat began vibrating like a frog's. Tess had noticed that this was how a contraction first showed itself with her. It was a peculiarly funny aspect of her labor. All women labored differently. For some reason, she'd visualized Bolivia laboring silently, stoically. But this wasn't going to be an easy birth. The girl just wasn't built wide.

Tess made her drink some liquor from Charles's flask—just a few drops. Bolivia didn't speak to her, only squeezed her hand and stared blue-lipped at the ceiling.

By nightfall, the contractions were coming a minute apart,

but she wasn't even to nine fingers. Charles was in and out, chain-smoking, and patting Bolivia's forehead with his big hands. He asked Tess if she was hungry, and she said she wasn't.

"Weren't you going to the hospital this evening?" he asked her.

"I can go later," she said.

"You need me to tell your boy anything?" he asked, and Bolivia looked at him.

"No, he's up at the hospital with his daddy."

"Sure you aren't hungry?"

"I'm sure," she replied, feeling once again up under the sheets between Bolivia's thighs. "Could you tie my hair back, though, with that shoelace?" she asked.

The room was growing dark. She felt Charles clumsily gather her hair up, his big hands awkwardly drawing the loose strands from under the collar of her dress. There were things she needed to tell him. He'd been at the mine practically around the clock, organizing volunteers, manning the telephone, and taking care of Keller. She wanted to thank him. Bolivia's throat rose in its hummingbird quiver, and Tess pinned her wrists to the sheets, fearing that the onset of a contraction was going to activate the Tennessee plans. It was too far into labor for Bolivia to begin leaping into the closet again.

"Thank you, Charles," Tess said, as he secured the last bit of hair.

"Your hair," he said.

"Is spectacular," she completed.

He smiled and sauntered over to the window that faced the creek. The stone wall was draped with crusty vines. A few bright stars were mirrored in the water.

"Come look at this," he whispered to Tess.

She rose and went to his side.

Bolivia screamed. Tess listened and heard the change in pitch that she'd been waiting for. The hard, grunting finale. "She's at the end of transition," she told Charles. "She's ready to push."

He fled.

Tess called, "Charles, get the liquor."

He returned, ashen, with the flask.

"Push!" Tess told her firmly. "Push."

Charles held the flask to her lips. "Wait," Tess said. "Wait till she's finished this one."

When she'd collapsed, her brown face alive with work and sweat, Tess instructed her to drink. Nodding, she took a sip. Women, Tess knew, were easier to deal with at the end. Charles sat at the foot of the bed, towels in hand.

"Isn't she bleeding a lot?" he asked.

"Yes."

Tess wasn't sure why uncertainty was taking over her gut, but she was conceding the fact that this wasn't turning into an easy delivery. After another hour of pushing, Tess checked her once more. She was still at seven or eight fingers. Yet her body was telling her to push. The baby's head wasn't crowning, was hardly within reaching distance. Tess gestured for Charles to follow her to the other room. Pushing a tendril of hair from her brow, she instructed Charles to go find Dr. Tate.

He stood still.

The fire was blazing orange behind his body.

"She told me not to," he said.

"Do you want this baby?"

He looked at her. There was something in his eyes, something she understood from a distance. There were things that separated neighbors, family members, that even separated her from herself, from her capacity to see truth. There were things going on all around her, in her, that she refused to see.

Charles's ice-blue eyes held firm.

"Yes?" she said.

"It's the one thing I promised her," he hedged. "Not to bring a doctor into this."

"Into what?"

His eyes filled.

"Oh, Jesus," Tess said and took him to her arms. She hated to see men cry. It made her relinquish authority. "Just stop this," she scolded. "Stop it this minute. Forget the doctor."

"No, I'm going to get him," he said, got his coat, and left.

The green of Bolivia's Christmas tree was beginning to turn brown, but the fire was reflected in the bottlecaps, making designs of light cross the room. Tess looked at the dried peppers strung wall to wall, the ball of cats sleeping beside the hearth, the rocker, the blue-green hooked rug. Christmas, she thought, Christmas 1941—come and gone.

She went back to Bolivia's bedroom, where she lay placid, ready to push with the new contraction. Tess felt again with her fingers, and believed she felt a slight bit of increased dilation. "You may be up to ten," she told Bolivia. Bolivia nodded.

"Where's Charles?" she asked. It was the first thing she'd said in hours.

"Out for a walk," Tess lied.

Bolivia asked for water. Tess got the metal cup from the table and filled it. Bolivia drank a few sips. "Where's Keller?" she asked, and Tess told her he was at the hospital with his father.

"Where you ought to be," Bolivia said. "I'm sorry."

Tess shushed her. "Don't be silly," she said. "I've got Ben Ray for the rest of my life," she told her and marveled at the words as she said them.

Bolivia pushed through a series of contractions before Charles came back with the doctor. Hearing the front door quietly shut, Tess walked out to the family room. Dr. Tate was wearing a light-brown hat and carrying his bag. He was tall and handsome.

Tess shook his hand.

"Your husband?" he inquired.

"Doing fine," she said.

Tate removed his hat. "We tried to get the best surgeon," he offered, and Tess smiled at the apology in his eyes—as if she cared whether or not Ben Ray had one or two legs. He was alive, wasn't he?

"She's back here," Tess said. She halted his progress toward the bedroom. "She's nine or ten, I can't tell. A lot of bleeding. Baby hasn't crowned, that's why I'm worried."

"When did her water break?"

"This afternoon. Three o'clock maybe?"

Tess hesitated, looking at Charles. "She, ah, doesn't know you're coming. She didn't want to have to call you. She's . . ." Tess searched for a kind word, "independent."

"Aren't you all?" he offered, handing Tess his hat.

She smiled and let him pass.

Tess and Charles stood at the door and watched Bolivia accept the doctor's presence, her dark face surrendering as if in relief. Then they went quietly into Bolivia's family room.

"Tea?" Charles asked.

Tess sat on the sofa, running her fingers over the tapestry while he boiled water for the tea. "Where did she get this?" Tess asked.

"Same place she got everything," he replied.

She looked at him.

"From me."

"And me," Tess added.

Charles poured the water up. Tess looked at his blue overalls and polar-bear face. He sat opposite her, in the rocker. Mud from his boots flaked to the floor, threatening to dirty up Bolivia's hooked rug. Tess brushed bits of coal dust from the cotton-sheet drapes behind the sofa, thinking she ought to wash them after the baby was born. Then she untied the shoelace from her hair, letting it fall. Charles watched her.

"He was a sight when we got to him," Charles said.

She'd been waiting for this conversation. She leaned forward eagerly.

"Tell me," she said.

"Hadn't lost his sense of humor."

She nodded.

"Called his boy's name. I had the boy by the shirt collar, damn near strangled him dragging him over to that hole so his daddy could holler at him. Cut the boy's knees up. Tore his overalls." Charles looked at her. "Who told Reba Hatfield about Jake?"

"I did. Was it his heart, Charles?"

"I reckon."

"They're burying him in the morning," Tess said.

Charles shook his head.

"They're taking Ben Ray to Birmingham on Monday," she went on. "It'll be quite some time before he gets a leg, but they want to see him over at the V.A."

"He fight in the war?"

"Yes."

Charles looked at the fire. "This new war," he began.

Tess got up. "We been fighting our own wars, haven't we?" she asked him, staring at the fire. She stoked it, making the embers glow. The idea of losing Keller to a war she didn't even understand was beyond considering. "You know," she said, turning to Charles, "My daddy fancied himself a scrap iron man once."

He smiled. "That so?"

"He got it in his head that if he collected enough junk metal, he could drive the family to Miami in his pickup. We went all over the place searching for scrap, and when the back was full, he loaded us up—me, Mama, and him, and headed for Florida. We drove two days running, and when he couldn't drive another mile, he just stopped right in the middle of the Everglades somewhere near the Tamiami Trail. I was sure alligators and crocodiles were going to eat me under that moon. And when we finally got to Miami, he drove straight onto the beach, and we got stuck in the sand right beside the ocean."

Charles smiled.

"Daddy liked liquor."

She watched Charles light a cigaret. She'd smoked a bit when she was younger, and for a moment she recalled what it was like—the bite of nicotine, the rush of heartbeat, and the jaded image you got of yourself as you smoked, as if you were suddenly able to see yourself from a distance, sitting there posed and questioning all kinds of things. She wished, not for a cigaret, but for that kind of distance. Her life had been shoved so fiercely into her face that she felt pinned against the wall, suffocated.

Tate came to the door.

"You want to come in here," he said.

Tess and Charles bolted.

He stopped them at the door. "I was able to turn the head. The baby was trying to be born sunnyside-up. It's turned right now. Just a couple more pushes, and that's it."

Tess searched his face. Something wasn't right.

"We'll see," he said. "She says she's been laboring for days."

Tess went to her side. Bolivia's cocoa skin was free from torment. A wistful calm crossed her eyes as she took Tess's hand and pushed, while the doctor held her upraised feet in his hands like stirrups. And even before Tess heard the doctor groan, even before she allowed herself to understand the real reason she was here, why Bolivia's pregnancy had become the focal point of her life, even before she looked at the baby girl's face and beheld Keller's image, even before she let herself believe for a split instant that she was a grandmother—even before she turned to see Charles's sad eyes, she knew the baby was dead.

"I'm giving you some morphine," the doctor told her.

It coursed through her like sweet milk. Floating dreamlike, she watched how Tess and Charles wrapped the baby in the ivory dress with turquoise and red rick-rack and laid her in a basket.

"Where did you get that?" she asked Tess, but her words were garbled by the medicine. Tess brushed the tears from Bolivia's cheeks. Because she was numb, she didn't know she was crying until Tess did this. "The basket," she went on.

"It's your basket," Tess said.

"Am I dreaming?"

"No, baby," Tess replied.

"Is this what I collect berries in?" she asked Charles. He was covering the baby girl's face. "Is it morning?" she asked, con-

228 --- NIGHT RIDE HOME

fused over the crisscrossed rays of light that streamed in the window.

"No, baby," Tess whispered. "It's midnight."

It was prism light, broken into tiny particles of color.

"She's hallucinating," Dr. Tate told Charles, as if Bolivia weren't listening. "It's the medicine, honey," the doctor told her.

But she knew better. *Mother?* She wasn't sure if she said it or thought it.

"Angels can fly because they take themselves lightly," Bolivia told Charles. Working deftly as if to comfort the baby, he glanced over.

"An old Scottish saying," Tess replied. She was standing like a nurse at Dr. Tate's side as he cleaned Bolivia's bloody legs.

"Is the baby dead?" Bolivia asked Tess.

Tess leaned over, touched her hair.

"Yes," she whispered. Angels' reflections stood in the green irises of Tess's eyes. Cherubim are guardians of fixed stars, Bolivia thought. Where had she heard that? *Where were you when the morning stars sang together and the angels shouted for joy?*

"That's from the book of Job, isn't it?" she asked Tess.

"What, baby?"

Dr. Tate looked over at Tess, a bloodstained towel in hand. "The medicine," he reminded her.

Tess assisted his every move, handing him gauze and iodine, tossing bloody towels to the floor, pressing hard on Bolivia's stomach as he instructed while he worked on her.

"Press hard," he told Tess.

"What're they doing?" Bolivia asked Charles, who sat near the bureau with the basket of baby.

"The afterbirth," Tess told her.

Bolivia vaguely recalled this from the births she'd witnessed. Tess bore down, heaving all her weight onto Bolivia's belly, which looked flat, empty, flabby, and fleshy. The doctor's hands disappeared up into her body cavity and when he brought them out, he was holding the placenta.

"Healthy," he pronounced, as if it were the baby.

"Then it was just the cord?" Tess asked him.

"Right."

Dr. Tate looked at Bolivia. "The cord was tangled," he said gently to her. "The baby couldn't get oxygen just before she came out. Otherwise . . ." he said, but he didn't finish. Otherwise didn't matter.

Bolivia looked at Tess. "Am I dead?" she asked.

"No," Tess replied. "You're alive. And I'm right here with you."

"Jacob wrestled an angel," Bolivia said.

"Yes, he did."

"Was it a man, the angel?"

"I don't know, baby."

"Get her some water," Dr. Tate instructed Tess. "We need to flush her system."

Charles was taking the basketed baby from the room.

"Stop," Bolivia told him.

He turned, his eyes warm.

"Can't I see her?"

Charles brought the basket to her bedside. Tess and the doctor moved away to allow him plenty of space. Peeling the blanket from the baby's face, Bolivia touched her lips. Keller, she thought. Everybody would have known. Every feature was his.

She lay back.

Charles covered the baby's face.

Mother? she began.

Tess returned to the room with a pitcher of water. Bolivia looked at her and panicked. Tess knew the truth. The father's name was written, like an epitath, on the baby's face.

Bolivia turned to the wall. Tess took her hand. "I'm seeing angels," she said to Tess, but she couldn't look at her.

"When you pray for somebody, an angel sits on the shoulder of that person," Tess said. "I'm praying for you."

Bolivia kept her face to the wall. *Mother?*

"I'm right here," Tess said.

—— ——

At daybreak, when the doctor was satisfied that she was stable, and Charles had returned from the morgue over in Fairfield, Tess and Dr. Tate left Bolivia's place. Charles fixed tea and toast. She sat up in bed and ate the toast with an appetite so fierce it scared her. "Labor," Charles told her. She drank gallons of water. Charles gave her paregoric all morning.

At noon, she sat up again.

"Build a pavilion," she told him.

He sat beside her, wearing his blue overalls and boots, with blond stubble sprouting from his unshaven face.

"What's that?"

"It's what Melungeons put over gravesites."

He remembered the photograph she'd shown him of her mother's grave. It had a white latticework arch over the marker like half an inverted gazebo. He wasn't certain just how he'd make it work, but he'd try.

"When," she asked him, her face tormented, "will we bury her?"

"When do you think?"

"Day after tomorrow," she told him.

By nightfall, she was hungry again. He made beans and rice. Tess brought over spoonbread. And by morning, the women were coming in hordes, bearing casseroles, corn pudding, pecan pies, and words of kindness. He let them come straight to her room, and she raised her brown hand to be kissed, which they did, awed by the fact that they were in Bolivia Ivey's bedroom and it contained not a whore but a mother who'd lost her child.

He spent the night beside her. Once, she woke and reached for his hands. "I want to have another baby," she whispered. He looked at her. "I want seven babies," she went on.

Charles turned and tried to look at her, but it was too dark.

He reached down to make sure the towels were secure under her body. He'd never loved her so much.

"It's strange," she said, "but all I can think about is having another one."

Charles put his arm around her and drew her up.

She touched his face.

"I want to move out of here," she whispered.

"When?"

"Tomorrow."

He got up, pulled the dropcord to turn on the lamp, and adjusted his eyes to the light.

"Not *now*," she said and tried to sit up. When she did, she winced.

"You hurting, baby?"

"Yes," she said and lay back down.

Charles threw on his overalls and went to the kitchen for the paregoric and water. He gave her a spoonful and checked the towels under her. She wasn't bleeding.

He went to the kitchen and made coffee. He looked at his watch. It was almost five, but the sky was dark.

"Charles!" she called.

He went to the bedroom.

"Come here," she said. He sat on the edge of the bed. She opened her eyes. They were dark, glazed by the narcotic.

"I didn't love Keller," she said.

Charles looked at the floor.

"Did you think I loved him?"

"Yes," he said.

"Why did you think it?"

He studied his hands.

"When he was over here and had his head in your lap. The way you were holding his head."

"He needed a mother," she said.

"He has a mother."

"But I was carrying his child," she said and put a hand on Charles's thigh.

He didn't understand what she was saying.

"It was that night, when he was crying in my lap, that I understood that I loved *you*," she said.

"Why do you love me?"

She took her hand from his thigh. "Why does anybody love anybody?"

He hated it when she did this—when she didn't answer his questions.

"Why?" he persisted.

She rolled to her side.

"Because you aren't looking for anything in me."

He glanced up at the sky. Dawn was near.

"You just love me," she whispered. "You aren't looking."

She lay back down and looked at the ceiling. "Why do you love me?" she asked.

He shook his head. He felt like he might cry. How could anybody *not* love her?

At daybreak, Charles began packing her things, her pots and pans, her metal cup that had held miner's clacker and Scotty Sandifer's liquor, her clothes and underwear, the canning jars, the gourds, and the brass angel Tess had given her. Because she still wasn't able to walk very much, he carried her like a child past the stream, beyond the stone wall where passionflower was going to sprout come summer, over the pasture, and up to his place. Later, in his flatbed truck, he collected her furniture and cats. He was going to marry her. But first he needed to find Keller. He had, after all, come to love the boy.

In the barn, they fed the horses, tossing hay and sidestepping manure. Keller didn't know how to build things. Carpentry, Charles noted, was as foreign to him as war, career, and fathering—all those things that lay on his road up ahead. Still, he had been jarred loose from youth, and from the idea that everything would always be easy, that he was in charge. He had learned that people depended on one another. Charles could see it in the way he concentrated on the task at hand, how he struggled to hammer nails neatly, securing the wood-framed canopy that would form an arc over his baby's grave, how he smoked his cigaret thoughtlessly, without posing.

His hands were becoming bruised and cut, just like they'd been the day he'd cut cedar trees for Graham's commissary. Charles turned to slap the cow's rump and began working the tits to get a morning's worth of milk. The burial was tomorrow.

Inside, Bolivia lay on his bed, reading a book Tess had given her. Sometimes, without any seeming provocation, she'd start to cry.

"Sorry," she'd say, like a girl caught taking something that didn't belong to her.

Keller had arrived this morning, pallid and tired.

Charles stood at the door, ready to give him instructions, knowing he was going to be desperate for absolution and eager to work off his penance. Constructing the burial canopy was the perfect task.

Now, he hammered diligently, and the sound of his labor echoed along the ridge. Charles had asked Bolivia to describe the canopy. She'd called it a shelter house and said it looked like an old-fashioned latticework spring house, painted white or white-washed, either square or in an arc. "Some people make them with cinder and they got a tin roof, but that's sinful," she'd told him.

"Sinful?"

"God meant graves to be simple."

She told him the shelters were important, and that a Melun-geon would paint his family's burial shelter before he'd paint his own house because the dead were more important than the living.

Charles hoped they were building it right. When they got the frame assembled, they sat on his porch. Keller leaned forward, resting his arms on the banister, his breath a puff of vapor in the cold.

"What did she look like?" he asked, staring at the land.

"You," Charles told him.

Keller looked at his feet, flicked ashes, looked up again.

"I told my daddy," he said.

"Good," Charles replied.

"I told him over at the hospital. He was eating soup and crackers. He was propped up in bed. A nurse came in and gave him a shot of something in the hip and I saw where his leg had been. It was bandaged up."

Charles said nothing, just looked ahead to where his land joined his brother's.

"He said he was sorry for Bolivia. He didn't say he was sorry for me. That was good. He told me that while he was down under he was thinking about me."

Keller looked over to the compost heap, where volunteer potato plants were leafing despite the cold. Charles knew they'd die in January.

"Any of your buddies signed up yet?" Charles asked him.

Keller looked at him curiously. "For what?"

"This war we're in."

Keller shook his head. "Why does she want to bury the baby up by the colored church?" he asked.

"Maybe because she's a bit colored herself," Charles replied.

Keller looked at him. "I got to ask you one more thing," he said. "Did Mom know? Do you think she knew the truth?"

"Yes."

Keller got up, opened the screen door, and went inside.

The Indian tapestry from her sofa was draped over the bedpost. Cats scurried about. Charles had moved her in; the company wasn't going to have to evict her. On the dresser was her metal cup and the brass angel Tess had given her for Christmas. In the open closet were all her dresses. Keller's eyes lingered over all the things. He knew he'd never again enter her place.

He didn't speak to her at first.

She put her book aside. The window shade was pulled down, muting the morning light. He didn't move closer, because he was afraid of her.

"I'm building the shelter," he told her, fingering his cap.

Her eyes filled.

He looked down.

"I'm glad your daddy is alive," she said.

He nodded, looking at the imperfections in Charles's floor.

"Come over here," she said, holding her arms forward like a mother.

He shook his head. A kitten rubbed his legs, first lightly, then harder, and he picked it up. The kitten, appreciative of the way his hands moved over her ears, looked him squarely in the face.

"I saw some angels," she whispered.

He got up. He wasn't going to listen to her. He went to Charles's kitchen, dodging the hanging gourds. The yellow bowls of milk were empty where the kittens had licked them clean, so clean they shone like porcelain. In the sink were plates with remnants of grits. Leaning against the butcher block, he looked out the window. A crow sat on the tire swing.

In the distance, smoke rose from Ranger Avery's chimney.

"Please." He heard her voice and turned.

She was wearing a flimsy nightgown, and he shrank back at the sight of her flat belly. "What're you doing?" he asked, moving toward her to get her back to bed, but then stopping because he was afraid to touch her. "You shouldn't be up."

"I am up. I'm going to bury my baby in the morning. I better be up."

He turned back to the window. "Don't say anything else to me about ghosts," he told her.

She leaned against the doorjamb, and morning light shone through her gown. "I wasn't talking about ghosts, Keller. I was talking about angels, spirits."

"What's the difference?"

"Ghosts are people trapped between worlds. An angel is an idea of God."

"You can't see an idea," he said.

Her eyes widened and, for an instant, he felt like he saw something rise like an apron in her nut-brown irises.

He backed up against the sink.

"I'm sorry," he told her.

She held a strand of hair between her fingers, turning it as if to knot it. He stared at her nightgown. It was the color of sand.

"I'm sorry about the baby," he said, but even as he said it, he knew it was a lie. The instant he'd heard the news, he'd been flooded with relief.

"Dr. Tate told me the angels were because of the medicine he gave me, but that can't be true, because they're here with us, right this moment. They're big, Keller."

"Stop it."

"You don't have to see them."

"I *don't* see them."

"They never make themselves known to people who're afraid."

"You're crazy as sin!"

What was she? What was a Melungeon? They were, he was certain, a cult, a band of half-colored gypsy witches who roamed Tennessee and Alabama in search of white boys to haunt.

She moved closer. "You've got to let them help you," she told him.

"I don't need any help," he said.

She reached for his jacket sleeves, and he stepped away, knocking over one of the kittens' yellow bowls. She was moving like a sleepwalker, her arms outstretched in front of her.

"Please," he said. "Charles is out there."

"He understands."

"Understands what?"

"How much you're hurting."

"I'm not hurting," he told her, moving against the wall like a man being held at gunpoint, hands up to shield himself from the bullets.

She was moving closer, then retreating, over and over as if dancing a waltz that only she was hearing.

She stopped moving and put her hand on the icebox. "I just want you to understand," she said.

"Understand *what?*"

"I just want you to understand that you're forgiven," she told him.

She smiled and moved away, back to the doorway, a dark mystic starting to vanish. "I don't mean that *I* forgive you; I mean that God has already forgiven you, and me, too. That's all." And she smiled in the way he loved, like an ordinary girl. "You'll need to know that someday," she went on.

He nodded, wanting suddenly to know more, but she was backing away toward the bedroom.

There were moments when she didn't believe it herself, but the yellow light of her mother shone all over Charles's place, in the barn where she stood at dusk, sore and bleeding and hurting as if her abdomen were threatening to come barreling down her legs, but determined to gain enough strength to make the trip up to the colored church in the morning to bury the baby. She watched as Charles fed and brushed the horses, tossed fresh hay, and whispered quietly to the animals. Moonlight fell over Charles's big body as he carried her like a baby to bed.

During the night, she dreamed that they were carrying the baby to Tennessee. In the distance, she could see the state like a huge boulder, a wall of mountain. It had a definable shape as if she were seeing it on the map—a long, flat rock. Lookout Mountain was like the map's jutting edge of Tennessee where Virginia and Carolina kissed it. In the dream, Kimbrall's Crossing was a corridor, crunched up between the ridges. "We're close, Charles," she told him, in the dream. A small sign said SE-QUATCHIE. "Turn beside that barn," she told him. The church came into view.

Charles took the coffin to the graveyard and started digging.

Her mother appeared, in the dream, and started telling her the old stories. There was the story of a Mediterranean ship that got lost westbound on the trade winds and dashed up on the North Carolina shore. Its timbers were of cedar from the Holy Land, her mother told her. The shipwrecked survivors struggled ashore and headed west into the green valleys of Tennessee and settled on Newman's Ridge, Mulberry Gap, and Powell Mountain. "And they were the first Melungeons," her mother said. She told the Lost Tribe of Israel story, and the Lost Colony of white people story, where they landed on the Carolina coast and married Indians and taught their mixed-blood children the legends of the lost colony with all its dancing and art and stories. "And *these* were the first Melungeons," her mother concluded. But then there were the Shakers, who were supposed to have been blessed by Indians and Melungeons who entered the Shakers' spirits and imparted songs to them and entered their bodies at church and caused them to dance and demand succotash to eat. And finally there was the mutiny of the Portuguese ship, and the successful mutineers who settled in Tennessee and retreated to the mountains, where they married Indians.

Her mother told her there was no solid truth, but then nobody knew where they'd come from, did they? Weren't all families lost tribes, her mother argued, mutineers westbound on the trade winds, survivors looking for green valleys, people surrounded by light, capable of imparting songs and causing one another to dance, led by the youngest acolyte—herself—who would carry the story like a candle, forward in time?

"But where do we bury her?" she'd asked her mother.

"In the sinners' pen," she said and smiled, pointing to the rusty fenced-in place where sinners came during camp revivals, from Wilder and Newman's Ridge. They were all there, in the dream—all the miners.

The following morning, Charles brought her breakfast in bed: grits and fruit served on a two-by-four. He'd made new sculptures with scrap and wire, odd-shaped figurines designed for the baby. They now sat beside the bed, sad and real. When Scotty Sandifer arrived in his truck, sunlight bounced from the chrome, making lightning on the wall.

"Who is it?" she called to Charles, who was in the kitchen.

He came to the bedroom. "It's Scotty," he replied.

She looked at him.

"He's come to help me load the grave shelter in my truck."

A few minutes later, he returned from the yard. "There's a caravan, baby," he told her.

She didn't say anything. She knew what he meant.

"It's how they pay homage. They're your neighbors."

"It makes me feel bad," she told him.

Charles shrugged. She got up, washed her face at the basin, put on her calico dress, and braided her hair. When she got into his truck, she was queasy and in more pain than she'd imagined. The very act of climbing into the cab had the feel of skin breaking.

At the base of the hill, she saw them gathering—a cluster of trucks and Fords. Scotty Sandifer and his wife. Keller, Laura, and Tess in the Studebaker. Ranger Avery and his daughter, and Miriam O'Cadlin with a nun she'd never seen before, along with a host of miners whose bodies she knew inside out.

Charles drove past them all in order to lead the caravan.

"I dreamed about them," Bolivia told him, looking back at the cars behind them. "I dreamed we buried the baby in Sequatchie, and they were all there."

Keller turned on his headlights.

In the backseat, Tess was going over the song she was going to sing at the funeral, humming lightly.

Laura turned to her. "What's the name of that?"

"It's an old Shaker hymn," she said.

They crossed the railroad tracks and began winding up the snaking road to the colored church. The winter sun made the car warm, but Keller was cold. Laura put her hand on his leg. She was wearing dark gloves.

Whatever she knew for certain about the baby, she wasn't saying. But something about her mood—the need to comfort him—caused Keller to think that she knew. Tess hadn't said a word to him about it. Keller could see the latticework shelter in the back of Charles's truck. He felt proud of his carpentry.

The caravan streamed forward, up the hill. In his rearview mirror, Keller saw them coming, their headlights bright. The entire neighborhood was coming to bury his baby. Other vehicles stopped by the roadside in respect. Black men took off their caps and held them over their hearts as if the flag were passing by.

"Bolivia," Laura said.

He turned to her. "What?"

"Everybody loves Bolivia," she said.

In the backseat, Tess kept humming the haunting tune. Keller turned the Studebaker into the churchyard. He parked under an oak.

"I'm going to help them with the coffin," he said to Laura. She nodded.

"You and Mom go on inside."

He went to Charles's truck and helped Scotty lift the grave shelter from the back. It still smelled of fresh paint.

Charles and Keller carried the shelter to a plot of dug-up ground.

The marker read MARQUITA IVEY.

"Is that the baby's name?" Keller asked Charles.

Charles nodded. "It's Bolivia's mother's name."

The chapel was tiny. A rusty cast-iron bell hung near the entrance. The cars kept coming up the hill. Keller put his hands

242 —— NIGHT RIDE HOME

in his pockets and watched the miners slam the car doors shut, take off their hats.

"What do we do?" he asked Charles.

"Go inside."

"The coffin?"

"Those colored men over there are going to carry it to the grave while we're inside."

Keller looked over at them. They were big. They were wearing overalls, holding shovels.

The chapel was filling up. Keller saw Miriam O'Cadlin, Reba Hatfield, Grace Sandifer, Lila Green, miners, farmers, and some old friends he'd known in school. Laura sat up on the first pew with Tess. Brother O'Flynn, who'd married them only three weeks ago, was shaking hands with some colored women. Keller had never been in church with colored folks. It gave the place a charged feeling, as if the world had been shaken up.

The feeling grew stronger as he made his way to Laura. He sat beside her on the pew. Tess rose to sing. When she did, Scotty and Grace came down the aisle and sat on the other side of Laura. Charles led Bolivia to the front. She was wearing a familiar ivory-colored dress and shawl.

They sat close to one another in the pew—Bolivia, Charles, Keller, Laura, Scotty, Grace, Reba Hatfield, and the colored women.

Brother O'Flynn stood behind the altar.

Some black men—deacons from the church, Keller reasoned—came forward with trays of bread crumbs and a jar of wine. One of the deacons moved to the far side of the first pew and handed a tray to Bolivia.

Keller watched her dark hands as they gathered bits of bread. He remembered how her hands had made love.

"And Jesus, the same night in which he was betrayed," Brother O'Flynn was saying, "took bread."

Charles held the tray for Bolivia to get bread. Keller held it, in turn, for Charles. Laura held it for Keller. Scotty held it for Laura, Grace for Scotty, Reba Hatfield for Grace, a colored woman for Reba.

Keller watched the tray pass over to the other side of the chapel. The pews held black and white miners suddenly together in the same church for the first time. He knew that they'd never shared Communion with each other, and might never again. He knew, too, that Bolivia—herself both colored and white—was the reason they were here, able to do this.

"And when he had given thanks," Brother O'Flynn went on, "he brake it, and said, 'Take eat: this is my body, which is broken for you.' "

Keller looked at Bolivia's hands bringing the bread up to her lips. He brought the bread to his own lips.

"Do this in remembrance of me," the preacher said.

He looked up at his mother, who was singing, " 'Tis a gift to be simple, 'tis a gift to be free ..."

He looked at Laura's folded hands, pale against her dark dress. He saw Scotty take one of Laura's hands, saw Grace take Scotty's other hand. He saw this family holding hands.

He thought of his school buddies somewhere behind him, taking Communion. Would they fire a weapon, sink a ship, love war, come home? He wasn't going to forget them. Or the miners, or the accident, or the baby. "Remember," the preacher kept saying. Keller looked at him as if he'd never seen him before—this preacher he'd been looking at every Sunday for all his life. "Remember," Brother O'Flynn said. "Just remember. That's all we're asked to do, is to remember," he said.

Keller watched Bolivia bring the jar of wine to her lips. He knew he wasn't going to forget, ever.

III

The drapes blew in and out. A pale light fell over the brown sweater. Tess picked it back up and started to knit. She'd turned thirty-eight in April. The neighborhood was emptying. Mothers whose boys were already gone had started doing odd things. The Lawler boys' mother was working at the steel plant. One was taking a night course in Birmingham. Grace Sandifer had set up a quilting frame at the station, and the mothers gathered there to quilt and pump gas. They were starting to dress like Grace.

Keller was smoking beside his father on the sofa.

"Did you buy new trousers today?" Tess asked him.

"Yes."

"Where's Laura?"

"Home."

"You got everything from Lila Green's place?"

"There wasn't much to get, Mom."

"I know, baby."

She held up some brown yarn.

"A sweater," Ben Ray clarified.

"Mom," Keller said. "It's July."

"But where you're going it may be cold," she said.

She looked at him.

After a while, he rose and moved toward the door. "We'll see you in the morning," he said to Ben Ray, "in Bessemer. Train leaves at eight. I think we'll be there around seven-fifteen." To Tess he said, "Set the alarm, Mom. Don't let him sleep late."

Knowing that she wasn't going to make a scene at the depot, she grabbed him up and held him tight, resting her chest on his shoulder.

"Don't think," he instructed her. "Don't think about anything yet."

Tess and Ben Ray stood at the window, watching the Studebaker spin from the yard, barely missing her tomato plants in the square garden. They went to the porch and sat on the steps.

"You going to be all right?" Ben Ray asked.

She watched Keller's car disappear up the hill. The trees, full and green, blocked her view.

Ben Ray looked at the sky.

"How long's this war going to last anyhow?"

He looked at her. "Wars are unpredictable. That's the worst thing about wars. You can't predict a thing."

"So you think maybe a few months?" she asked him. "You think Keller might be home in a few months?"

He shook his head. The crickets were loud now. The sky was darkening. "No, it'll be longer than that."

"A year?" she pressed.

"Yeah," he said and took her hand. "It'll be a year at best."

She sighed. "You hungry?"

"Starved," he said.

But they didn't get up. They sat still, holding hands, their fingers interlocked, palms pressed. The neighborhood grew dark as ink, and inside the houses across the road you could see, in the lighted rooms, women carrying bowls to tables, toddlers in diapers and T-shirts, miners reading newspapers. You couldn't see the headlines but you knew it was war. Tess moved closer to Ben Ray and let her dress fall between her parted legs.

"How short will dresses get?" she asked Ben Ray.

He glanced over, smiled.

"Do you think they'll ever be up to here?" she asked and pulled the cotton dress up a few inches above her knee.

"Hard to predict," he said.

"You think women will ever fight in wars?"

"Hard to say," he said and put a hand on her knee.

"When Keller comes home, maybe he and Laura can open a store."

Ben Ray smiled. "What kind of store?"

"Oh." She shrugged and let her dress fall back below her knees, looking at her bare feet. She liked how they looked. "Oh, maybe they could sell tires."

Ben Ray chuckled.

"Cars are big business. You can't go wrong selling tires."

Ben Ray nodded and yawned.

But they still didn't get up. They sat until the women in the houses across the street began clearing dishes from the table, and the neighborhood dogs started to howl for scraps.

Tess waited. Overhead the stars were bright. Finally, she asked the question. "You think Keller loved Bolivia?" She looked into Ben Ray's brown eyes. In the light of evening, they were like dark sugar.

"I don't know, babe."

"But did he talk to you about her ever?"

"Just that it was his baby," he replied.

"You ever go to the grave?" she asked him.

"No."

"I do every now and then," she said and touched the rickrack on the apron that lay across her lap.

After a while, they went inside and made supper. She tore

some grapes from the stems and dropped them into a green bowl of sliced bananas. Then she made iced tea, heated some beans, and opened a can of sardines. It was a strange kind of meal. But they ate it and talked at the table. They talked about war and coal and their son. They talked about the accident and the baby. They talked about the past and the present and all that might come their way.

Keller passed the stadium and turned the car into the yard.

Laura was on the steps, wearing shorts. Her hair had grown longer. In recent days, she'd been gathering it up in pastel scarves. It made her look like a woman. But as now she rose from the steps and walked toward him, the bare, muscled legs reminded him that she was still Laura Sandifer.

"Where were you?" she asked.

"Mom's."

Laura led him inside. Scotty was in the parlor, cleaning his guns.

He smiled. Since he'd quit drinking, he smiled frequently, although you got the feeling it was forced—as if he were trying hard to be cordial when, at heart, he was still on fire.

Grace called from the kitchen. "We're having fried chicken, Keller."

"Thank you, ma'am, that's my favorite," he called back.

Laura started putting books on the shelves in the parlor. Since they'd moved back in and the weather had warmed, she'd become domestic—cleaning the fireplace, painting the bookshelves, and spending less time at the station.

"They're kicking me out of here," Scotty joked, motioning to his pile of hunting and fishing gear. "Little by little."

He got up, wiped his hands on his jeans, smiled a tight smile, and went outside.

Laura kept stacking books, her back to him. The shorts weren't baggy like the workpants. He thought she'd put on some weight, something she'd needed to do. Since she'd known he was leaving, though, she'd become busy, distant, and chipper.

"Turn around," he said.

When she did, he saw that she was crying. He'd never seen her cry.

Later, he held her in the bed upstairs in her old room, and they didn't make love. Instead, they got up, went downstairs, and walked over to the stadium by the Sandifers' house. They sat in the bleachers and talked about who had already left, who was preparing to leave, who was going to get out of it for medical reasons, and who was going to have a hard time. They didn't talk about the war itself, because they didn't understand what the war was. They didn't talk about geography, because they didn't know any. They didn't talk about the past, because they were still in it. They didn't talk about the future, because they didn't have one. They didn't talk about what they were losing, because they hadn't lost it yet. They were barefoot under the stars, and eventually they walked out onto the field, past each marker, yardline by yardline, until they got to the goalposts, where they turned and faced each other.

When the train left the station, Keller had been amazed at how fast things sailed by—his parents' faces gone in a flash, the town of Bessemer erased after a fleeting glimpse of the five-and-dime, the dry goods store, and the library. The train picked up speed quickly, and the landscape grew rural and flat, as they passed fields of cows, scrap yards, houses painted aqua and chartreuse. White church steeples rose here and there. In backyards, women hung wash on clotheslines beside pickups.

American flags flew by.

A short distance past Tuscaloosa, the hills of Moundville rose. "Indians buried there," he heard a soldier behind him say. Next came wetlands where swamp cabbage was growing near the knees of cypress trees.

Catfish farms, shacks, and acacia trees were here and gone

like a a series of watercolor pictures being thumbed through so quickly you never had time to focus on the object at hand. Occasionally the train cut through a forest, and Keller's view narrowed to a tunnel of pines. Then the landscape opened again to fields of horses, hawks atop oak trees.

The soldier behind him snored, then woke with a jolt.

They made stops at Tuscaloosa, Laurel, Hattiesburg, Picayune, and Slidell. But Keller hardly acquainted himself with the facade of each station before they were once more flying over the rails. They crossed Lake Pontchartrain and he saw startling above-ground graveyards.

"Elysian Fields," the soldier said.

The train raced on, faster and faster. Keller reached for his bag of clothes. He'd packed light like the navy told him to do. Yet he knew there were things he'd always carry with him—his baby daughter, the morning his father walked out of his grave, wounded but alive. If you have a baby with a man, you can always predict his future, Bolivia had told him. He'd believed her when she said that Laura would give him children, sons. He also believed her later when she said he'd come home, though he knew somehow that home wouldn't be the same place. He pictured himself living in Birmingham—a steel mill executive or a scientist or an engineer. He and Laura would take their boys to the baseball games. On Saturday nights, they'd ride home to Sweetgum Flat to see their parents. They'd go by Charles and Bolivia's place, spread a quilt on the summer grass, and watch all their children—his and Laura's, Charles and Bolivia's—play together in the field, under the stars. But his thoughts were flying by as fast as the landscape. He was traveling at the speed of light. The train was without reason, persistent and teeming with the seduction of new scenes, so that even when he stepped out at New Orleans, reported to the naval station, and made his way to the hotel, he still felt it moving, carrying him away.